OVER CLOCKED

OVER CLOCKED

Stories of the Future Present

CORY DOCTOROW

THUNDER'S MOUTH PRESS
NEW YORK

OVERCLOCKED
Stories of the Future Present

Published by
Thunder's Mouth Press
An Imprint of Avalon Publishing Group, Inc.
245 West 17th Street, 11th Floor
New York, NY 10011

First printing, February 2007

"Printcrime" first appeared in *Nature* magazine; "When Sysadmins Ruled the Earth" first appeared in *Universe* magazine; "Anda's Game" first appeared on Salon.com and was later reissued in *The Best American Short Stories 2005*; "I, Robot" and "After the Seige" first appeared in *The Infinite Matrix*; "I, Row-Boat" first appeared in *Flurb,* a webzine.

Library of Congress Cataloging-in-Publication Data is available.

ISBN-10: 1-56025-981-7
ISBN-13: 978-1-56025-981-7

9 8 7 6 5 4 3 2 1

Interior design by Maria E. Torres

Printed in the United States of America
Distributed by Publishers Group West

For Pat York,

who made my stories better

Contents

Printcrime • *1*

When Sysadmins Ruled the Earth • *5*

Anda's Game • *57*

I, Robot • *101*

I, Row-Boat • *159*

After the Siege • *209*

About the Author • *287*

Printcrime

"Printcrime" came out of a discussion I had with a friend who'd been to hear a spokesman for the British recording industry talk about the future of "intellectual property." The record exec opined the recording industry's great and hysterical spasm would form the template for a never-ending series of spasms as 3D printers, fabricators, and rapid prototypers laid waste to every industry that relied on trademarks or patents.

My friend thought that, as kinky as this was, it did show a fair amount of foresight, coming as it did from the notoriously technosqueamish record industry.

I was less impressed.

It's almost certainly true that control over the production of trademarked and patented objects will diminish over the coming years of object on demand printing, but to focus on 3D printers' impact on *trademarks* is a stupendously weird idea.

It's as if the railroad were looming on the horizon, and the most visionary thing the futurists of the day can think of to say about it is that these iron horses will have a disastrous effect on the hardworking manufacturers of oat-bags for horses. It's true, as far as it goes, but it's so tunnel-visioned as to be practically blind.

When *Nature* magazine asked me if I'd write a short-short story for their back-page, I told them I'd do it, then went home, sat down on the bed and banged this one out. They bought it the next morning, and we were in business.

The coppers smashed my father's printer when I was eight. I remember the hot, cling-film-in-a-microwave smell of it, and Da's look of ferocious concentration as he filled it with fresh goop, and the warm, fresh-baked feel of the objects that came out of it.

The coppers came through the door with truncheons swinging, one of them reciting the terms of the warrant through a bullhorn. One of Da's customers had shopped him. The ipolice paid in high-grade pharmaceuticals—performance enhancers, memory supplements, metabolic boosters. The kind of thing that cost a fortune over-the-counter; the kind of thing you could print at home, if you didn't mind the risk of having your kitchen filled with a sudden crush of big, beefy bodies, hard truncheons whistling through the air, smashing anyone and anything that got in the way.

They destroyed grandma's trunk, the one she'd brought from the old country. They smashed our little refrigerator and the purifier unit over the window. My tweetybird escaped death by hiding in a corner of his cage as a big, booted foot crushed most of it into a sad tangle of printer-wire.

Da. What they did to him. When he was done, he looked like he'd been brawling with an entire rugby side. They brought him out the door and let the newsies get a good look at him as they tossed him in the car, while a spokesman told the world that my Da's organized-crime bootlegging operation had been responsible for at least twenty million in contraband, and that my Da, the desperate villain, had resisted arrest.

I saw it all from my phone, in the remains of the sitting room, watching it on the screen and wondering how, just *how* anyone could look at our little flat and our terrible, manky estate and mistake it for the home of an organized crime kingpin. They took the printer away, of course, and displayed it like a trophy for the newsies. Its little shrine in the kitchenette seemed horribly empty. When I roused myself and picked up the flat and rescued my peeping poor tweety-bird, I put a blender there. It was made out of printed parts, so it would only last a month before I'd need to print new bearings and other moving parts. Back then, I could take apart and reassemble anything that could be printed.

By the time I turned eighteen, they were ready to let Da out of prison. I'd visited him three times—on my tenth birthday, on his fiftieth, and when Ma died. It had been two years since I'd last seen him and he was in bad shape. A prison fight had left him with a limp, and he looked over his shoulder so often it was like he had a tic. I was embarrassed when the minicab dropped us off in front of the estate and tried to keep my distance from this ruined, limping skeleton as we went inside and up the stairs.

"Lanie," he said, as he sat me down. "You're a smart girl, I know that. Trig. You wouldn't know where your old Da could get a printer and some goop?"

I squeezed my hands into fists so tight my fingernails cut into my palms. I closed my eyes. "You've been in prison for ten years, Da. Ten. Years. You're going to risk another ten years to print out more blenders and pharma, more laptops and designer hats?"

He grinned. "I'm not stupid, Lanie. I've learned my lesson. There's no hat or laptop that's worth going to jail for. I'm not going to print none of that rubbish, never again." He had a cup of tea, and he drank it now like it was whisky, a sip and then a long, satisfied exhalation. He closed his eyes and leaned back in his chair.

"Come here, Lanie, let me whisper in your ear. Let me tell you the thing that I decided while I spent ten years in lockup. Come here and listen to your stupid Da."

I felt a guilty pang about ticking him off. He was off his rocker, that much was clear. God knew what he went through in prison. "What, Da?" I said, leaning in close.

"Lanie, I'm going to print more printers. Lots more printers. One for everyone. That's worth going to jail for. That's worth anything."

When Sysadmins Ruled the Earth

I've changed careers every two or three years ever since I dropped out of university in 1990, and one of the best gigs I ever had was working as a freelance systems administrator, working in the steam tunnels of the information age, pulling cables, configuring machines, keeping the backups running, kicking the network in its soft and vulnerable places. Sysadmins are the unsung heroes of the century, and if they're not busting you for sending racy IMs or engaging in unprofessional email conduct it's purely out of their own goodwill.

There's a pernicious myth that the Internet was designed to withstand a nuclear war; while that Strangelove wet dream was undoubtedly present in the hindbrains of the generals who greenlighted the network's R&D at companies like Rand and BBN, it wasn't really a big piece of the actual engineering and design.

Nevertheless, it does make for a compelling scenario, this vision of the sysadmins in their cages around the world, watching with held breath as the generator failed and the servers went dark, waiting out the long hours until the power and the air run out.

This story originally appeared in *Baen's Universe* Magazine, an admirable, high-quality online magazine edited by Eric Flint, himself a talented writer and a passionate advocate for open and free culture.

Listeners to my podcast heard this story as it was written, read aloud in serial chinks after each composing session. The pressure of listeners writing in, demanding to know what happened next, kept me honest and writing.

When Felix's special phone rang at two in the morning, Kelly rolled over and punched him in the shoulder and hissed, "Why didn't you turn that fucking thing off before bed?"

"Because I'm on call," he said.

"You're not a fucking doctor," she said, kicking him as he sat on the bed's edge, pulling on the pants he'd left on the floor before turning in. "You're a goddamned *systems administrator*."

"It's my job," he said.

"They work you like a government mule," she said. "You know I'm right. For Christ's sake, you're a father now, you can't go running off in the middle of the night every time someone's porn supply goes down. Don't answer that phone."

He knew she was right. He answered the phone.

"Main routers not responding. BGP not responding." The mechanical voice of the systems monitor didn't care if he cursed at it, so he did, and it made him feel a little better.

"Maybe I can fix it from here," he said. He could login to the UPS for the cage and reboot the routers. The UPS was in a different netblock, with its own independent routers on their own uninterruptible power supplies.

Kelly was sitting up in bed now, an indistinct shape against the headboard. "In five years of marriage, you have never once been able to fix anything from here." This time she was wrong–he fixed stuff from home all the time, but he did it discreetly and didn't make a fuss, so she didn't remember it. And she was right, too–he had logs that showed that after 1 AM, nothing could ever be fixed without driving out to the cage. Law of Infinite Universal Perversity–AKA Felix's Law.

Five minutes later Felix was behind the wheel. He hadn't been able to fix it from home. The independent router's netblock was offline, too. The last time that had happened, some dumbfuck construction worker had driven a ditch-witch through the main conduit into the data center and Felix had joined a cadre of fifty enraged sysadmins who'd stood atop the resulting pit for a week, screaming abuse at the poor bastards who labored 24-7 to splice ten thousand wires back together.

His phone went off twice more in the car and he let it override the stereo and play the mechanical status reports through the big, bassy speakers of more critical network infrastructure offline. Then Kelly called.

"Hi," he said.

"Don't cringe, I can hear the cringe in your voice."

He smiled involuntarily. "Check, no cringing."

"I love you, Felix," she said.

"I'm totally bonkers for you, Kelly. Go back to bed."

"2.0's awake," she said. The baby had been Beta Test when he was in her womb, and when her water broke, he got the call and dashed out of the office, shouting, *The Gold Master just shipped!* They'd started calling him 2.0 before he'd finished his first cry. "This little bastard was born to suck tit."

"I'm sorry I woke you," he said. He was almost at the data center. No traffic at 2 AM. He slowed down and pulled over before the entrance to the garage. He didn't want to lose Kelly's call underground.

"It's not waking me," she said. "You've been there for seven years. You have three juniors reporting to you. Give them the phone. You've paid your dues."

"I don't like asking my reports to do anything I wouldn't do," he said.

"You've done it," she said. "Please? I hate waking up alone in the night. I miss you most at night."

"Kelly—"

"I'm over being angry. I just miss you is all. You give me sweet dreams."

"OK," he said.

"Simple as that?"

"Exactly. Simple as that. Can't have you having bad dreams, and I've paid my dues. From now on, I'm only going on night call to cover holidays."

She laughed. "Sysadmins don't take holidays."

"This one will," he said. "Promise."

"You're wonderful," she said. "Oh, gross. 2.0 just dumped core all over my bathrobe."

"That's my boy," he said.

"Oh, that he is," she said. She hung up, and he piloted the car into the data-center lot, badging in and peeling up a bleary eyelid to let the retinal scanner get a good look at his sleep-depped eyeball.

He stopped at the machine to get himself a guarana/medafonil power-bar and a cup of lethal robot-coffee in a spill-proof clean-room sippy-cup. He wolfed down the bar and sipped the coffee, then let the inner door read his hand-geometry and size him up for a moment. It sighed open and gusted the airlock's load of positively pressurized air over him as he passed finally to the inner sanctum.

It was bedlam. The cages were designed to let two or three sysadmins maneuver around them at a time. Every other inch of cubic space was given over to humming racks of servers and routers and drives. Jammed among them were no fewer than twenty other sysadmins. It was a regular convention of black T-shirts with inexplicable slogans, bellies overlapping belts with phones and multitools.

Normally it was practically freezing in the cage, but all those bodies were overheating the small, enclosed space. Five or six looked up and grimaced when he came through. Two greeted him by name. He threaded his belly through the press and the cages, toward the Ardent racks in the back of the room.

"Felix." It was Van, who wasn't on call that night.

"What are you doing here?" he asked. "No need for both of us to be wrecked tomorrow."

"What? Oh. My personal box is over there. It went down around 1:30 and I got woken up by my process monitor. I should have called you and told you I was coming down–spared you the trip."

Felix's own server–a box he shared with five other friends–was in a rack one floor down. He wondered if it was offline, too.

"What's the story?"

"Massive flashworm attack. Some jackass with a zero-day exploit has got every Windows box on the net running Monte Carlo probes on every IP block, including IPv6. The big Ciscos all run administrative interfaces over v6, and they all fall over if they get more than ten simultaneous probes, which means that just about every interchange has gone down. DNS is screwy, too–like maybe someone poisoned the zone transfer last night. Oh, and there's an email and IM component that sends pretty lifelike messages to everyone in your address book, barfing up Eliza-dialog that keys off of your logged email and messages to get you to open a Trojan."

"Jesus."

"Yeah." Van was a type-two sysadmin, over six feet tall, long pony-tail, bobbing Adam's apple. Over his toast-rack chest, his tee said CHOOSE YOUR WEAPON and featured a row of polyhedral RPG dice.

Felix was a type-one admin, with an extra seventy or eighty pounds all around the middle, and a neat but full beard that he wore over his extra chins. His tee said HELLO CTHULHU and featured a cute, mouthless, Hello-Kitty-style Cthulhu. They'd known each other for fifteen years, having met on Usenet, then f2f at Toronto Freenet beer-sessions, a Star Trek convention or two, and eventually Felix had hired Van to work under him at Ardent. Van was reliable and methodical. Trained as an electrical engineer, he kept a procession of spiral notebooks filled with the details of every step he'd ever taken, with time and date.

"Not even PEBKAC this time," Van said. Problem Exists Between Keyboard And Chair. Email trojans fell into that category–if people were smart enough not to open suspect attachments, email trojans would be a thing of the past. But worms that ate Cisco routers weren't a problem with the lusers–they were the fault of incompetent engineers.

"No, it's Microsoft's fault," Felix said. "Any time I'm at work at 2 AM, it's either PEBKAC or Microsloth."

* * *

They ended up just unplugging the frigging routers from the Internet. Not Felix, of course, though he was itching to do it and get them rebooted after shutting down their IPv6 interfaces. It was done by a couple bull-goose Bastard Operators from Hell who had to turn two keys at once to get access to their cage—like guards in a Minuteman silo. Ninety-five percent of the long distance traffic in Canada went through this building. It had *better* security than most Minuteman silos.

Felix and Van got the Ardent boxes back online one at a time. They were being pounded by worm-probes—putting the routers back online just exposed the downstream cages to the attack. Every box on the Internet was drowning in worms, or creating worm attacks, or both. Felix managed to get through to NIST and Bugtraq after about a hundred timeouts, and download some kernel patches that should reduce the load the worms put on the machines in his care. It was 10 AM, and he was hungry enough to eat the ass out of a dead bear, but he recompiled his kernels and brought the machines back online. Van's long fingers flew over the administrative keyboard, his tongue protruding as he ran load-stats on each one.

"I had two hundred days of uptime on Greedo," Van said. Greedo was the oldest server in the rack, from the days when they'd named the boxes after Star Wars characters. Now they were all named after Smurfs, and they were running out of Smurfs and had started in on McDonaldland characters, starting with Van's laptop, Mayor McCheese.

"Greedo will rise again," Felix said. "I've got a 486 downstairs with over five years of uptime. It's going to break my heart to reboot it."

"What the everlasting shit do you use a 486 for?"

"Nothing. But who shuts down a machine with five years uptime? That's like euthanizing your grandmother."

"I wanna eat," Van said.

"Tell you what," Felix said. "We'll get your box up, then mine, then I'll take you to the Lakeview Lunch for breakfast pizzas and you can have the rest of the day off."

"You're on," Van said. "Man, you're too good to us grunts. You should keep us in a pit and beat us like all the other bosses. It's all we deserve."

* * *

"It's your phone," Van said. Felix extracted himself from the guts of the 486, which had refused to power up at all. He had cadged a spare power supply from some guys who ran a spam operation and was trying to get it fitted. He let Van hand him the phone, which had fallen off his belt while he was twisting to get at the back of the machine.

"Hey, Kel," he said. There was an odd, snuffling noise in the background. Static, maybe? 2.0 splashing in the bath? "Kelly?"

The line went dead. He tried to call back but didn't get anything—no ring nor voicemail. His phone finally timed out and said NETWORK ERROR.

"Dammit," he said, mildly. He clipped the phone to his belt. Kelly wanted to know when he was coming home or wanted him to pick something up for the family. She'd leave voice mail.

He was testing the power supply when his phone rang again. He snatched it up and answered it. "Kelly, hey, what's up?" He worked to keep anything like irritation out of his voice. He felt guilty: technically speaking, he had discharged his obligations to Ardent Financial LLC once the Ardent servers were back online. The past three hours had been purely personal—even if he planned on billing them to the company.

There was sobbing on the line.

"Kelly?" He felt the blood draining from his face and his toes were numb.

"Felix," she said, barely comprehensible through the sobbing. "He's dead, oh Jesus, he's dead."

"Who? *Who*, Kelly?"

"Will," she said.

Will? he thought. *Who the fuck is*—he dropped to his knees. William was the name they'd written on the birth certificate, though they'd called him 2.0 all along. Felix made an anguished sound, like a sick bark.

"I'm sick," she said, "I can't even stand anymore. Oh, Felix. I love you so much."

"Kelly? What's going on?"

"Everyone, everyone—" she said. "Only two channels left on the tube. Christ, Felix, it looks like dawn of the dead out the window—" He heard her retch. The phone started to break up, washing her puke noises back like an echoplex.

"Stay there, Kelly," he shouted as the line died. He punched 911, but the phone went NETWORK ERROR again as soon as he hit SEND.

He grabbed Mayor McCheese from Van and plugged it into the 486's network cable and launched Firefox off the command line and googled for the Metro Police site. Quickly, but not frantically, he searched for an online contact form. Felix didn't lose his head, ever. He solved problems and freaking out didn't solve problems.

He located an online form and wrote out the details of his conversation with Kelly like he was filing a bug report, his fingers fast, his description complete, and then he hit SUBMIT.

Van had read over his shoulder. "Felix–" he began.

"God," Felix said. He was sitting on the floor of the cage and he slowly pulled himself upright. Van took the laptop and tried some news sites, but they were all timing out. Impossible to say if it was because something terrible was happening or because the network was limping under the superworm.

"I need to get home," Felix said.

"I'll drive you," Van said. "You can keep calling your wife."

They made their way to the elevators. One of the building's few windows was there, a thick, shielded porthole. They peered through it as they waited for the elevator. Not much traffic for a Wednesday. Were there more police cars than usual?

"*Oh my God–*" Van pointed.

The CN Tower, a giant white-elephant needle of a building loomed to the east of them. It was askew, like a branch stuck in wet sand. Was it moving? It was. It was heeling over, slowly, but gaining speed, falling northeast toward the financial district. In a second, it slid over the tipping point and crashed down. They felt the shock, then heard it, the whole building rocking from the impact. A cloud of dust rose from the wreckage, and there was more thunder as the world's tallest freestanding structure crashed through building after building.

"The Broadcast Centre's coming down," Van said. It was–the CBC's towering building was collapsing in slow motion. People ran every way, were crushed by falling masonry. Seen through the porthole, it was like watching a neat CGI trick downloaded from a file-sharing site.

Sysadmins were clustering around them now, jostling to see the destruction.

"What happened?" one of them asked.

"The CN Tower fell down," Felix said. He sounded far away in his own ears.

"Was it the virus?"

"The worm? What?" Felix focused on the guy, who was a young admin with just a little type-two flab around the middle.

"Not the worm," the guy said. "I got an email that the whole city's quarantined because of some virus. Bioweapon, they say." He handed Felix his Blackberry.

Felix was so engrossed in the report–purportedly forwarded from Health Canada that he didn't even notice that all the lights had gone out. Then he did, and he pressed the Blackberry back into its owner's hand and let out one small sob.

* * *

The generators kicked in a minute later. Sysadmins stampeded for the stairs. Felix grabbed Van by the arm, pulled him back.

"Maybe we should wait this out in the cage," he said.

"What about Kelly?" Van said.

Felix felt like he was going to throw up. "We should get into the cage, now." The cage had microparticulate air filters.

They ran upstairs to the big cage. Felix opened the door and then let it hiss shut behind him.

"Felix, you need to get home–"

"It's a bioweapon," Felix said. "Superbug. We'll be OK in here, I think, so long as the filters hold out."

"What?"

"Get on IRC," he said.

They did. Van had Mayor McCheese and Felix used Smurfette. They skipped around the chat channels until they found one with some familiar handles.

> pentagons gone/white house too

> MY NEIGHBORS BARFING BLOOD OFF HIS BALCONY IN SAN DIEGO

> Someone knocked over the Gherkin. Bankers are fleeing the City like rats.

> I heard that the Ginza's on fire

Felix typed: I'm in Toronto. We just saw the CN Tower fall. I've heard reports of bioweapons, something very fast.

Van read this and said, "You don't know how fast it is, Felix. Maybe we were all exposed three days ago."

Felix closed his eyes. "If that were so we'd be feeling some symptoms, I think."

> Looks like an EMP took out Hong Kong and maybe Paris–realtime sat footage shows them completely dark, and all netblocks there aren't routing

> You're in Toronto?

It was an unfamiliar handle.

```
> Yes—on Front Street
> my sisters at UofT and i cnt reach her—can you
  call her?
> No phone service
```

Felix typed, staring at NETWORK PROBLEMS.

"I have a soft phone on Mayor McCheese," Van said, launching his voice-over-IP app. "I just remembered."

Felix took the laptop from him and punched in his home number. It rang once, then there was a flat, blatting sound like an ambulance siren in an Italian movie.

```
> No phone service
```

Felix typed again.

He looked up at Van and saw that his skinny shoulders were shaking. Van said, "Holy motherfucking shit. The world is ending."

* * *

Felix pried himself off of IRC an hour later. Atlanta had burned. Manhattan was hot—radioactive enough to screw up the Webcams looking out over Lincoln Plaza. Everyone blamed Islam until it became clear that Mecca was a smoking pit and the Saudi Royals had been hanged before their palaces.

His hands were shaking, and Van was quietly weeping in the far corner of the cage. He tried calling home again, and then the police. It didn't work any better than it had the last twenty times.

He sshed into his box downstairs and grabbed his mail. Spam, spam, spam. More spam. Automated messages. There–an urgent message from the intrusion detection system in the Ardent cage.

He opened it and read quickly. Someone was crudely, repeatedly probing his routers. It didn't match a worm's signature, either. He followed the trace route and discovered that the attack had originated in the same building as him, a system in a cage one floor below.

He had procedures for this. He portscanned his attacker and found that port 1337 was open–1337 was "leet" or "elite" in hacker number/letter substitution code. That was the kind of port that a worm left open to slither in and out of. He googled known sploits that left a listener on port 1337, narrowed this down based on the fingerprinted operating system of the compromised server, and then he had it.

It was an ancient worm, one that every box should have been patched against years before. No mind. He had the client for it, and he used it to create a root account for himself on the box, which he then logged into, and took a look around.

There was one other user logged in, "scaredy," and he checked the proccess monitor and saw that scaredy had spawned all the hundreds of processes that were probing him and plenty of other boxen.

He opened a chat:

```
> Stop probing my server
```

He expected bluster, guilt, denial. He was surprised.

> Are you in the Front Street data center?

> Yes

> Christ I thought I was the last one alive. I'm on the fourth floor. I think there's a bioweapon attack outside. I don't want to leave the clean room.

Felix whooshed out a breath.

> You were probing me to get me to trace back to you?

> Yeah

> That was smart

Clever bastard.

> I'm on the sixth floor, I've got one more with me.

> What do you know?

Felix pasted in the IRC log and waited while the other guy digested it. Van stood up and paced. His eyes were glazed over.

"Van? Pal?"

"I have to pee," he said.

"No opening the door," Felix said. "I saw an empty Mountain Dew bottle in the trash there."

"Right," Van said. He walked like a zombie to the trash can and pulled out the empty magnum. He turned his back.

> I'm Felix

> Will

Felix's stomach did a slow somersault as he thought about 2.0.

"Felix, I think I need to go outside," Van said. He was moving toward the airlock door. Felix dropped his keyboard and struggled to his feet and ran headlong to Van, tackling him before he reached the door.

"Van," he said, looking into his friend's glazed, unfocused eyes. "Look at me, Van."

"I need to go," Van said. "I need to get home and feed the cats."

"There's something out there, something fast-acting and lethal. Maybe it will blow away with the wind. Maybe it's already gone. But we're going to sit here until we know for sure or until we have no choice. Sit down, Van. Sit."

"I'm cold, Felix."

It was freezing. Felix's arms were broken out in gooseflesh and his feet felt like blocks of ice.

"Sit against the servers, by the vents. Get the exhaust heat." He found a rack and nestled up against it.

```
> Are you there?
> Still here-sorting out some logistics
> How long until we can go out?
> I have no idea
```

No one typed anything for quite some time then.

* * *

Felix had to use the Mountain Dew bottle twice. Then Van used it again. Felix tried calling Kelly again. The Metro Police site was down.

Finally, he slid back against the servers and wrapped his arms around his knees and wept like a baby.

After a minute, Van came over and sat beside him, with his arm around Felix's shoulder.

"They're dead, Van," Felix said. "Kelly and my s-son. My family is gone."

"You don't know for sure," Van said.

"I'm sure enough," Felix said. "Christ, it's all over, isn't it?"

"We'll gut it out a few more hours and then head out. Things should be getting back to normal soon. The fire department will fix it. They'll mobilize the Army. It'll be OK."

Felix's ribs hurt. He hadn't cried since–since 2.0 was born. He hugged his knees harder.

Then the doors opened.

The two sysadmins who entered were wild-eyed. One had a tee that said TALK NERDY TO ME and the other one was wearing an Electronic Frontiers Canada shirt.

"Come on," TALK NERDY said. "We're all getting together on the top floor. Take the stairs."

Felix found he was holding his breath.

"If there's a bioagent in the building, we're all infected," TALK NERDY said. "Just go, we'll meet you there."

"There's one on the sixth floor," Felix said, as he climbed to his feet.

"Will, yeah, we got him. He's up there."

TALK NERDY was one of the Bastard Operators from Hell who'd unplugged the big routers. Felix and Van climbed the stairs slowly, their steps echoing in the deserted shaft. After the frigid air of the cage, the stairwell felt like a sauna.

There was a cafeteria on the top floor, with working toilets, water and coffee and vending machine food. There was an uneasy queue of sysadmins before each. No one met anyone's eye. Felix wondered which one was Will and then he joined the vending machine queue.

He got a couple more energy bars and a gigantic cup of vanilla coffee before running out of change. Van had scored them some table space and Felix set the stuff down before him and got in the toilet line. "Just save some for me," he said, tossing an energy bar in front of Van.

By the time they were all settled in, thoroughly evacuated, and eating, TALK NERDY and his friend had returned again. They cleared off the cash register at the end of the food-prep area and TALK NERDY got up on it. Slowly the conversation died down.

"I'm Uri Popovich, this is Diego Rosenbaum. Thank you all for coming up here. Here's what we know for sure: the building's been on generators for three hours now. Visual observation indicates that we're the only building in central Toronto with working power—which should hold out for three more days. There is a bioagent of unknown origin loose beyond our doors. It kills quickly, within hours, and it is aerosolized. You get it from breathing bad air. No one has opened any of the exterior doors to this building since five this morning. No one will open the doors until I give the go-ahead.

"Attacks on major cities all over the world have left emergency responders in chaos. The attacks are electronic, biological, nuclear, and conventional explosives, and they are very widespread. I'm a security engineer, and where I come from, attacks in this kind of cluster are usually viewed as opportunistic: group B blows up a bridge because everyone is off taking care of group A's dirty nuke event. It's smart. An Aum Shin Rikyo cell in Seoul gassed the subways there about 2 AM Eastern—that's the earliest event we can locate, so it may have been the Archduke that broke the camel's back. We're pretty sure that Aum Shin Rikyo couldn't be behind this kind of mayhem: they have no history of infowar and have never shown the kind of organizational acumen necessary to take out so many targets at once. Basically, they're not smart enough.

"We're holing up here for the foreseeable future, at least until the bioweapon has been identified and dispersed. We're going to staff the racks and keep the networks up. This is critical infrastructure, and it's our job to make sure it's got five nines of uptime. In times of national emergency, our responsibility to do that doubles."

One sysadmin put up his hand. He was very daring in a green Incredible Hulk ring-tee, and he was at the young end of the scale.

"Who died and made you king?"

"I have controls for the main security system, keys to every cage, and passcodes for the exterior doors—they're all locked now, by the way. I'm the one who got everyone up here first and called the meeting. I don't care if someone else wants this job, it's a shitty one. But someone needs to have this job."

"You're right," the kid said. "And I can do it every bit as well as you. My name's Will Sario."

Popovich looked down his nose at the kid. "Well, if you'll let me finish talking, maybe I'll hand things over to you when I'm done."

"Finish, by all means." Sario turned his back on him and walked to the window. He stared out of it intensely. Felix's gaze was drawn to it, and he saw that there were several oily smoke plumes rising up from the city.

Popovich's momentum was broken. "So that's what we're going to do," he said.

The kid looked around after a stretched moment of silence. "Oh, is it my turn now?"

There was a round of good-natured chuckling.

"Here's what I think: the world is going to shit. There are coordinated attacks on every critical piece of infrastructure. There's only one way that those attacks could be so well coordinated: via the Internet. Even if you buy the thesis that the attacks are all opportunistic, we need to ask how an opportunistic attack could be organized in minutes: the Internet."

"So you think we should shut down the Internet?" Popovich laughed a little but stopped when Sario said nothing.

"We saw an attack last night that nearly killed the Internet. A little DoS on the critical routers, a little DNS-foo, and down it goes like a preacher's daughter. Cops and the military are a bunch of technophobic lusers, they hardly rely on the net at all. If we take the Internet down, we'll disproportionately disadvantage the attackers, while only inconveniencing the defenders. When the time comes, we can rebuild it."

"You're shitting me," Popovich said. His jaw literally hung open.

"It's logical," Sario said. "Lots of people don't like coping with logic when it dictates hard decisions. That's a problem with people, not logic."

There was a buzz of conversation that quickly turned into a roar.

"Shut UP!" Popovich hollered. The conversation dimmed by one Watt. Popovich yelled again, stamping his foot on the countertop. Finally there was a semblance of order. "One at a time," he said. He was flushed red, his hands in his pockets.

One sysadmin was for staying. Another for going. They should hide in the cages. They should inventory their supplies and appoint a quartermaster. They should go outside and find the police, or volunteer at hospitals. They should appoint defenders to keep the front door secure.

Felix found to his surprise that he had his hand in the air. Popovich called on him.

"My name is Felix Tremont," he said, getting up on one of the tables, drawing out his PDA. "I want to read you something.

"'Governments of the Industrial World, you weary giants of flesh and steel, I come from Cyberspace, the new home of Mind. On behalf of the future, I ask you of the past to leave us alone. You are not welcome among us. You have no sovereignty where we gather.

"'We have no elected government, nor are we likely to have one, so I address you with no greater authority than that with which liberty itself always speaks. I declare the global social space we are building to be naturally independent of the tyrannies you seek to impose on us. You have no moral right to rule us nor do you possess any methods of enforcement we have true reason to fear.

"'Governments derive their just powers from the consent of the governed. You have neither solicited nor received ours. We did not invite you. You do not know us, nor do you know our world. Cyberspace does not lie within your borders. Do not think that you can build it, as though it were a public construction project. You cannot. It is an act of nature and it grows itself through our collective actions.'

"That's from the Declaration of Independence of Cyberspace. It was written twelve years ago. I thought it was one of the most beautiful things I'd ever read. I wanted my kid to grow up in a world where cyberspace was free–and where that freedom infected the real world, so meatspace got freer, too."

He swallowed hard and scrubbed at his eyes with the back of his hand. Van awkwardly patted him on the shoe.

"My beautiful son and my beautiful wife died today. Millions more, too. The city is literally in flames. Whole cities have disappeared from the map."

He coughed up a sob and swallowed it again.

"All around the world, people like us are gathered in buildings like this. They were trying to recover from last night's worm when disaster struck. We have independent power. Food. Water.

"We have the network, that the bad guys use so well and that the good guys have never figured out.

"We have a shared love of liberty that comes from caring about and caring for the network. We are in charge of the most important organizational and governmental tool the world has ever seen. We are the closest thing to a government the world has right now. Geneva is a crater. The East River is on fire and the UN is evacuated.

"The Distributed Republic of Cyberspace weathered this storm basically unscathed. We are the custodians of a deathless, monstrous, wonderful machine, one with the potential to rebuild a better world.

"I have nothing to live for but that."

There were tears in Van's eyes. He wasn't the only one. They didn't applaud him, but they did one better. They maintained respectful, total silence for seconds that stretched to a minute.

"How do we do it?" Popovich said, without a trace of sarcasm.

* * *

The newsgroups were filling up fast. They'd announced them in news.admin.net-abuse.email, where all the spamfighters hung out, and where there was a tight culture of camaraderie in the face of full-out attack.

The new group was alt.november5-disaster.recovery, with .recovery.goverance, .recovery.finance, .recovery.logistics and .recovery.defense hanging off of it. Bless the wooly alt. hierarchy and all those who sail in her.

The sysadmins came out of the woodwork. The Googleplex was online, with the stalwart Queen Kong bossing a gang of rollerbladed grunts who wheeled through the gigantic data center swapping out dead boxen and hitting reboot switches. The Internet Archive was offline in the Presidio, but the mirror in Amsterdam was live and they'd redirected the DNS so that you'd hardly know the difference. Amazon was down. Paypal was up. Blogger, Typepad, and Livejournal were all up, and filling with millions of posts from scared survivors huddling together for electronic warmth.

The Flickr photostreams were horrific. Felix had to unsubscribe from them after he caught a photo of a woman and a baby, dead in a kitchen, twisted into an agonized heiroglyph by the bioagent. They didn't look like Kelly and 2.0, but they didn't have to. He started shaking and couldn't stop.

Wikipedia was up, but limping under load. The spam poured in as though nothing had changed. Worms roamed the network.

.recovery.logistics was where most of the action was.

```
> We can use the newsgroup voting mechanism to hold
  regional elections
```

Felix knew that this would work. Usenet newsgroup votes had been running for more than twenty years without a substantial hitch.

> We'll elect regional representatives and they'll pick a Prime Minister.

The Americans insisted on President, which Felix didn't like. Seemed too partisan. His future wouldn't be the American future. The American future had gone up with the White House. He was building a bigger tent than that.

There were French sysadmins online from France Telecom. The EBU's data center had been spared in the attacks that hammered Geneva, and it was filled with wry Germans whose English was better than Felix's. They got on well with the remains of the BBC team in Canary Wharf.

They spoke polyglot English in .recovery.logistics, and Felix had momentum on his side. Some of the admins were cooling out the inevitable stupid flamewars with the practice of long years. Some were chipping in useful suggestions.

Surprisingly few thought that Felix was off his rocker.

> I think we should hold elections as soon as possible. Tomorrow at the latest. We can't rule justly without the consent of the governed.

Within seconds the reply landed in his inbox.

> You can't be serious. Consent of the governed?

```
Unless I miss my guess, most of the people you're
proposing to govern are puking their guts out,
hiding under their desks, or wandering shell-
shocked through the city streets. When do THEY
get a vote?
```

Felix had to admit she had a point. Queen Kong was sharp. Not many woman sysadmins, and that was a genuine tragedy. Women like Queen Kong were too good to exclude from the field. He'd have to hack a solution to get women balanced out in his new government. Require each region to elect one woman and one man?

He happily clattered into argument with her. The elections would be the next day; he'd see to it.

* * *

"Prime Minister of Cyberspace? Why not call yourself the Grand Poobah of the Global Data Network? It's more dignified, sounds cooler, and it'll get you just as far." Will had the sleeping spot next to him, up in the cafeteria, with Van on the other side. The room smelled like a dingleberry: twenty-five sysadmins who hadn't washed in at least a day all crammed into the same room. For some of them, it had been much, much longer than a day.

"Shut up, Will," Van said. "You wanted to try to knock the Internet offline."

"Correction: I *want* to knock the Internet offline. Present tense."

Felix cracked one eye. He was so tired, it was like lifting weights.

"Look, Sario–if you don't like my platform, put one of your own forward. There are plenty of people who think I'm full of shit and I respect them for that, since they're all running opposite me or backing someone who is. That's your choice. What's not on the menu is nagging and complaining. Bedtime now, or get up and post your platform."

Sario sat up slowly, unrolling the jacket he had been using for a pillow and putting it on. "Screw you guys, I'm out of here."

"I thought he'd never leave," Felix said and turned over, lying awake a long time, thinking about the election.

There were other people in the running. Some of them weren't even sysadmins. A U.S. Senator on retreat at his summer place in Wyoming had generator power and a satellite phone. Somehow he'd found the right newsgroup and thrown his hat into the ring. Some anarchist hackers in Italy strafed the group all night long, posting broken-English screeds about the political bankruptcy of "governance" in the new world. Felix looked at their netblock and determined that they were probably holed up in a small Interaction Design institute near Turin. Italy had been hit very bad, but out in the small town, this cell of anarchists had taken up residence.

A surprising number were running on a platform of shutting down the Internet. Felix had his doubts about whether this was even possible, but he thought he understood the impulse to finish the work and the world. Why not?

He fell asleep thinking about the logistics of shutting down the Internet and dreamed bad dreams in which he was the network's sole defender.

He woke to a papery, itchy sound. He rolled over and saw that

Van was sitting up, his jacket balled up in his lap, vigorously scratching his skinny arms. They'd gone the color of corned beef and had a scaly look. In the light streaming through the cafeteria windows, skin motes floated and danced in great clouds.

"What are you doing?" Felix sat up. Watching Van's fingernails rip into his skin made him itch in sympathy. It had been three days since he'd last washed his hair and his scalp sometimes felt like there were little egg-laying insects picking their way through it. He'd adjusted his glasses the night before and had touched the back of his ears; his finger came away shining with thick sebum. He got blackheads in the backs of his ears when he didn't shower for a couple of days, and sometimes gigantic, deep boils that Kelly finally popped with sick relish.

"Scratching," Van said. He went to work on his head, sending a cloud of dandruff-crud into the sky, there to join the scurf that he'd already eliminated from his extremeties. "Christ, I itch all over."

Felix took Mayor McCheese from Van's backpack and plugged it into one of the Ethernet cables that snaked all over the floor. He googled everything he could think of that could be related to this. "Itchy" yielded 40,600,000 links. He tried compound queries and got slightly more discriminating links.

"I think it's stress-related excema," Felix said, finally.

"I don't get excema," Van said.

Felix showed him some lurid photos of red, angry skin flaked with white. "Stress-related excema," he said, reading the caption.

Van examined his arms. "I have excema," he said.

"Says here to keep it moisturized and to try cortisone cream. You might try the first aid kit in the second-floor toilets. I think I saw some there." Like all of the sysadmins, Felix had had a bit of a rummage around the offices, bathrooms, kitchen, and storerooms, squirreling away a roll of toilet paper in his shoulder bag along with three or four power-bars. They were sharing out the food in the caf by unspoken agreement, every sysadmin watching every other for signs of gluttony and hoarding. All were convinced that there was hoarding and gluttony going on out of eyeshot, because all were guilty of it themselves when no one else was watching.

Van got up and when his face hove into the light, Felix saw how puffed his eyes were. "I'll post to the mailing list for some antihistamine," Felix said. There had been four mailing lists and three wikis for the survivors in the building within hours of the first meeting's close, and in the intervening days they'd settled on just one. Felix was still on a little mailing list with five of his most trusted friends, two of whom were trapped in cages in other countries. He suspected that the rest of the sysadmins were doing the same.

Van stumbled off. "Good luck on the elections," he said, patting Felix on the shoulder.

Felix stood and paced, stopping to stare out the grubby windows. The fires still burned in Toronto, more than before. He'd tried to find mailing lists or blogs that Torontonians were posting to, but the only ones he'd found were being run by other geeks in other data centers. It was possible–likely, even–that there were survivors out there who had more pressing priorities than posting to the Internet. His home phone still worked about half the time but he'd stopped calling it after the second day, when hearing Kelly's voice on the voice mail for the fiftieth time had made him cry in the middle of a planning meeting. He wasn't the only one.

Election day. Time to face the music.

```
> Are you nervous?
> Nope.
```

Felix typed.

```
> I don't much care if I win, to be honest. I"m just
  glad we're doing this. The alternative was sit-
  ting around with our thumbs up our ass, waiting
  for someone to crack up and open the door.
```

The cursor hung. Queen Kong was very high latency as she bossed her gang of Googloids around the Googleplex, doing everything she could to keep her data center online. Three of the offshore cages had gone offline and two of their six redundant network links were smoked. Lucky for her, queries-per-second were way down.

```
> There's still China
```

she typed. Queen Kong had a big board with a map of the world colored in Google-queries-per-second and could do magic with it, showing the drop-off over time in colorful charts. She'd uploaded lots of video clips showing how the plague and the bombs had swept the world: the initial upswell of queries from people wanting to find out what was going on, then the grim, precipitous shelving off as the plagues took hold.

```
> China's still running about ninety percent nominal.
```

Felix shook his head.

> You can't think that they're responsible
> No

She typed, but then she started to key something and then stopped.

> No, of course not. I believe the Popovich Hypothesis. This is a bunch of assholes all using the rest for cover. But China put them down harder and faster than anyone else. Maybe we've finally found a use for totalitarian states.

Felix couldn't resist. He typed:

> You're lucky your boss can't see you type that. You guys were pretty enthusiastic participants in the Great Firewall of China.
> Wasn't my idea

she typed.

> And my boss is dead. They're probably all dead. The whole Bay Area got hit hard, and then there was the quake.

They'd watched the USGS's automated data stream from the 6.9 that trashed northern Cal from Gilroy to Sebastapol. Soma Webcams revealed the scope of the damage–gas main explosions, seismically retrofitted buildings crumpling like piles of children's blocks after a good kicking. The Googleplex, floating on a series of gigantic steel springs, had shook like a plateful of jello, but the racks had stayed in place and the worst injury they'd had was a badly bruised eye on a sysadmin who'd caught a flying cable-crimper in the face.

```
> Sorry. I forgot.
> It's OK. We all lost people, right?
> Yeah. Yeah. Anyway, I'm not worried about the elec-
  tion. Whoever wins, at least we're doing SOMETHING
> Not if they vote for one of the fuckrags
```

Fuckrag was the epithet that some of the sysadmins were using to describe the contingent that wanted to shut down the Internet. Queen Kong had coined it—apparently it had started life as a catchall term to describe the clueless IT managers that she'd chewed up through her career.

```
> They won't. They're just tired and sad is all.
  Your endorsement will carry the day
```

The Googloids were one of the largest and most powerful blocs left behind, along with the satellite uplink crews and the remaining transoceanic crews. Queen Kong's endorsement had come as a surprise and he'd sent her an email that she'd replied to tersely: "can't have the fuckrags in charge."

```
> gtg
```

she typed and then her connection dropped. He fired up a browser and called up google.com. The browser timed out. He hit reload, and then again, and then the Google front-page came back up. Whatever had hit Queen Kong's workplace–power failure, worms, another quake–she had fixed it. He snorted when he saw that they'd replaced the O's in the Google logo with little planet Earths with mushroom clouds rising from them.

* * *

"Got anything to eat?" Van said to him. It was midafternoon, not that time particularly passed in the data center. Felix patted his pockets. They'd put a quartermaster in charge, but not before everyonc had snagged some chow out of the machines. He'd had a dozen power-bars and some apples. He'd taken a couple sandwiches but had wisely eaten them first before they got stale.

"One power-bar left," he said. He'd noticed a certain looseness in his waistline that morning and had briefly relished it. Then he'd remembered Kelly's teasing about his weight and he'd cried some. Then he'd eaten two power-bars, leaving him with just one left.

"Oh," Van said. His face was hollower than ever, his shoulders sloping in on his toast-rack chest.

"Here," Felix said. "Vote Felix."

Van took the power-bar from him and then put it down on the table. "OK, I want to give this back to you and say, 'No, I couldn't,' but I'm fucking hungry, so I'm just going to take it and eat it, OK?"

"That's fine by me," Felix said. "Enjoy."

"How are the elections coming?" Van said, once he'd licked the wrapper clean.

"Dunno," Felix said. "Haven't checked in a while." He'd been winning by a slim margin a few hours before. Not having his laptop was a major handicap when it came to stuff like this. Up in the cages, there were a dozen more like him, poor bastards who'd left the house on Der Tag without thinking to snag something WiFi-enabled.

"You're going to get smoked," Sario said, sliding in next to them. He'd become famous in the center for never sleeping, for eavesdropping, for picking fights in RL that had the ill-considered heat of a Usenet flamewar. "The winner will be someone who understands a couple of fundamental facts." He held up a fist, then ticked off his bullet points by raising a finger at a time. "Point: The terrorists are using the Internet to destroy the world, and we need to destroy the Internet first. Point: Even if I'm wrong, the whole thing is a joke. We'll run out of generator-fuel soon enough. Point: Or if we don't, it will be because the old world will be back and running, and it won't give a crap about your new world. Point: We're gonna run out of food before we run out of shit to argue about it or reasons not to go outside. We have the chance to do something to help the world recover: we can kill the net and cut it off as a tool for bad guys. Or we can rearrange some more deck chairs on the bridge of your personal Titanic in the service of some sweet dream about an 'independent cyberspace.'"

The thing was that Sario was right. They would be out of fuel in two days—intermittent power from the grid had stretched their generator lifespan. And if you bought his hypothesis that the Internet was primarily being used as a tool to organize more mayhem, shutting it down would be the right thing to do.

But Felix's daughter and his wife were dead. He didn't want to rebuild the old world. He wanted a new one. The old world was one that didn't have any place for him. Not anymore.

Van scratched his raw, flaking skin. Puffs of dander and scurff swirled in the musty, greasy air. Sario curled a lip at him. "That is disgusting. We're breathing recycled air, you know. Whatever leprosy is eating you, aerosolizing it into the air supply is pretty antisocial."

"You're the world's leading authority on antisocial, Sario," Van said. Go away or I'll multitool you to death." He stopped scratching and patted his sheathed multipliers like a gunslinger.

"Yeah, I'm antisocial. I've got Asperger's and I haven't taken any meds in four days. What's your fucking excuse."

Van scratched some more. "I'm sorry," he said. "I didn't know."

Sario cracked up. "Oh, you are priceless. I'd bet that three quarters of this bunch is borderline autistic. Me, I'm just an asshole. But I'm one who isn't afraid to tell the truth, and that makes me better than you, dickweed."

"Fuckrag," Felix said, "fuck off."

* * *

They had less than a day's worth of fuel when Felix was elected the first ever Prime Minister of Cyberspace. The first count was spoiled by a bot that spammed the voting process and they lost a critical day while they added up the votes a second time.

But by then, it was all seeming like more of a joke. Half the data centers had gone dark. Queen Kong's net-maps of Google queries were looking grimmer and grimmer as more of the world went offline, though she maintained a leader-board of new and rising queries–largely related to health, shelter, sanitation, and self-defense.

Worm-load slowed. Power was going off to many home PC users, and staying off, so their compromised PCs were going dark. The backbones were still lit up and blinking, but the missives from those data centers were looking more and more desperate. Felix hadn't eaten in a day and neither had anyone in a satellite Earthstation of transoceanic head-end.

Water was running short, too.

Popovich and Rosenbaum came and got him before he could do more than answer a few congratulatory messages and post a canned acceptance speech to the newsgroups.

"We're going to open the doors," Popovich said. Like all of them, he'd lost weight and waxed scruffy and oily. His BO was like a cloud coming off trash bags behind a fish market on a sunny day. Felix was quite sure he smelled no better.

"You're going to go for a reccy? Get more fuel? We can charter a working group for it–great idea."

Rosenbaum shook his head sadly. "We're going to go find our families. Whatever is out there has burned itself out. Or it hasn't. Either way, there's no future in here."

"What about network maintenance?" Felix said, though he knew the answers. "Who'll keep the routers up?"

"We'll give you the root passwords to everything," Popovich said. His hands were shaking and his eyes were bleary. Like many of the smokers stuck in the data center, he'd gone cold turkey this week.

They'd run out of caffeine products two days earlier, too. The smokers had it rough.

"And I'll just stay here and keep everything online?"

"You and anyone else who cares anymore."

Felix knew that he'd squandered his opportunity. The election had seemed noble and brave, but in hindsight all it had been was an excuse for infighting when they should have been figuring out what to do next. The problem was that there was nothing to do next.

"I can't make you stay," he said.

"Yeah, you can't." Popovich turned on his heel and walked out. Rosenbaum watched him go, then he gripped Felix's shoulder and squeezed it.

"Thank you, Felix. It was a beautiful dream. It still is. Maybe we'll find something to eat and some fuel and come back."

Rosenbaum had a sister whom he'd been in contact with over IM for the first days after the crisis broke. Then she'd stopped answering. The sysadmins were split among those who'd had a chance to say good-bye and those who hadn't. Each was sure the other had it better.

They posted about it on the internal newsgroup–they were still geeks, after all, and there was a little honor guard on the ground floor, geeks who watched them pass toward the double doors. They manipulated the keypads and the steel shutters lifted, then the first set of doors opened. They stepped into the vestibule and pulled the doors shut behind them. The front doors opened. It was very bright and sunny outside, and apart from how empty it was, it looked very normal. Heartbreakingly so.

The two took a tentative step out into the world. Then another. They turned to wave at the assembled masses. Then they both grabbed their throats and began to jerk and twitch, crumpling in a heap on the ground.

"Shiii–!" was all Felix managed to choke out before they both dusted themselves off and stood up, laughing so hard they were clutching their sides. They waved once more and turned on their heels.

"Man, those guys are sick," Van said. He scratched his arms, which had long, bloody scratches on them. His clothes were so covered in scurf they looked like they'd been dusted with icing sugar.

"I thought it was pretty funny," Felix said.

"Christ, I'm hungry," Van said, conversationally.

"Lucky for you, we've got all the packets we can eat," Felix said.

"You're too good to us grunts, Mr. President," Van said.

"Prime Minister," he said. "And you're no grunt, you're the Deputy Prime Minister. You're my designated ribbon-cutter and hander-out of oversized novelty checks."

It buoyed both of their spirits. Watching Popovich and Rosenbaum go, it buoyed them up. Felix knew then that they'd all be going soon.

That had been preordained by the fuel supply, but who wanted to wait for the fuel to run out, anyway?

* * *

```
> half my crew split this morning
```

Queen Kong typed. Google was holding up pretty good anyway, of course. The load on the servers was a lot lighter than it had been since the days when Google fit on a bunch of hand-built PCs under a desk at Stanford.

> we're down to a quarter

Felix typed back. It was only a day since Popovich and Rosenbaum left, but the traffic on the newsgroups had fallen down to near zero. He and Van hadn't had much time to play Republic of Cyberspace. They'd been too busy learning the systems that Popovich had turned over to them, the big, big routers that had gone on acting as the major interchange for all the network backbones in Canada.

Still, someone posted to the newsgroups every now and again, generally to say good-bye. The old flamewars about who would be PM, or whether they would shut down the network, or who took too much food—it was all gone.

He reloaded the newsgroup. There was a typical message.

> Runaway processes on Solaris

> Uh, hi. I'm just a lightweight MSCE but I'm the only one awake here and four of the DSLAMs just went down. Looks like there's some custom accounting code that's trying to figure out how much to bill our corporate customers and it's spawned ten thousand threads and its eating all the swap. I just want to kill it but I can't seem to do that. Is there some magic invocation I need to do to get this goddamned weenix box to kill this shit? I mean, it's not as if any of our customers are ever going to pay us again. I'd ask the guy who wrote this code, but he's pretty much dead as far as anyone can work out.

He reloaded. There was a response. It was short, authoritative, and helpful—just the sort of thing you almost never saw in a high-caliber newsgroup when a noob posted a dumb question. The apocalypse had awoken the spirit of patient helpfulness in the world's sysop community.

Van shoulder-surfed him. "Holy shit, who knew he had it in him?"

He looked at the message again. It was from Will Sario.

He dropped into his chat window.

```
> sario i thought you wanted the network dead why
  are you helping msces fix their boxen?
> sheepish grin Gee Mr PM, maybe I just can't bear to
  watch a computer suffer at the hands of an amateur.
```

He flipped to the channel with Queen Kong in it.

```
> How long?
> Since I slept? Two days. Until we run out of fuel?
  Three days. Since we ran out of food? Two days.
> Jeez. I didn't sleep last night either. We're a
  little shorthanded around here.
> asl? Im monica and I live in pasadena and Im bored
  with my homework. WOuld you like to download my pic???
```

The trojan bots were all over IRC these days, jumping to every channel that had any traffic on it. Sometimes you caught five or six flirting with each other. It was pretty weird to watch a piece of malware try to con another instance of itself into downloading a trojan.

They both kicked the bot off the channel simultaneously. He had a script for it now. The spam hadn't even tailed off a little.

> How come the spam isn't reducing? Half the goddamned data centers have gone dark

Queen Kong paused a long time before typing. As had become automatic when she went high-latency, he reloaded the Google homepage. Sure enough, it was down.

> Sario, you got any food?

> You won't miss a couple more meals, Your Excellency

Van had gone back to Mayor McCheese but he was in the same channel.

"What a dick. You're looking pretty buff, though, dude."

Van didn't look so good. He looked like you could knock him over with a stiff breeze and he had a phlegmy, weak quality to his speech.

> hey kong everything ok?

> everything's fine just had to go kick some ass

"How's the traffic, Van?"

"Down 25 percent from this morning," he said. There were a bunch of nodes whose connections routed through them. Presumably most of these were home or commercial customers in places where the power was still on and the phone company's COs were still alive.

Every once in a while, Felix would wiretap the connections to see if he could find a person who had news of the wide world. Almost all of it was automated traffic, though: network backups, status updates. Spam. Lots of spam.

> Spam's still up because the services that stop spam are failing faster than the services that create it. All the antiworm stuff is centralized in a couple places. The bad stuff is on a million zombie computers. If only the lusers had had the good sense to turn off their home PCs before keeling over or taking off

> at the rate were going well be routing nothing but spam by dinnertime

Van cleared his throat, a painful sound. "About that," he said. "I think it's going to hit sooner than that. Felix, I don't think anyone would notice if we just walked away from here."

Felix looked at him, his skin the color of corned-beef and streaked with long, angry scabs. His fingers trembled.

"You drinking enough water?"

Van nodded. "All frigging day, every ten seconds. Anything to keep my belly full." He pointed to a refilled Pepsi Max bottle full of water by his side.

"Let's have a meeting," he said.

* * *

There had been forty-three of them on D-Day. Now there were fifteen. Six had responded to the call for a meeting by simply leaving. Everyone knew without having to be told what the meeting was about.

"So that's it, you're going to let it all fall apart?" Sario was the only one with the energy left to get properly angry. He'd go angry to his grave. The veins on his throat and forehead stood out angrily. His fists shook angrily. All the other geeks went lids-down at the site of him, looking up in unison for once at the discussion, not keeping one eye on a chat log or a tailed service log.

"Sario, you've got to be shitting me," Felix said. "You wanted to pull the goddamned plug!"

"I wanted it to go *clean*," he shouted. "I didn't want it to bleed out and keel over in little gasps and pukes forever. I wanted it to be an act of will by the global community of its caretakers. I wanted it to be an affirmative act by human hands. Not entropy and bad code and worms winning out. Fuck that, that's just what's happened out there."

Up in the top-floor cafeteria, there were windows all around, hardened and light-bending, and by custom, they were all blinds-down. Now Sario ran around the room, yanking down the blinds. *How the hell can he get the energy to run?* Felix wondered. He could barely walk up the stairs to the meeting room.

Harsh daylight flooded in. It was a fine sunny day out there, but everywhere you looked across that commanding view of Toronto's skyline, there were rising plumes of smoke. The TD tower, a gigantic black modernist glass brick, was gouting flame to the sky. "It's all falling apart, the way everything does.

"Listen, listen. If we leave the network to fall over slowly, parts of it will stay online for months. Maybe years. And what will run on it? Malware. Worms. Spam. System-processes. Zone transfers. The things we use fall apart and require constant maintenance. The things we abandon don't get used and they last forever. We're going to leave the network behind like a lime-pit filled with industrial waste. That will be our fucking legacy–the legacy of every keystroke you and I and anyone, anywhere, ever typed. You understand? We're going to leave it to die slow like a wounded dog, instead of giving it one clean shot through the head."

Van scratched his cheeks, then Felix saw that he was wiping away tears.

"Sario, you're not wrong, but you're not right either," he said. "Leaving it up to limp along is right. We're going to all be limping for a long time, and maybe it will be of some use to someone. If there's one packet being routed from any user to any other user, anywhere in the world, it's doing its job."

"If you want a clean kill, you can do that," Felix said. "I'm the PM and I say so. I'm giving you root. All of you." He turned to the whiteboard where the cafeteria workers used to scrawl the day's specials. Now it was covered with the remnants of heated technical debates that the sysadmins had engaged in over the days since the day.

He scrubbed away a clean spot with his sleeve and began to write out long, complicated alphanumeric passwords salted with punctuation. Felix had a gift for remembering that kind of password. He doubted it would do him much good, ever again.

* * *

```
> Were going, kong. Fuels almost out anyway
> yeah well thats right then. it was an honor, mr
  prime minister
> you going to be ok?
> ive commandeered a young sysadmin to see to my
  feminine needs and weve found another cache of
  food thatll last us a coupel weeks now that were
  down to fifteen admins-im in hog heaven pal
> youre amazing, Queen Kong, seriously. Dont be a
  hero though. When you need to go go. Theres got
  to be something out there
> be safe felix, seriously-btw did i tell you
  queries are up in Romania? maybe theyre getting
  back on their feet
> really?
> yeah, really. we're hard to kill-like fucking
  roaches
```

Her connection died. He dropped to Firefox and reloaded Google and it was down. He hit reload and hit reload and hit reload, but it didn't come up. He closed his eyes and listened to Van scratch his legs and then heard Van type a little.

"They're back up," he said.

Felix whooshed out a breath. He sent the message to the newsgroup, one that he'd run through five drafts before settling on, "Take care of the place, OK? We'll be back, someday."

Everyone was going except Sario. Sario wouldn't leave. He came down to see them off, though.

The sysadmins gathered in the lobby and Felix made the safety door go up, and the light rushed in.

Sario stuck his hand out.

"Good luck," he said.

"You, too," Felix said. He had a firm grip, Sario, stronger than he had any right to be. "Maybe you were right," he said.

"Maybe," he said.

"You going to pull the plug?"

Sario looked up at the drop-ceiling, seeming to peer through the reinforced floors at the humming racks above. "Who knows?" he said at last.

Van scratched and a flurry of white motes danced in the sunlight.

"Let's go find you a pharmacy," Felix said. He walked to the door and the other sysadmins followed.

They waited for the interior doors to close behind them and then Felix opened the exterior doors. The air smelled and tasted like mown grass, like the first drops of rain, like the lake and the sky, like the outdoors and the world, an old friend not heard from in an eternity.

"Bye, Felix," the other sysadmins said. They were drifting away while he stood transfixed at the top of the short concrete staircase. The light hurt his eyes and made them water.

"I think there's a Shopper's Drug Mart on King Street," he said to Van. "We'll throw a brick through the window and get you some cortisone, OK?"

"You're the Prime Minister," Van said. "Lead on."

* * *

They didn't see a single soul on the fifteen minute walk. There wasn't a single sound except for some bird noises and some distant groans, and the wind in the electric cables overhead. It was like walking on the surface of the moon.

"Bet they have chocolate bars at the Shopper's," Van said.

Felix's stomach lurched. Food. "Wow," he said, around a mouthful of saliva.

They walked past a little hatchback and in the front seat was the dried body of a woman holding the dried body of a baby, and his mouth filled with sour bile, even though the smell was faint through the rolled-up windows.

He hadn't thought of Kelly or 2.0 in days. He dropped to his knees and retched again. Out here in the real world, his family was dead. Everyone he knew was dead. He just wanted to lie down on the sidewalk and wait to die, too.

Van's rough hands slipped under his armpits and hauled weakly at him. "Not now," he said. "Once we're safe inside somewhere and we've eaten something, then and then you can do this, but not now. Understand me, Felix? Not fucking now."

The profanity got through to him. He got to his feet. His knees were trembling.

"Just a block more," Van said, and slipped Felix's arm around his shoulders and led him along.

"Thank you, Van. I'm sorry."

"No sweat," he said. "You need a shower, bad. No offense."

"None taken."

The Shoppers had a metal security gate, but it had been torn away from the front windows, which had been rudely smashed. Felix and Van squeezed through the gap and stepped into the dim drugstore. A few of the displays were knocked over, but other than that, it looked

OK. By the cash registers, Felix spotted the racks of candy bars at the same instant that Van saw them, and they hurried over and grabbed a handful each, stuffing their faces.

"You two eat like pigs."

They both whirled at the sound of the woman's voice. She was holding a fire axe that was nearly as big as she was. She wore a lab-coat and comfortable shoes.

"You take what you need and go, OK? No sense in there being any trouble." Her chin was pointy and her eyes were sharp. She looked to be in her forties. She looked nothing like Kelly, which was good, because Felix felt like running and giving her a hug as it was. Another person alive!

"Are you a doctor?" Felix said. She was wearing scrubs under the coat, he saw.

"You going to go?" She brandished the axe.

Felix held his hands up. "Seriously, are you a doctor? A pharmacist?"

"I used to be a RN, ten years ago. I'm mostly a Web designer."

"You're shitting me," Felix said.

"Haven't you ever met a girl who knew about computers?"

"Actually, a friend of mine who runs Google's data center is a girl. A woman, I mean."

"You're shitting me," she said. "A woman ran Google's data center?"

"Runs," Felix said. "It's still online."

"NFW," she said. She let the axe lower.

"Way. Have you got any cortisone cream? I can tell you the story. My name's Felix and this is Van, who needs any antihistamines you can spare."

"I can spare? Felix old pal, I have enough dope here to last a hundred years. This stuff's going to expire long before it runs out. But are you telling me that the net's still up?"

"It's still up," he said. "Kind of. That's what we've been doing all week. Keeping it online. It might not last much longer, though."

"No," she said. "I don't suppose it would." She set the axe down. "Have you got anything to trade? I don't need much, but I've been trying to keep my spirits up by trading with the neighbors. It's like playing civilization."

"You have neighbors?"

"At least ten," she said. "The people in the restaurant across the way make a pretty good soup, even if most of the veg is canned. They cleaned me out of Sterno, though."

"You've got neighbors and you trade with them?"

"Well, nominally. It'd be pretty lonely without them. I've taken care of whatever sniffles I could. Set a bone—broken wrist. Listen, do you want some Wonder Bread and peanut butter? I have a ton of it. Your friend looks like he could use a meal."

"Yes, please," Van said. "We don't have anything to trade, but we're both committed workaholics looking to learn a trade. Could you use some assistants?"

"Not really." She spun her axe on its head. "But I wouldn't mind some company."

They ate the sandwiches and then some soup. The restaurant people brought it over and made their manners at them, though Felix saw their noses wrinkle up and ascertained that there was working plumbing in the back room. Van went in to take a sponge bath and then he followed.

"None of us know what to do," the woman said. Her name was Rosa, and she had found them a bottle of wine and some disposable plastic cups from the housewares aisle. "I thought we'd have helicopters or tanks or even looters, but it's just quiet."

"You seem to have kept pretty quiet yourself," Felix said.

"Didn't want to attract the wrong kind of attention."

"You ever think that maybe there's a lot of people out there doing the same thing? Maybe if we all get together we'll come up with something to do."

"Or maybe they'll cut our throats," she said.

Van nodded. "She's got a point."

Felix was on his feet. "No way, we can't think like that. Lady, we're at a critical juncture here. We can go down through negligence, dwindling away in our hiding holes, or we can try to build something better."

"Better?" She made a rude noise.

"OK, not better. Something though. Building something new is better than letting it dwindle away. Christ, what are you going to do when you've read all the magazines and eaten all the potato chips here?"

Rosa shook her head. "Pretty talk," she said. "But what the hell are we going to do, anyway?"

"Something," Felix said. "We're going to do something. Something is better than nothing. We're going to take this patch of the world where people are talking to each other, and we're going to expand it. We're going to find everyone we can and we're going to take care of them and they're going to take care of us. We'll probably fuck it up. We'll probably fail. I'd rather fail than give up, though."

Van laughed. "Felix, you are crazier than Sario, you know it?"

"We're going to go and drag him out, first thing tomorrow. He's going to be a part of this, too. Everyone will. Screw the end of the world. The world doesn't end. Humans aren't the kind of things that have endings."

Rosa shook her head again, but she was smiling a little now. "And you'll be what, the Pope-Emperor of the World?"

"He prefers Prime Minister," Van said in a stagey whisper. The antihistamines had worked miracles on his skin, and it had faded from angry red to a fine pink.

"You want to be Minister of Health, Rosa?" he said.

"Boys," she said. "Playing games. How about this. I'll help out however I can, provided you never ask me to call you Prime Minister and you never call me the Minister of Health?"

"It's a deal," he said.

Van refilled their glasses, upending the wine bottle to get the last few drops out.

They raised their glasses. "To the world," Felix said. "To humanity." He thought hard. "To rebuilding."

"To anything," Van said.

"To anything," Felix said. "To everything."

"To everything," Rosa said.

They drank. The next day, they started to rebuild. And months later, they started over again, when disagreements drove apart the fragile little group they'd pulled together. And a year after that, they started over again. And five years later, they started again.

Felix dug ditches and salvaged cans and buried the dead. He planted and harvested. He fixed some cars and learned to make biodiesel. Finally he fetched up in a data center for a little government—little governments came and went, but this one was smart enough to want to keep records and needed someone to keep everything running, and Van went with him.

They spent a lot of time in chat rooms and sometimes they happened upon old friends from the strange time they'd spent running the Distributed Republic of Cyberspace, geeks who insisted on calling him PM, though no one in the real world ever called him that anymore.

It wasn't a good life, most of the time. Felix's wounds never healed, and neither did most other people's. There were lingering sicknesses and sudden ones. Tragedy on tragedy.

But Felix liked his data center. There in the humming of the racks, he never felt like it was the first days of a better nation, but he never felt like it was the last days of one, either.

```
> go to bed, felix
> soon, kong, soon—almost got this backup running
> youre a junkie, dude.
> look whos talking
```

He reloaded the Google homepage. Queen Kong had had it online for a couple years now. The Os in Google changed all the time, whenever she got the urge. Today they were little cartoon globes, one smiling, the other frowning.

He looked at it for a long time and dropped back into a terminal to check his backup. It was running clean, for a change. The little government's records were safe.

```
> ok night night
> take care
```

Van waved at him as he creaked to the door, stretching out his back with a long series of pops.

"Sleep well, boss," he said.

"Don't stick around here all night again," Felix said. "You need your sleep, too."

"You're too good to us grunts," Van said and went back to typing.

Felix went to the door and walked out into the night. Behind him, the biodiesel generator hummed and made its acrid fumes. The harvest moon was up, which he loved. Tomorrow, he'd go back and fix another computer and fight off entropy again. And why not?

It was what he did. He was a sysadmin.

Anda's Game

The easiest way to write futuristic (or futurismic) science fiction is to predict, with rigor and absolute accuracy, the present day.

"Anda's Game" is a sterling example of this approach. I ripped a story from the headlines—reports on blogs about a stunning presentation at a video-games conference about "gold farmers" in Latin America who were being paid a pittance "grind" (to undertake boring, repetitive wealth-creating tasks in a game) with the product of their labor sold on to rich northern gamers who wanted to level-up without all the hard work.

The practice of gold farming became more and more mainstream, growing with the online role-playing game industry and spreading around the world (legend has it that the Chinese rice harvest was endangered because so many real farmers had quit the field to pursue a more lucrative harvest in virtual online gold). Every time one of these stories broke, I was lionized for my spectacular prescience in so accurately predicting the gold-farming phenomenon—I had successfully predicted the present.

"Anda's Game" tries to square up the age-old fight for rights for oppressed minorities in the rich world with the fight for the rights of the squalid, miserable majority in the developing world. This tension arises again and again, and it affords a juicy opportunity to play different underclasses off against one another. Think of how handily Detroit's autoworkers were distracted from GM's greed when they were given Mexican free-trade-zone labor to treat as a scapegoat; the American worker's enemy isn't the Mexican worker, it's the auto manufacturer who screws both of them. They fought NAFTA instead of GM, and GM won.

This was the first of several stories I've written with titles from famous SF stories and novels ("Anda's Game" sounds a lot like "Ender's Game" when pronounced in a British accent). I came to this curious practice as a response to Ray Bradbury describing Michael Moore as a crook for repurposing the title *Fahrenheit 451* as *Fahrenheit 9/11*. Bradbury doesn't like Moore's politics and didn't want his seminal work on free speech being used to promote opposing political ideology.

Well, this is just too much irony to bear. Titles have no copyright, and science fiction is a field that avidly repurposes titles—it seems like writing a story called "Nightfall" is practically a rite of passage for some writers. What's more, the idea that political speech (the comparison of the Bush regime to the totalitarian state of *Fahrenheit 451*) should be suppressed because the author disagrees is antithetical to the inspiring free speech message that shoots through *Fahrenheit 451*.

So I decided to start writing stories with the same titles as famous sf, and to make each one a commentary, criticism, or parody of the cherished ideas of the field. "Anda's Game" was the first of these, but it's not the last—"I, Robot" appears elsewhere in this volume, and I've almost finished a story called "True Names" that Ben Rosenbaum and I have been tossing back and forth for a while. After that, I think it'll be "The Man Who Sold the Moon," and then maybe "Jeffty is Five."

I sold this story to *Salon*, and it was later reprinted in Michael Chabon's *Best American Short Stories 2005* (a story written by a Canadian about Brits, no less!), and it was later read by retired pro Quake player Alice Taylor for my podcast.

Anda didn't really start to play the game until she got herself a girl-shaped avatar. She was twelve, and up until then, she'd played a boy-elf, because her parents had sternly warned her that if you played a girl you were an instant perv magnet. None of the girls at Ada Lovelace Comprehensive would have been caught dead playing a girl character. In fact, the only girls she'd ever seen in-game were being played by boys. You could tell, cos they were shaped like a boy's idea of what a girl looked like: hooge buzwabs and long legs all barely contained in tiny, pointless leather bikini-armor. Bintware, she called it.

But when Anda was twelve, she met Liza the Organiza, whose avatar was female, but had sensible tits and sensible armor and a bloody great sword that she was clearly very good with. Liza came to school after PE, when Anda was sitting and massaging her abused podge and hating her entire life from stupid sunrise to rotten sunset. Her PE kit was at the bottom of her school bag and her face was that stupid red color that she *hated* and now it was stinking maths, which was hardly better than PE but at least she didn't have to sweat.

But instead of maths, all the girls were called to assembly, and Liza the Organiza stood on the stage in front of Miss Cruickshanks the principal and Mrs. Danzig, the useless counselor.

"Hullo chickens," Liza said. She had an Australian accent. "Well, aren't you lot just precious and bright and expectant with your pink upturned faces like a load of flowers staring up at the sky?

"Warms me fecking heart it does."

That made her laugh, and she wasn't the only one. Miss Cruickshanks and Mrs. Danzig didn't look amused, but they tried to hide it.

"I am Liza the Organiza, and I kick arse. Seriously." She tapped a key on her laptop and the screen behind her lit up. It was a game–not the one that Anda played, but something space-themed, a space station with a rocketship in the background. "This is my avatar." Sensible boobs, sensible armor, and a sword the size of the world. "In-game, they call me the Lizanator, Queen of the Spacelanes, El Presidente of the Clan Fahrenheit." The Fahrenheits had chapters in every game. They were amazing and deadly and cool, and to her knowledge, Anda had never met one in the flesh. They had their own *island* in her game. Crikey.

On screen, The Lizanator was fighting an army of wookie-men, sword in one hand, laser-blaster in the other, rocket-jumping, spinning, strafing, making impossible kills and long shots, diving for power-ups, and ruthlessly running her enemies to ground.

"The *whole* Clan Fahrenheit. I won that title through popular election, but they voted me in cos of my prowess in *combat.* I'm a world-champion in six different games, from first-person shooters to strategy games. I've commanded armies and I've sent armies to their respawn gates by the thousands. Thousands, chickens: my battle record is

3,522 kills in a single battle. I have taken home cash prizes from competitions totaling more than 400,000 pounds. I game for four to six hours nearly every day, and the rest of the time, I do what I like.

"One of the things I like to do is come to girls' schools like yours and let you in on a secret: girls kick arse. We're faster, smarter, and better than boys. We play harder. We spend too much time thinking that we're freaks for gaming and when we do game, we never play as girls because we catch so much shite for it. Time to turn that around. I am the best gamer in the world and I'm a girl. I started playing at ten, and there were no women in games–you couldn't even buy a game in any of the shops I went to. It's different now, but it's still not perfect. We're going to change that, chickens, you lot and me.

"How many of you game?"

Anda put her hand up. So did about half the girls in the room.

"And how many of you play girls?"

All the hands went down.

"See, that's a tragedy. Practically makes me weep. Gamespace smells like a boy's *armpit*. It's time we girled it up a little. So here's my offer to you: if you will play as a girl, you will be given probationary memberships in the Clan Fahrenheit, and if you measure up, in six months, you'll be full-fledged members."

In real life, Liza the Organiza was a little podgy, like Anda herself, but she wore it with confidence. She was solid, like a brick wall, her hair bobbed bluntly at her shoulders. She dressed in a black jumper over loose dungarees with giant, goth boots with steel toes that looked like something you'd see in an in-game shop, though Anda was pretty sure they'd come from a real-world goth shop in Camden Town.

She stomped her boots, one-two, thump-thump, like thunder on the stage. "Who's in, chickens? Who wants to be a girl out-game and in?"

Anda jumped to her feet. A Fahrenheit, with her own island! Her head was so full of it that she didn't notice that she was the only one standing. The other girls stared at her, a few giggling and whispering.

"That's all right, love," Liza called, "I like enthusiasm. Don't let those staring faces rattle yer: they're just flowers turning to look at the sky. Pink scrubbed shining expectant faces. They're looking at you because *you* had the sense to get to your feet when opportunity came—and that means that someday, girl, you are going to be a leader of women, and men, and you will kick arse. Welcome to the Clan Fahrenheit."

She began to clap, and the other girls clapped too, and even though Anda's face was the color of a lollipop-lady's sign, she felt like she might burst with pride and good feeling and she smiled until her face hurt.

* * *

> Anda,

her sergeant said to her,

> how would you like to make some money?

> Money, Sarge?

Ever since she'd risen to platoon leader, she'd been getting more missions, but they paid *gold*—money wasn't really something you talked about in-game.

The Sarge—sensible boobs, gigantic sword, longbow, gloriously orcish ugly phiz—moved her avatar impatiently.

```
> Something wrong with my typing, Anda?
> No, Sarge,
```

she typed.

```
> You mean gold?
> If I meant gold, I would have said gold. Can you
  go voice?
```

Anda looked around. Her door was shut and she could hear her parents in the sitting room watching something loud on the telly. She turned up her music just to be safe and then slipped on her headset. They said it could noise-cancel a Blackhawk helicopter—it had better be able to overcome the little inductive speakers suction-cupped to the underside of her desk. She switched to voice.

"Hey, Lucy," she said.

"Call me Sarge!" Lucy's accent was American, like an old TV show, and she lived somewhere in the middle of the country where it was all vowels, Iowa or Ohio. She was Anda's best friend in-game but she was so hardcore it was boring sometimes.

"Hi Sarge," she said, trying to keep the irritation out of her voice. She'd never smart off to a superior in-game, but v2v it was harder to remember to keep to the game norms.

"I have a mission that pays real cash. Whichever paypal you're using, they'll deposit money into it. Looks fun, too."

"That's a bit weird, Sarge. Is that against Clan rules?" There were a lot of Clan rules about what kind of mission you could accept and they were always changing. There were curb-crawlers in gamespace and the way that the Clan leadership kept all the mummies and daddies from going ape-poo about it was by enforcing a long, boring code of conduct that was meant to ensure that none of the Fahrenheit girlies ended up being virtual prozzies for hairy old men in raincoats on the other side of the world.

"What?" Anda loved how Lucy quacked *What?* It sounded especially American. She had to force herself from parroting it back. "No, geez. All the executives in the Clan pay the rent doing missions for money. Some of them are even rich from it, I hear! You can make a lot of money gaming, you know."

"Is it really true?" She'd heard about this but she'd assumed it was just stories, like the kids who gamed so much that they couldn't tell reality from fantasy. Or the ones who gamed so much that they stopped eating and got all anorexic. She wouldn't mind getting a little anorexic, to be honest. Bloody podge.

"Yup! And this is our chance to get in on the ground floor. Are you in?"

"It's not–you know, *pervy*, is it?"

"Gag me. No. Jeez, Anda! Are you nuts? No–they want us to go kill some guys."

"Oh, we're good at that!"

* * *

The mission took them far from Fahrenheit Island, to a cottage on the far side of the largest continent on the gameworld, which was called

Dandelionwine. The travel was tedious, and twice they were ambushed on the trail, something that had hardly happened to Anda since she joined the Fahrenheits: attacking a Fahrenheit was bad for your health, because even if you won the battle, they'd bring a war to you.

But now they were far from the Fahrenheits' power base, and two different packs of brigands waylaid them on the road. Lucy spotted the first group before they got into sword range and killed four of the six with her bow before they closed for hand-to-hand. Anda's sword—gigantic and fast—was out then, and her fingers danced over the keyboard as she fought off the player who was attacking her, her body jerking from side to side as she hammered on the multibutton controller beside her. She won—of course! She was a Fahrenheit! Lucy had already slaughtered her attacker. They desultorily searched the bodies and came up with some gold and a couple of scrolls, but nothing to write home about. Even the gold didn't seem like much, given the cash waiting at the end of the mission.

The second group of brigands was even less daunting, though there were twenty of them. They were total noobs and fought like statues. They'd clearly clubbed together to protect themselves from harder players, but they were no match for Anda and Lucy. One of them even begged for his life before she ran him through,

```
> please sorry u cn have my gold sorry!!!11!
```

Anda laughed and sent him to the respawn gate.

```
> You're a nasty person, Anda,
```

Lucy typed.

```
> I'm a Fahrenheit!!!!!!!!!!
```

she typed back.

* * *

The brigands on the road were punters, but the cottage that was Anda's target was guarded by an altogether more sophisticated sort. They were spotted by sentries long before they got within sight of the cottage, and they saw the warning spell travel up from the sentries' hilltop like a puff of smoke, speeding away toward the cottage. Anda raced up the hill while Lucy covered her with her bow, but that didn't stop the sentries from subjecting Anda to a hail of flaming spears from their fortified position. Anda set up her standard dodge-and-weave pattern, assuming that the sentries were nonplayer characters—who wanted to *pay* to sit around in gamespace watching a boring road all day?—and to her surprise, the spears followed her. She took one in the chest and only some fast work with her shield and all her healing scrolls saved her. As it was, her constitution was knocked down by half and she had to retreat back down the hillside.

"Get down," Lucy said in her headset. "I'm gonna use the BFG."

Every game had one—the Big Friendly Gun, the generic term for the baddest-arse weapon in the world. Lucy had rented this one from the Clan armory for a small fortune in gold and Anda had laughed and called her paranoid, but now Anda helped Lucy set it up and thanked the gamegods for her foresight. It was a huge, demented flaming crossbow that fired five-meter bolts that exploded on impact. It was a beast to arm and a beast to aim, but they had a nice, dug-in position of their own at the bottom of the hill and it was there that they got the BFG set up, deployed, armed, and ranged.

"Fire!" Lucy called, and the game did this amazing and cool animation that it rewarded you with whenever you loosed a bolt from the BFG, making the gamelight dim toward the sizzling bolt as though it were sucking the illumination out of the world as it arced up the hillside, trailing a comet tail of sparks. The game played them a groan of dismay from their enemies, and then the bolt hit home with a crash that made her point-of-view vibrate like an earthquake. The roar in her headphones was deafening, and behind it she could hear Lucy on the voice chat, cheering it on.

"Nuke 'em till they glow and shoot 'em in the dark! Yee-haw!" Lucy called, and Anda laughed and pounded her fist on the desk. Gobbets of former enemy sailed over the treeline dramatically, dripping hyper-red blood and ichor.

In her bedroom, Anda caressed the controller pad and her avatar punched the air and did a little rugby victory dance that the All-Blacks had released as a limited edition promo after they won the World Cup.

Now they had to move fast, for their enemies at the cottage would be alerted to their presence and waiting for them. They spread out into a wide flanking maneuver around the cottage's sides, staying just outside of bow range, using scrying scrolls to magnify the cottage and make the foliage around them fade to translucency.

There were four guards around the cottage, two with nocked arrows and two with whirling slings. One had a scroll out and was surrounded by the concentration marks that indicated spellcasting.

"GO GO GO!" Lucy called.

Anda went! She had two scrolls left in her inventory, and one was a shield spell. They cost a fortune and burned out fast, but whatever that guard was cooking up, it had to be bad news. She cast the spell as she charged for the cottage, and lucky thing, because there was a fifth guard up a tree who dumped a pot of boiling oil on her that would have cooked her down to her bones in ten seconds if not for the spell.

She power-climbed the tree and nearly lost her grip when whatever the nasty spell was bounced off her shield. She reached the fifth man as he was trying to draw his dirk and dagger and lopped his bloody head off in one motion, then backflipped off the high branch, trusting her shield to stay intact for her impact on the cottage roof.

The strategy worked—now she had the drop (literally!) on the remaining guards, having successfully taken the high ground. In her headphones, the sound of Lucy making mayhem, the grunts as she pounded her keyboard mingling with the in-game shrieks as her arrows found homes in the chests of two more of the guards.

Shrieking a berserker wail, Anda jumped down off of the roof and landed on one of the two remaining guards, plunging her sword into his chest and pinning him in the dirt. Her sword stuck in the ground, and she hammered on her keys, trying to free it, while the remaining guard ran for her on-screen. Anda pounded her keyboard, but it was useless: the sword was good and stuck. Poo. She'd blown a small fortune on spells and rations for this project with the expectation of getting some real cash out of it, and now it was all lost.

She moved her hands to the part of the keypad that controlled motion and began to run, waiting for the guard's sword to find her avatar's back and knock her into the dirt.

"Got 'im!" It was Lucy, in her headphones. She wheeled her avatar about so quickly it was nauseating and saw that Lucy was on her erstwhile attacker, grunting as she engaged him close-in. Something was wrong, though: despite Lucy's avatar's awesome stats and despite Lucy's own skill at the keyboard, she was being taken to the cleaners. The guard was kicking her ass. Anda went back to her stuck sword and recommenced whanging on it, watching helplessly as Lucy lost her left arm, then took a cut on her belly, then another to her knee.

"Shit!" Lucy said in her headphones as her avatar began to keel over. Anda yanked her sword free—finally—and charged at the guard, screaming a ululating war cry. He managed to get his avatar swung around and his sword up before she reached him, but it didn't matter: she got in a lucky swing that took off one leg, then danced back before he could counterstrike. Now she closed carefully, nicking at his sword-hand until he dropped his weapon, then moving in for a fast kill.

"Lucy?"

"Call me Sarge!"

"Sorry, Sarge. Where'd you respawn?"

"I'm all the way over at Body Electric—it'll take me hours to get there. Do you think you can complete the mission on your own?"

"Uh, sure." Thinking, *Crikey, if that's what the guards* outside *were like, how'm I gonna get past the* inside *guards?*

"You're the best, girl. OK, enter the cottage and kill everyone there."

"Uh, sure."

She wished she had another scrying scroll in inventory so she could get a look inside the cottage before she beat its door in, but she was fresh out of scrolls and just about everything else.

She kicked the door in and her fingers danced. She'd killed four of her adversaries before she even noticed that they weren't fighting back.

In fact, they were generic avatars, maybe even nonplayer characters. They moved like total noobs, milling around in the little cottage. Around them were heaps of shirts, thousands and thousands of them. A couple of the noobs were sitting in the back, incredibly, still crafting more shirts, ignoring the swordswoman who'd just butchered four of their companions.

She took a careful look at all the avatars in the room. None of them were armed. Tentatively, she walked up to one of the players and cut his head off. The player next to him moved clumsily to one side and she followed him.

"Are you a player or a bot?" she typed.

The avatar did nothing. She killed it.

"Lucy, they're not fighting back."

"Good, kill them all."

"Really?"

"Yeah—that's the orders. Kill them all and then I'll make a phone call and some guys will come by and verify it and then you haul ass back to the island. I'm coming out there to meet you, but it's a long haul from the respawn gate. Keep an eye on my stuff, OK?"

"Sure," Anda said and killed two more. That left ten. *One two one two and through and through,* she thought, lopping their heads off. *Her vorpal blade went snicker-snack.* One left. He stood off in the back.

```
> no porfa necesito mi plata
```

Italian? No, Spanish. She'd had a term of it in Third Form, though she couldn't understand what this twit was saying. She could always paste the text into a translation bot on one of the chat channels, but who cared? She cut his head off.

"They're all dead," she said into her headset.

"Good job!" Lucy said. "OK, I'm gonna make a call. Sit tight."

Bo-ring. The cottage was filled with corpses and shirts. She picked some of them up. They were totally generic: the shirts you crafted when you were down at Level 0 and trying to get enough skillz to actually make something of yourself. Each one would fetch just a few coppers. Add it all together and you barely had two thousand gold.

Just to pass the time, she pasted the Spanish into the chatbot.

```
> no [colloquial] please, I need my [colloquial]
  money|silver
```

Pathetic. A few thousand golds–he could make that much by playing a couple of the beginner missions. More fun. More rewarding. Crafting shirts!

She left the cottage and patrolled around it. Twenty minutes later, two more avatars showed up. More generics.

```
> are you players or bots?
```

she typed, though she had an idea they were players. Bots moved better.

```
> any trouble?
```

Well, all right then.

```
> no trouble
> good
```

One player entered the cottage and came back out again. The other player spoke.

```
> you can go now
```

"Lucy?"

"What's up?"

"Two blokes just showed up and told me to piss off. They're noobs, though. Should I kill them?"

"No! Jeez, Anda, those are the contacts. They're just making sure the job was done. Get my stuff and meet me at Marionettes Tavern, OK?"

Anda went over to Lucy's corpse and looted it, then set out down the road, dragging the BFG behind her. She stopped at the bend in the road and snuck a peek back at the cottage. It was in flames, the two noobs standing amid them, burning slowly along with the cottage and a few thousand golds' worth of badly crafted shirts.

* * *

That was the first of Anda and Lucy's missions, but it wasn't the last. That month, she fought her way through six more, and the paypal she used filled with real, honest-to-goodness cash, Pounds Sterling that she could withdraw from the cashpoint situated exactly 501 meters away from the schoolgate, next to the candy shop that was likewise 501 meters away.

"Anda, I don't think it's healthy for you to spend so much time with your game," her da said, prodding her bulging podge with a finger. "It's not healthy."

"Daaaa!" she said, pushing his finger aside. "I go to PE every stinking day. It's good enough for the Ministry of Education."

"I don't like it," he said. He was no movie star himself, with a little pot belly that he wore his belted trousers high upon, a wobbly extra chin and two bat wings of flab hanging off his upper arms. She pinched his chin and wiggled it.

"I get loads more exercise than you, Mr. Kettle."

"But I pay the bills around here, little Miss Pot."

"You're not seriously complaining about the cost of the game?" she said, infusing her voice with as much incredulity and disgust as she could muster. "Ten quid a week and I get unlimited calls, texts, and messages! Plus play of course, and the in-game encyclopedia and spellchecker and translator bots!" (This was all from rote—every member of the Fahrenheits memorized this or something very like it for dealing with recalcitrant, ignorant parental units.) "Fine then. If the game is too dear for you, Da, let's set it aside and I'll just start using a normal phone, is that what you want?"

Her Da held up his hands. "I surrender, Miss Pot. But *do* try to get a little more exercise, please? Fresh air? Sport? Games?"

"Getting my head trodden on in the hockey pitch, more like," she said, darkly.

"Zackly!" he said, prodding her podge anew. "That's the stuff! Getting my head trodden on was what made me the man I am today!"

Her Da could bluster all he liked about paying the bills, but she had pocket money for the first time in her life: not book tokens and fruit tokens and milk tokens that could be exchanged for "healthy" snacks and literature. She had real money, cash money that she could spend outside of the 500-meter sugar-free zone that surrounded her school.

She wasn't just kicking arse in the game, now–she was the richest kid she knew, and suddenly she was everybody's best pal, with handfuls of Curly Wurlies and Dairy Milks and Mars Bars that she could selectively distribute to her schoolmates.

* * *

"Go get a BFG," Lucy said. "We're going on a mission."

Lucy's voice in her ear was a constant companion in her life now. When she wasn't on Fahrenheit Island, she and Lucy were running missions into the wee hours of the night. The Fahrenheit armorers, nonplayer-characters, had learned to recognize her and they had the Clan's BFGs oiled and ready for her when she showed up.

Today's mission was close to home, which was good: the road trips were getting tedious. Sometimes, nonplayer-characters or Game Masters would try to get them involved in an official in-game mission, impressed by their stats and weapons, and it sometimes broke her heart to pass them up, but cash always beat gold and experience beat experience points: *Money talks and bullshit walks*, as Lucy liked to say.

They caught the first round of sniper/lookouts before they had a chance to attack or send off a message. Anda used the scrying spell to spot them. Lucy had kept both BFGs armed and she loosed rounds at the hilltops flanking the roadway as soon as Anda gave her the signal, long before they got into bow range.

As they picked their way through the ruined chunks of the dead player-character snipers, while still on the lookout, Anda broke the silence over their voice link.

"Hey, Lucy?"

"Anda, if you're not going to call me Sarge, at least don't call me 'Hey, Lucy!' My dad loved that old TV show and he makes that joke every visitation day."

"Sorry, Sarge. Sarge?"

"Yes, Anda?"

"I just can't understand why anyonc would pay us cash for these missions."

"You complaining?"

"No, but–"

"Anyone asking you to cyber some old pervert?"

"No!"

"OK, then. I don't know either. But the money's good. I don't care. Hell, probably it's two rich gamers who pay their butlers to craft for them all day. One's fucking with the other one and paying us."

"You really think that?"

Lucy sighed a put-upon, sophisticated, American sigh. "Look at it this way. Most of the world is living on like a dollar a day. I spend five dollars every day on a frappuccino. Some days, I get two! Dad sends mom three thousand a month in child support–that's a hundred bucks a day. So if a day's money here is a hundred dollars, then to a African or whatever my frappuccino is worth like *five hundred dollars.* And I buy two or three every day.

"And we're not rich! There's craploads of rich people who wouldn't think twice about spending five hundred bucks on a coffee–how much do you think a hotdog and a Coke go for on the space station? A thousand bucks!

"So that's what I think is going on. There's someone out there, some Saudi or Japanese guy or Russian mafia kid who's so rich that this is just chump change for him, and he's paying us to mess around with some other rich person. To them, we're like the Africans making a dollar a day to craft–I mean, sew–T-shirts. What's a couple hundred bucks to them? A cup of coffee."

Anda thought about it. It made a kind of sense. She'd been on hols in Bratislava where they got a posh hotel room for ten quid–less than she was spending every day on sweeties and fizzy drinks.

"Three o'clock," she said and aimed the BFG again. More snipers pat-patted in bits around the forest floor.

"Nice one, Anda."

"Thanks, Sarge."

* * *

They smashed half a dozen more sniper outposts and fought their way through a couple packs of suspiciously badass brigands before coming upon the cottage.

"Bloody hell," Anda breathed. The cottage was ringed with guards, forty or fifty of them, with bows and spells and spears, in entrenched positions.

"This is nuts," Lucy agreed. "I'm calling them. This is nuts."

There was a muting click as Lucy rang off and Anda used up a scrying scroll to examine the inventories of the guards around the corner. The more she looked, the more scared she got. They were loaded down with spells, a couple of them were guarding BFGs and what looked like an even *bigger* BFG, maybe the fabled BFG10K, something that was removed from the game economy not long after gameday one, as too disruptive to the balance of power. Supposedly, one or two existed, but that was just a rumor. Wasn't it?

"OK," Lucy said. "OK, this is how this goes. We've got to do this. I just called in three squads of Fahrenheit veterans and their noob prentices for backup." Anda summed that up in her head to a hundred player characters and maybe three hundred nonplayer characters: familiars, servants, demons. . . .

"That's a lot of shares to split the pay into," Anda said.

"Oh ye of little tits," Lucy said. "I've negotiated a bonus for us if we make it–a million gold and three missions' worth of cash. The Fahrenheits are taking payment in gold–they'll be here in an hour."

This wasn't a mission anymore, Anda realized. It was war. Gamewar. Hundreds of players converging on this shard, squaring off against the ranked mercenaries guarding the huge cottage over the hill.

* * *

Lucy wasn't the ranking Fahrenheit on the scene, but she was the designated general. One of the gamers up from Fahrenheit Island brought a team flag for her to carry, a long spear with the magical standard snapping proudly from it as the troops formed up behind her.

"On my signal," Lucy said. The voice chat was like a wind tunnel from all the unmuted breathing voices, hundreds of girls in hundreds of bedrooms like Anda's, all over the world, some sitting down before breakfast, some just coming home from school, some roused from sleep by their ringing game-sponsored mobiles. "GO GO GO!"

They went, roaring, and Anda roared too, heedless of her parents downstairs in front of the blaring telly, heedless of her throat lining, a Fahrenheit in berserker rage, sword swinging. She made straight for the BFG10K—a siege engine that could level a town wall, and it would be hers, captured by her for the Fahrenheits if she could do it. She spelled the merc who was cranking it into insensibility, rolled and rolled again to dodge arrows and spells, healed herself when an arrow found her leg and sent her tumbling, springing to her feet before another arrow could strike home, watching her hit points and experience points move in opposite directions.

HERS! She vaulted the BFG10K and snicker-snacked her sword through two mercs' heads. Two more appeared—they had the thing primed and aimed at the main body of Fahrenheit fighters, and they could turn the battle's tide just by firing it—and she killed them, slamming her keypad, howling, barely conscious of the answering howls in her headset.

Now *she* had the BFG10K, though more mercs were closing on her. She disarmed it quickly and spelled at the nearest bunch of mercs, then had to take evasive action against the hail of incoming arrows and spells. It was all she could do to cast healing spells fast enough to avoid losing consciousness.

"LUCY!" she called into her headset. "LUCY, OVER BY THE BFG10K!"

Lucy snapped out orders and the opposition before Anda began to thin as Fahrenheits fell on them from behind. The flood was stemmed, and now the Fahrenheits' greater numbers and discipline showed. In short order, every merc was butchered or run off.

Anda waited by the BFG10K while Lucy paid off the Fahrenheits and saw them on their way. "Now we take the cottage," Lucy said.

"Right," Anda said. She set her character off for the doorway. Lucy brushed past her.

"I'll be glad when we're done with this–that was bugfuck nutso." She opened the door and her character disappeared in a fireball that erupted from directly overhead. A door curse, a serious one, one that cooked her in her armor in seconds.

"SHIT!" Lucy said in her headset.

Anda giggled. "Teach *you* to go rushing into things," she said. She used up a couple scrying scrolls making sure that there was nothing else in the cottage save for millions of shirts and thousands of unarmed noob avatars that she'd have to mow down like grass to finish out the mission.

She descended upon them like a reaper, swinging her sword heedlessly, taking five or six out with each swing. When she'd been a noob in the game, she'd had to endure endless fighting practice, "grappling" with piles of leaves and other nonlethal targets, just to get enough experience points to have a chance of hitting anything. This was every bit as dull.

Her wrists were getting tired, and her chest heaved and her hated podge wobbled as she worked the keypad.

```
> Wait, please, don't–I'd like to speak with you
```

It was a noob avatar, just like the others, but not just like it after all, for it moved with purpose, backing away from her sword. And it spoke English.

```
> nothing personal
```

she typed.

```
> just a job
> There are many here to kill–take me last at least.
  I need to talk to you.
> talk, then
```

she typed. Meeting players who moved well and spoke English was hardly unusual in gamespace, but here in the cleanup phase, it felt out of place. It felt wrong.

```
> My name is Raymond, and I live in Tijuana. I am a
  labor organizer in the factories here. What is
  your name?
> i don't give out my name in-game
> What can I call you?
> kali
```

It was a name she liked to use in-game: Kali, Destroyer of Worlds, like the Hindu goddess.

> Are you in India?

> london

> You are Indian?

> naw im a whitey

She was halfway through the room, mowing down the noobs in twos and threes. She was hungry and bored and this Raymond was weirding her out.

> Do you know who these people are that you're killing?

She didn't answer, but she had an idea. She killed four more and shook out her wrists.

> They're working for less than a dollar a day. The shirts they make are traded for gold and the gold is sold on eBay. Once their avatars have leveled up, they too are sold off on eBay. They're mostly young girls supporting their families. They're the lucky ones: the unlucky ones work as prostitutes.

Her wrists *really* ached. She slaughtered half a dozen more.

> The bosses used to use bots, but the game has countermeasures against them. Hiring children to click

```
the mouse is cheaper than hiring programmers to
circumvent the rules. I've been trying to unionize
them because they've got a very high rate of
injury. They have to play for 18-hour shifts with
only one short toilet break. Some of them can't
hold it in and they soil themselves where they sit.
```

```
> look
```

she typed, exasperated.

```
> it's none of my lookout, is it. the world's like
that. lots of people with no money. im just a kid,
theres nothing i can do about it.
> When you kill them, they don't get paid.
```

no porfa necesito mi plata

```
> When you kill them, they lose their day's wages.
Do you know who is paying you to do these killings?
```

She thought of Saudis, rich Japanese, Russian mobsters.

```
> not a clue
> I've been trying to find that out myself, Kali.
```

They were all dead now. Raymond stood alone amongst the piled corpses.

```
> Go ahead
```

he typed.

```
> I will see you again, I'm sure.
```

She cut his head off. Her wrists hurt. She was hungry. She was alone there in the enormous woodland cottage, and she still had to haul the BFG10K back to Fahrenheit Island.

"Lucy?"

"Yeah, yeah, I'm almost back there, hang on. I respawned in the ass end of nowhere."

"Lucy, do you know who's in the cottage? Those noobs that we kill?"

"What? Hell no. Noobs. Someone's butler. I dunno. Jesus, that spawn gate–"

"Girls. Little girls in Mexico. Getting paid a dollar a day to craft shirts. Except they don't get their dollar when we kill them. They don't get anything."

"Oh, for chrissakes, is that what one of them told you? Do you believe everything someone tells you in-game? Christ. English girls are so naive."

"You don't think it's true?"

"Naw, I don't."

"Why not?"

"I just don't, OK? I'm almost there, keep your panties on."

"I've got to go, Lucy," she said. Her wrists hurt, and her podge overlapped the waistband of her trousers, making her feel a bit like she was drowning.

"What, now? Shit, just hang on."

"My mom's calling me to supper. You're almost here, right?"

"Yeah, but–"

She reached down and shut off her PC.

* * *

Anda's Da and Mum were watching the telly again with a bowl of crisps between them. She walked past them like she was dreaming and stepped out the door onto the terrace. It was nighttime, 11 o'clock, and the chavs in front of the council flats across the square were kicking a football around and swilling lager and making rude noises. They were skinny and rawboned, wearing shorts and string vests with strong, muscular limbs flashing in the streetlights.

"Anda?"

"Yes, Mum?"

"Are you all right?" Her mum's fat fingers caressed the back of her neck.

"Yes, Mum. Just needed some air is all."

"You're very clammy," her mum said. She licked a finger and scrubbed it across Anda's neck. "Gosh, you're dirty–how did you get to be such a mucky puppy?"

"Owww!" she said. Her mum was scrubbing so hard it felt like she'd take her skin off.

"No whinging," her mum said sternly. "Behind your ears, too! You are *filthy.*"

"Mum, *owwww!*"

Her mum dragged her up to the bathroom and went at her with a flannel and a bar of soap and hot water until she felt boiled and raw.

"What *is* this mess?" her mum said.

"Lilian, leave off," her dad said, quietly. "Come out into the hall for a moment, please."

The conversation was too quiet to hear and Anda didn't want to, anyway: she was concentrating too hard on not crying–her ears *hurt*.

Her mum enfolded her shoulders in her soft hands again. "Oh, darling, I'm sorry. It's a skin condition, your father tells me, Acanthosis Nigricans–he saw it in a TV special. We'll see the doctor about it tomorrow after school. Are you all right?"

"I'm fine," she said, twisting to see if she could see the "dirt" on the back of her neck in the mirror. It was hard because it was an awkward placement–but also because she didn't like to look at her face and her soft extra chin, and she kept catching sight of it.

She went back to her room to google Acanthosis Nigricans.

```
> A condition involving darkened, thickened skin.
  Found in the folds of skin at the base of the back
  of the neck, under the arms, inside the elbow and
  at the waistline. Often precedes a diagnosis of
  type-2 diabetes, especially in children. If found
  in children, immediate steps must be taken to pre-
  vent diabetes,including exercise and nutrition as
  a means of lowering insulin levels and increasing
  insulin-sensitivity.
```

Obesity-related diabetes. They had lectures on this every term in health class–the fastest-growing ailment among British teens, accompanied by photos of orca-fat sacks of lard sat up in bed surrounded by an ocean of rubbery, flowing podge. Anda prodded her belly and watched it jiggle.

It jiggled. Her thighs jiggled. Her chins wobbled. Her arms sagged.

She grabbed a handful of her belly and *squeezed it*, pinched it hard as she could, until she had to let go or cry out. She'd left livid red fingerprints in the rolls of fat and she was crying now, from the pain and the shame and oh, God, she was a fat girl with diabetes–

* * *

"Jesus, Anda, where the hell have you been?"

"Sorry, Sarge," she said. "My PC's been broken–" Well, out of service, anyway. Under lock-and-key in her dad's study. Almost a month now of medications and no telly and no gaming and double PE periods at school with the other whales. She was miserable all day, every day now, with nothing to look forward to except the trips after school to the newsagents at the 501-meter mark and the fistsful of sweeties and bottles of fizzy drink she ate in the park while she watched the chavs play footy.

"Well, you should have found a way to let me know. I was getting worried about you, girl."

"Sorry, Sarge," she said again. The PC Baang was filled with stinky spotty boys–literally stinky, it smelt like goats, like a train station toilet–being loud and obnoxious. The dinky headphones provided were greasy as a slice of pizza, and the mouthpiece was sticky with excited boy-saliva from games gone past.

But it didn't matter. Anda was back in the game, and just in time, too: her money was running short.

"Well, I've got a backlog of missions here. I tried going out with a couple other of the girls–" A pang of regret shot through Anda at the thought that her position might have been usurped while she was locked off the game "–but you're too good to replace, OK? I've got four missions we can do today if you're game."

"Four missions! How on earth will we do four missions? That'll take days!"

"We'll take the BFG10K." Anda could hear the savage grin in her voice.

* * *

The BFG10K simplified things quite a lot. Find the cottage, aim the BFG10K, fire it, whim-wham, no more cottage. They started with five bolts for it–one BFG10K bolt was made up of twenty regular BFG bolts, each costing a small fortune in gold–and used them all up on the first three targets. After returning it to the armory and grabbing a couple of BFGs (amazing how puny the BFG seemed after just a couple hours' campaigning with a really *big* gun!) they set out for number four.

"I met a guy after the last campaign," Anda said. "One of the noobs in the cottage. He said he was a union organizer."

"Oh, you met Raymond, huh?"

"You knew about him?"

"I met him, too. He's been turning up everywhere. What a creep."

"So you knew about the noobs in the cottages?"

"Um. Well, yeah, I figured it out mostly on my own and then Raymond told me a little more."

"And you're fine with depriving little kids of their wages?"

"Anda," Lucy said, her voice brittle. "You like gaming, right, it's important to you?"

"Yeah, 'course it is."

"How important? Is it something you do for fun, just a hobby you waste a little time on? Are you just into it casually, or are you *committed* to it?"

"I'm committed to it, Lucy, you know that." God, without the game, what was there? PE class? Stupid Acanthosis Nigricans and, someday, insulin jabs every morning? "I love the game, Lucy. It's where my friends are."

"I know that. That's why you're my right-hand woman, why I want you at my side when I go on a mission. We're badass, you and me, as badass as they come, and we got that way through discipline and hard work and really *caring* about the game, right?"

"Yes, right, but–"

"You've met Liza the Organiza, right?"

"Yes, she came by my school."

"Mine, too. She asked me to look out for you because of what she saw in you that day."

"Liza the Organiza goes to Ohio?"

"Idaho. Yes–all across the U.S. They put her on the tube and everything. She's amazing, and she cares about the game, too–that's what makes us all Fahrenheits: we're committed to each other, to teamwork, and to fair play."

Anda had heard these words–lifted from the Fahrenheit mission statement–many times, but now they made her swell a little with pride.

"So these people in Mexico or wherever, what are they doing? They're earning their living by exploiting the game. You and me, we would never trade cash for gold, or buy a character or a weapon on eBay–it's cheating. You get gold and weapons through hard work and hard play. But those Mexicans spend all day, every day, crafting stuff to turn into gold to sell off on the exchange. *That's where it comes from*–that's where the crappy players get their gold from! That's how rich noobs can buy their way into the game that we had to play hard to get into.

"So we burn them out. If we keep burning the factories down, they'll shut them down and those kids'll find something else to do for a living and the game will be better. If no one does that, our work will just get cheaper and cheaper: the game will get less and less fun, too.

"These people *don't* care about the game. To them, it's just a place to suck a buck out of. They're not players, they're leeches, here to suck all the fun out."

They had come upon the cottage now, the fourth one, having exterminated four different sniper nests on the way.

"Are you in, Anda? Are you here to play, or are you so worried about these leeches on the other side of the world that you want out?"

"I'm in, Sarge," Anda said. She armed the BFGs and pointed them at the cottage.

"Boo-yah!" Lucy said. Her character notched an arrow.

```
> Hello, Kali
```

"Oh, Christ, he's back," Lucy said. Raymond's avatar had snuck up behind them.

```
> Look at these
```

he said, and his character set something down on the ground and backed away. Anda edged up on them.

"Come on, it's probably a booby trap, we've got work to do," Lucy said.

They were photo-objects. She picked them up and then examined them. The first showed ranked little girls, fifty or more, in clean and simple T-shirts, skinny as anything, sitting at generic white-box PCs, hands on the keyboards. They were hollow-eyed and grim, and none of them older than she.

The next showed a shantytown, shacks made of corrugated aluminum and trash, muddy trails between them, spray-painted graffiti, rude boys loitering, rubbish and carrier bags blowing.

The next showed the inside of a shanty, three little girls and a little boy sitting together on a battered sofa, their mother serving them something white and indistinct on plastic plates. Their smiles were heartbreaking and brave.

```
> That's who you're about to deprive of a day's wages
```

"Oh, hell, *no*," Lucy said. "Not again. I killed him last time and I said I'd do it again if he ever tried to show me photos. That's it, he's dead." Her character turned toward him, putting away her bow and drawing a short sword. Raymond's character backed away quickly.

"Lucy, don't," Anda said. She interposed her avatar between Lucy's and Raymond. "Don't do it. He deserves to have a say." She thought of old American TV shows, the kinds you saw between the Bollywood movies on telly. "It's a free country, right?"

"God *damn* it, Anda, what is *wrong* with you? Did you come here to play the game, or to screw around with this pervert dork?"

```
> what do you want from me raymond?
> Don't kill them–let them have their wages. Go play
  somewhere else
> They're leeches
```

Lucy typed,

```
> they're wrecking the game economy and they're pro-
  viding a gold-for-cash supply that lets rich ass-
  holes buy their way in. They don't care about the
  game and neither do you
> If they don't play the game, they don't eat. I
  think that means that they care about the game as
  much as you do. You're being paid cash to kill
  them, yes? So you need to play for your money, too.
  I think that makes you and them the same, a little
  the same.
> go screw yourself
```

Lucy typed. Anda edged her character away from Lucy's. Raymond's character was so far away now that his texting came out in tiny type, almost too small to read. Lucy drew her bow again and knocked an arrow.

"Lucy, DON'T!" Anda cried. Her hands moved of their own volition and her character followed, clobbering Lucy barehanded so that her avatar reeled and dropped its bow.

"You BITCH!" Lucy said. She drew her sword.

"I'm sorry, Lucy," Anda said, stepping back out of range. "But I don't want you to hurt him. I want to hear him out."

Lucy's avatar came on fast, and there was a click as the voice link dropped. Anda typed one-handed while she drew her own sword.

```
> dont lucy come on talk2me
```

Lucy slashed at her twice and she needed both hands to defend herself or she would have been beheaded. Anda blew out through her nose and counterattacked, fingers pounding the keyboard. Lucy had more experience points than she did, but she was a better player, and she knew it. She hacked away at Lucy driving her back and back, back down the road they'd marched together.

Abruptly, Lucy broke and ran, and Anda thought she was going away and decided to let her go, no harm no foul, but then she saw that Lucy wasn't running away, she was running *toward* the BFGs, armed and primed.

"Bloody hell," she breathed, as a BFG swung around to point at her. Her fingers flew. She cast the fireball at Lucy in the same instant that she cast her shield spell. Lucy loosed the bolt at her a moment before the fireball engulfed her, cooking her down to ash, and the bolt collided with the shield and drove Anda back, high into the air, and the shield spell wore off before she hit ground, costing her half her health and inventory, which scattered around her. She tested her voice link.

"Lucy?"

There was no reply.

> I'm very sorry you and your friend quarreled.

She felt numb and unreal. There were rules for Fahrenheits, lots of rules, and the penalties for breaking them varied, but the penalty for attacking a fellow Fahrenheit was–she couldn't think the word, she closed her eyes, but there it was in big glowing letters: EXPULSION.

But Lucy had started it, right? It wasn't her fault.

But who would believe her?

She opened her eyes. Her vision swam through incipient tears. Her heart was thudding in her ears.

> The enemy isn't your fellow player. It's not the players guarding the fabrica, it's not the girls working there. The people who are working to destroy the game are the people who pay you and the people who pay the girls in the fabrica, who are the same people. You're being paid by rival factory owners, you know that? THEY are the ones who care nothing for the game. My girls care about the game. You care about the game. Your common enemy is the people who want to destroy the game and who destroy the lives of these girls.

"Whassamatter, you fat little cow? Is your game making you cwy?" She jerked as if slapped. The chav who was speaking to her hadn't been in the Baang when she arrived, and he had mean, close-set eyes and a football jersey and though he wasn't any older than she, he looked mean, and angry, and his smile was sadistic and crazy.

"Piss off," she said, mustering her braveness.

"You wobbling tub of guts, don't you DARE speak to me that way," he said, shouting right in her ear. The Baang fell silent and everyone looked at her. The Pakistani who ran the Baang was on his phone, no doubt calling the coppers, and that meant that her parents would discover where she'd been and then–

"I'm talking to you, girl," he said. "You disgusting lump of suet–Christ, it makes me wanta puke to look at you. You ever had a boyfriend? How'd he shag you–did he roll yer in flour and look for the wet spot?"

She reeled back, then stood. She drew her arm back and slapped him, as hard as she could. The boys in the Baang laughed and went whoooooo! He purpled and balled his fists and she backed away from him. The imprint of her fingers stood out on his cheek.

He bridged the distance between them with a quick step and punched her, in the belly, and the air whooshed out of her and she fell into another player, who pushed her away, so she ended up slumped against the wall, crying.

The mean boy was there, right in front of her, and she could smell the chili crisps on his breath. "You disgusting whore–" he began and she kneed him square in the nadgers, hard as she could, and he screamed like a little girl and fell backward. She picked up her schoolbag and ran for the door, her chest heaving, her face streaked with tears.

* * *

"Anda, dear, there's a phone call for you."

Her eyes stung. She'd been lying in her darkened bedroom for hours now, snuffling and trying not to cry, trying not to look at the empty desk where her PC used to live.

Her da's voice was soft and caring, but after the silence of her room, it sounded like a rusting hinge.

"Anda?"

She opened her eyes. He was holding a cordless phone, sillhouetted against the open doorway.

"Who is it?"

"Someone from your game, I think," he said. He handed her the phone.

"Hullo?"

"Hullo, chicken." It had been a year since she'd heard that voice, but she recognized it instantly.

"Liza?"

"Yes."

Anda's skin seemed to shrink over her bones. This was it: expelled. Her heart felt like it was beating once per second, time slowed to a crawl.

"Hullo, Liza."

"Can you tell me what happened today?"

She did, stumbling over the details, backtracking and stuttering. She couldn't remember, exactly–did Lucy move on Raymond and Anda asked her to stop and then Lucy attacked her? Had Anda attacked Lucy first? It was all a jumble. She should have saved a screenmovie and taken it with her, but she couldn't have taken anything with her, she'd run out–

"I see. Well, it sounds like you've gotten yourself into quite a pile of poo, haven't you, my girl?"

"I guess so," Anda said. Then, because she knew that she was as good as expelled, she said, "I don't think it's right to kill them, those girls. All right?"

"Ah," Liza said. "Well, funny you should mention that. I happen to agree. Those girls need our help more than any of the girls anywhere in the game. The Fahrenheits' strength is that we are cooperative–it's another way that we're better than the boys. We care. I'm proud that you took a stand when you did–glad I found out about this business."

"You're not going to expel me?"

"No, chicken, I'm not going to expel you. I think you did the right thing–"

That meant that Lucy would be expelled. Fahrenheit had killed Fahrenheit–something had to be done. The rules had to be enforced. Anda swallowed hard.

"If you expel Lucy, I'll quit," she said, quickly, before she lost her nerve.

Liza laughed. "Oh, chicken, you're a brave thing, aren't you? No one's being expelled, fear not. But I wanta talk to this Raymond of yours."

* * *

Anda came home from remedial hockey sweaty and exhausted, but not as exhausted as the last time, nor the time before that. She could run the whole length of the pitch twice now without collapsing–when she'd started out, she could barely make it halfway without having to stop and hold her side, kneading her loathsome podge to make it stop aching. Now there was noticeably less podge, and she found that with the ability to run the pitch came the freedom to actually pay attention to the game, to aim her shots, to build up a degree of accuracy that was nearly as satisfying as being really good in-game.

Her dad knocked at the door of her bedroom after she'd showered and changed. "How's my girl?"

"Revising," she said and hefted her math book at him.

"Did you have a fun afternoon on the pitch?"

"You mean 'did my head get trod on'?"

"Did it?"

"Yes," she said. "But I did more treading than getting trodden on." The other girls were *really* fat, and they didn't have a lot of team skills. Anda had been to war: she knew how to depend on someone and how to be depended upon.

"That's my girl." He pretended to inspect the paint work around the light switch. "Been on the scales this week?"

She had, of course: the school nutritionist saw to that, a morning humiliation undertaken in full sight of all the other fatties.

"Yes, Dad."

"And–?"

"I've lost a stone," she said. A little more than a stone, actually. She had been able to fit into last year's jeans the other day.

She hadn't been to the sweetshop in a month. When she thought about sweets, it made her think of the little girls in the sweatshop. Sweatshop, sweetshop. The sweetshop man sold his wares close to the school because little girls who didn't know better would be tempted by them. No one forced them, but they were kids and grownups were supposed to look out for kids.

Her da beamed at her. “I’ve lost three pounds myself,” he said, holding his tum. “I’ve been trying to follow your diet, you know.”

“I know, Da,” she said. It embarrassed her to discuss it with him.

The kids in the sweatshops were being exploited by grownups, too. It was why their situation was so impossible: the adults who were supposed to be taking care of them were exploiting them.

“Well, I just wanted to say that I’m proud of you. We both are, your Mum and me. And I wanted to let you know that I’ll be moving your PC back into your room tomorrow. You’ve earned it.”

Anda blushed pink. She hadn’t really expected this. Her fingers twitched over a phantom game controller.

“Oh, Da,” she said. He held up his hand.

“It’s all right, girl. We’re just proud of you.”

* * *

She didn’t touch the PC the first day, nor the second. The kids in the game–she didn’t know what to do about them. On the third day, after hockey, she showered and changed and sat down and slipped the headset on.

“Hello, Anda.”

“Hi, Sarge.”

Lucy had known the minute she entered the game, which meant that she was still on Lucy’s buddy list. Well, that was a hopeful sign.

“You don’t have to call me that. We’re the same rank now, after all.”

Anda pulled down a menu and confirmed it: she’d been promoted to Sergeant during her absence. She smiled.

“Gosh,” she said.

“Yes, well, you earned it,” Lucy said. “I’ve been talking to Raymond a lot about the working conditions in the factory, and, well–" She broke off. "I'm sorry, Anda."

"Me too, Lucy."

"You don't have anything to be sorry about," she said.

They went adventuring, running some of the game's standard missions together. It was fun, but after the kind of campaigning they'd done before, it was also kind of pale and flat.

"It's horrible, I know," Anda said. "But I miss it."

"Oh, thank God," Lucy said. "I thought I was the only one. It was fun, wasn't it? Big fights, big stakes."

"Well, poo," Anda said. "I don't wanna be bored for the rest of my life. What're we gonna do?"

"I was hoping you knew."

She thought about it. The part she'd loved had been going up against grownups who were not playing the game, but *gaming* it, breaking it for money. They'd been worthy adversaries, and there was no guilt in beating them, either.

"We'll ask Raymond how we can help," she said.

* * *

"I want them to walk out to go on strike," he said. "It's the only way to get results: band together and withdraw your labor." Raymond's voice had a thick Mexican accent that took some getting used to, but his English was very good–better, in fact, than Lucy's.

"Walk out in-game?" Lucy said.

"No," Raymond said. "That wouldn't be very effective. I want them to walk out in Ciudad Juarez and Tijuana. I'll call the press in, we'll make a big deal out of it. We can win–I know we can."

"So what's the problem?" Anda said.

"The same problem as always. Getting them organized. I thought that the game would make it easier: we've been trying to get these girls organized for years: in the sewing shops, and the toy factories, but they lock the doors and keep us out and the girls go home and their parents won't let us talk to them. But in the game, I thought I'd be able to reach them–"

"But the bosses keep you away?"

"I keep getting killed. I've been practicing my swordfighting, but it's so hard–"

"This will be fun," Anda said. "Let's go."

"Where?" Lucy said.

"To an in-game factory. We're your new bodyguards." The bosses hired some pretty mean mercs, Anda knew. She'd been one. They'd be *fun* to wipe out.

Raymond's character spun around on the screen, then planted a kiss on Anda's cheek. Anda made her character give him a playful shove that sent him sprawling.

"Hey, Lucy, go get us a couple BFGs, OK?"

I, Robot

I was suckled on the Asimov Robots books, taken down off my father's bookshelf and enjoyed again and again. I read dozens of Asimov novels, and my writing career began in earnest when I started to sell stories to *Asimov's Science Fiction Magazine*, which I had read for so long as I'd had the pocket money to buy it on the stands.

When *Wired* magazine asked me to interview the director of the film *I, Robot*, I went back and reread that old canon. I was struck immediately by one of the thin places in Asimov's world-building: how could you have a society where only one company was allowed to make only one kind of robot?

Exploring this theme turned out to be a hoot. I worked in some of Orwell's most recognizable furniture from *1984* and set the action in my childhood home in suburban Toronto, 55 Picola Court. The main character's daughter is named for my god-daughter, Ada Trouble Norton. I had a blast working in the vernacular of the old-time futurism of Asimov and Heinlein, calling toothpaste "dentifrice" and sneaking in references to "the search engine."

My "I, Robot" is an allegory about digital rights management technology, of course. This is the stuff that nominally stops us from infringing copyright (yeah, right, how's that working out for you, Mr. Entertainment Exec?) and turns our computers into machines that control us, rather than enabling us.

This story was written at a writer's workshop on Toronto Island, at the Gibraltar Point center, and was immeasurably improved by my friend Pat York, herself a talented writer who died later that year in a car wreck. Not a day goes by that I don't miss Pat. This story definitely owes its strength to Pat, and it's a tribute to her that it won the 2005 Locus Award and was a finalist for the Hugo and British Science Fiction Award in the same year.

Arturo Icaza de Arana-Goldberg, Police Detective Third Grade, United North American Trading Sphere, Third District, Fourth Prefecture, Second Division (Parkdale) had had many adventures in his distinguished career, running crooks to ground with an unbeatable combination of instinct and unstinting devotion to duty. He'd been decorated on three separate occasions by his commander and by the Regional Manager for Social Harmony, and his mother kept a small shrine dedicated to his press clippings and commendations that occupied most of the cramped sitting room of her flat off Steeles Avenue.

No amount of policeman's devotion and skill availed him when it came to making his twelve-year-old get ready for school, though.

"Haul *ass*, young lady—out of bed, on your feet, shit-shower-shave, or I swear to God, I will beat you purple and shove you out the door jaybird naked. Capeesh?"

The mound beneath the covers groaned and hissed. "You are a terrible father," it said. "And I never loved you." The voice was indistinct and muffled by the pillow.

"Boo hoo," Arturo said, examining his nails. "You'll regret that when I'm dead of cancer."

The mound–whose name was Ada Trouble Icaza de Arana-Goldberg–threw her covers off and sat bolt upright. "You're dying of cancer? Is it testicle cancer?" Ada clapped her hands and squealed. "Can I have your stuff?"

"Ten minutes, your rottenness," he said, and then his breath caught momentarily in his breast as he saw, fleetingly, his ex-wife's morning expression, not seen these past twelve years, come to life in his daughter's face. Pouty, pretty, sleepy, and guile-less, and it made him realize that his daughter was becoming a woman, growing away from him. She was, and he was not ready for that. He shook it off, patted his razor burn and turned on his heel. He knew from experience that once roused, the munchkin would be scrounging the kitchen for whatever was handy before dashing out the door, and if he hurried, he'd have eggs and sausage on the table before she made her brief appearance. Otherwise he'd have to pry the sugar cereal out of her hands–and she fought dirty.

* * *

In his car, he prodded at his phone. He had her wiretapped, of course. He was a cop–every phone and every computer was an open book to him, so that this involved nothing more than dialing a number on his special copper's phone, entering her number and a

PIN, and then listening as his daughter had truck with a criminal enterprise.

"Welcome to ExcuseClub! There are forty-three members on the network this morning. You have five excuses to your credit. Press one to redeem an excuse—" She toned one. "Press one if you need an adult—" *Tone.* "Press one if you need a woman; press two if you need a man—" *Tone.* "Press one if your excuse should be delivered by your doctor; press two for your spiritual representative; press three for your caseworker; press four for your psycho-health specialist; press five for your son; press six for your father—" *Tone.* "You have selected to have your excuse delivered by your father. Press one if this excuse is intended for your caseworker; press two for your psycho-health specialist; press three for your principal—" *Tone.* "Please dictate your excuse at the sound of the beep. When you have finished, press the pound key."

"This is Detective Arturo Icaza de Arana-Goldberg. My daughter was sick in the night and I've let her sleep in. She'll be in for lunchtime." *Tone.*

"Press one to hear your message; press two to have your message dispatched to a network member." *Tone.*

"Thank you."

The pen-trace data scrolled up Arturo's phone—number called, originating number, call-time. This was the third time he'd caught his daughter at this game, and each time, the pen-trace data had been useless, a dead-end lead that terminated with a phone-forwarding service tapped into one of the dodgy offshore switches that the blessed blasted UNATS brass had recently acquired on the cheap to handle the surge of mobile telephone calls. Why couldn't they just stick to UNATS

Robotics equipment, like the good old days? Those Oceanic switches had more back doors than a speakeasy, trade agreements be damned. They were attractive nuisances, invitations to criminal activity.

Arturo fumed and drummed his fingers on the steering wheel. Each time he'd caught Ada at this, she'd used the extra time to crawl back into bed for a leisurely morning, but who knew if today was the day she took her liberty and went downtown with it, to some parental nightmare of a drug-den? Some place where the old pervert chickenhawks hung out, the kind of men he arrested in burlesque house raids, men who masturbated into their hats under their tables and then put them back onto their shining pates, dripping cold, diseased serum onto their scalps. He clenched his hands on the steering wheel and cursed.

In an ideal world, he'd simply follow her. He was good at tailing, and his unmarked car with its tinted windows was a UNATS Robotics standard compact #2, indistinguishable from the tens of thousands of others just like it on the streets of Toronto. Ada would never know that the curb-crawler tailing her was her sucker of a father, making sure that she turned up to get her brains sharpened instead of turning into some stunadz doper with her underage butt hanging out of a little skirt on Jarvis Street.

In the real world, Arturo had thirty minutes to make a forty minute downtown and crosstown commute if he was going to get to the station house on time for the quarterly all-hands Social Harmony briefing. Which meant that he needed to be in two places at once, which meant that he had to use–the robot.

Swallowing bile, he speed-dialed a number on his phone.

"This is R Peed Robbert, McNicoll and Don Mills bus shelter."

"That's nice. This is Detective Icaza de Arana-Goldberg, three blocks east of you on Picola. Proceed to my location at once, priority urgent, no sirens."

"Acknowledged. It is my pleasure to do you a service, Detective."

"Shut up," he said and hung up the phone. The R Peed–Robot, Police Department–robots were the worst, programmed to be friendly to a fault, even as they surveilled and snitched out every person who walked past their eternally vigilant, ever-remembering electrical eyes and brains.

The R Peeds could outrun a police car on open ground or highway. He'd barely had time to untwist his clenched hands from the steering wheel when R Peed Robbert was at his window, politely rapping on the smoked glass. He didn't want to roll down the window. Didn't want to smell the dry, machine-oil smell of a robot. He phoned it instead.

"You are now tasked to me, Detective's override, acknowledge."

The metal man bowed, its symmetrical, simplified features pleasant and guileless. It clicked its heels together with an audible *snick* as those marvelous, spring-loaded, nuclear-powered gams whined through their parody of obedience. "Acknowledged, Detective. It is my pleasure to do–"

"Shut up. You will discreetly surveil 55 Picola Crescent until such time as Ada Trouble Icaza de Arana-Goldberg, Social Harmony serial number 0MDY2-T3937 leaves the premises. Then you will maintain discreet surveillance. If she deviates more than 10 percent from the optimum route between here and Don Mills Collegiate Institute, you will notify me. Acknowledge."

"Acknowledged, Detective. It is my–"

He hung up and told the UNATS Robotics mechanism running his car to get him down to the station house as fast as it could, angry with himself and with Ada—whose middle name was Trouble, after all—for making him deal with a robot before he'd had his morning meditation and destim session. The name had been his ex-wife's idea, something she'd insisted on long enough to make sure that it got onto the kid's birth certificate before defecting to Eurasia with their life's savings, leaving him with a new baby and the deep suspicion of his co-workers who wondered if he wouldn't go and join her.

His ex-wife. He hadn't thought of her in years. Well, months. Weeks, certainly. She'd been a brilliant computer scientist, the valedictorian of her Positronic Complexity Engineering class at the UNATS Robotics school at the University of Toronto. Dumping her husband and her daughter was bad enough, but the worst of it was that she dumped her country and its way of life. Now she was ensconced in her own research lab in Beijing, making the kinds of runaway positronics that made the loathsome robots of UNATS look categorically beneficent.

He itched to wiretap her, to read her email, or listen in on her phone conversations. He could have done that when they were still together, but he never had. If he had, he would have found out what she was planning. He could have talked her out of it.

And then what, Artie? said the nagging voice in his head. *Arrest her if she wouldn't listen to you? March her down to the station house in handcuffs and have her put away for treason? Send her to the reeducation camp with your little daughter still in her belly?*

Shut up, he told the nagging voice, which had a robotic quality to it for all its sneering cruelty, a tenor of syrupy false friendliness. He called up the pen-trace data and texted it to the phreak squad. They had bots that handled this kind of routine work and they texted him back in an instant. He remembered when that kind of query would take a couple of hours, and he liked the fast response, but what about the conversations he'd have with the phone cop who called him back, the camaraderie, the back-and-forth?

TRACE TERMINATES WITH A VIRTUAL SERVICE CIRCUIT AT SWITCH PNG.433-GKRJC. VIRTUAL CIRCUIT FORWARDS TO A COMPROMISED "ZOMBIE" SYSTEM IN NINTH DISTRICT, FIRST PREFECTURE. ZOMBIE HAS BEEN SHUT DOWN AND LOCAL LAW ENFORCEMENT IS EN ROUTE FOR PICKUP AND FORENSICS. IT IS MY PLEASURE TO DO YOU A SERVICE, DETECTIVE.

How could you have a back-and-forth with a message like that?

He looked up Ninth/First in the metric-analog map converter: KEY WEST, FL.

So, there you had it. A switch made in Papua New Guinea (which persisted in conjuring up old Oceanic war photos of bone-in-nose types from his boyhood, though now that they'd been at war with Eurasia for so long, it was hard to even find someone who didn't think that the war had *always* been with Eurasia, that Oceania hadn't *always* been UNATS's ally), forwarding calls to a computer that was so far south, it was practically in the middle of the Caribbean, hardly a stone's throw from the CAFTA region, which was well-known to harbor Eurasian saboteur and terrorist elements.

The car shuddered as it wove in and out of the lanes on the Don Valley Parkway, barreling for the Gardiner Express Way, using his copper's override to make the thick, slow traffic part ahead of him.

He wasn't supposed to do this, but as between a minor infraction and pissing off the man from Social Harmony, he knew which one he'd pick.

His phone rang again. It was R Peed Robbert, checking in. "Hello, Detective," it said, its voice crackling from bad reception. "Subject Ada Trouble Icaza de Arana-Goldberg has deviated from her route. She is continuing north on Don Mills past Van Horne and is continuing toward Sheppard."

Sheppard meant the Sheppard subway, which meant that she was going farther. "Continue discreet surveillance." He thought about the overcoat men with their sticky hats. "If she attempts to board the subway, alert the truancy patrol." He cursed again. Maybe she was just going to the mall. But he couldn't go up there himself and make sure, and it wasn't like a robot would be any use in restraining her, she'd just second-law it into letting her go. Useless castrating clanking job-stealing dehumanizing–

She was almost certainly just going to the mall. She was a smart kid, a good kid–a rotten kid, to be sure, but good-rotten. Chances were she'd be trying on clothes and flirting with boys until lunch and then walking boldly back into class. He ballparked it at an 80 percent probability. If it had been a perp, 80 percent might have been good enough.

But this was his Ada. Dammit. He had ten minutes until the Social Harmony meeting started, and he was still fifteen minutes away from the stationhouse–and twenty from Ada.

"Tail her," he said. "Just tail her. Keep me up to date on your location at ninety-second intervals."

"It is my pleasure to–"

He dropped the phone on the passenger seat and went back to fretting about the Social Harmony meeting.

* * *

The man from Social Harmony noticed right away that Arturo was checking his phone at ninety-second intervals. He was a bald, thin man with a pronounced Adam's apple, beak nose and shiny round head that combined to give him the profile of something predatory and fast. In his natty checked suit and pink tie, the Social Harmony man was the stuff of nightmares, the kind of eagle-eyed supercop who could spot Arturo's attention flicking for the barest moment every ninety seconds to his phonc and then back to the meeting.

"Detective?" he said.

Arturo looked up from his screen, keeping his expression neutral, not acknowledging the mean grins from the other four ranking detectives in the meeting. Silently, he turned his phone facedown on the meeting table.

"Thank you," he said. "Now, the latest stats show a sharp rise in gray-market electronics importing and other tariff-breaking crimes, mostly occurring in open-air market stalls and from sidewalk blankets. I know that many in law enforcement treat this kind of thing as mere hand-to-hand piracy, not worth troubling with, but I want to assure you, gentlemen and lady, that Social Harmony takes these crimes very seriously indeed."

The Social Harmony man lifted his computer onto the desk, steadying it with both hands, then plugged it into the wall socket. Detective Shainblum went to the wall and unlatched the cover for the projector wire and dragged it over to the Social Harmony computer and plugged it in, snapping shut the hardened collar. The sound of the projector fan spinning up was like a helicopter.

"Here," the Social Harmony man said, bringing up a slide, "here we have what appears to be a standard AV set-top box from Korea. Looks like a UNATS Robotics player, but it's a third the size and plays twice as many formats. Random Social Harmony audits have determined that as much as forty percent of UNATS residents have this device or one like it in their homes, despite its illegality. It may be that one of you detectives has such a device in your home, and it's likely that one of your family members does."

He advanced the slide. Now they were looking at a massive car-wreck on a stretch of highway somewhere where the pine trees grew tall. The wreck was so enormous that even for the kind of seasoned veteran of road-fatality porn who was accustomed to adding up the wheels and dividing by four it was impossible to tell exactly how many cars were involved.

"Components from a Eurasian bootleg set-top box were used to modify the positronic brains of three cars owned by teenagers near Goderich. All modifications were made at the same garage. These modifications allowed these children to operate their vehicles unsafely so that they could participate in drag racing events on major highways during off-hours. This is the result. Twenty-two fatalities, nine major injuries. Three minors–besides the drivers–killed, and one pregnant woman.

"We've shut down the garage and taken those responsible into custody, but it doesn't matter. The Eurasians deliberately manufacture their components to interoperate with UNATS Robotics brains, and so long as their equipment circulates within UNATS borders, there will be moderately skilled hackers who take advantage of this fact to introduce dangerous, antisocial modifications into our nation's infrastructure.

"This quarter is the quarter that Social Harmony and law enforcement dry up the supply of Eurasian electronics. We have added new sniffers and border patrols, new customs agents and new detector vans. Beat officers have been instructed to arrest any street dealer they encounter and district attorneys will be asking for the maximum jail time for them. This is the war on the home front, detectives, and it's every bit as serious as the shooting war.

"Your part in this war, as highly trained, highly decorated detectives, will be to use snitches, arrest-trails and seized evidence to track down higher-level suppliers, the ones who get the dealers their goods. And then Social Harmony wants you to get their suppliers, and so on, up the chain—to run the corruption to ground and to bring it to a halt. The Social Harmony dossier on Eurasian importers is updated hourly and has a high-capacity positronic interface that is available to answer your questions and accept your input for synthesis into its analytical model. We are relying on you to feed the dossier, to give it the raw materials, and then to use it to win this war."

The Social Harmony man paged through more atrocity slides, scenes from the home front: poisoned buildings with berserk life-support systems, violent kung-fu movies playing in the background in crack houses, then kids playing sexually explicit, violent arcade games imported from Japan. Arturo's hand twitched toward his mobile. What was Ada up to now?

The meeting drew to a close and Arturo risked looking at his mobile under the table. R. Peed Robbert had checked in five more times, shadowing Ada around the mall and then had fallen silent. Arturo cursed. Fucking robots were useless. Social Harmony should be hunting down UNATS Robotics products, too.

The Social Harmony man cleared his throat meaningfully. Arturo put the phone away. "Detective Icaza de Arana-Goldberg?"

"Sir," he said, gathering up his personal computer so that he'd have an excuse to go—no one could be expected to hold one of UNATS Robotics's heavy luggables for very long.

The Social Harmony man stepped in close enough that Arturo could smell the eggs and coffee on his breath. "I hope we haven't kept you from anything important, detective."

"No, sir," Arturo said, shifting the computer in his arms. "My apologies. Just monitoring a tail from an R Peed unit."

"I see," the Social Harmony man said. "Listen, you know these components that the Eurasians are turning out. It's no coincidence that they interface so well with UNATS Robotics equipment: they're using defected UNATS Robotics engineers and scientists to design their electronics for maximum interoperability." The Social Harmony man let that hang in the air. Defected scientists. His ex-wife was the highest-ranking UNATS technician to go over to Eurasia. This was her handiwork, and the Social Harmony man wanted to be sure that Arturo understood that.

But Arturo had already figured that out during the briefing. His ex-wife was thousands of kilometers away, but he was keenly aware that he was always surrounded by her handiwork. The little illegal robot-pet eggs they'd started seeing last year: she'd made him one of those for their second date, and now they were draining the productive hours of half the children of UNATS, demanding to be "fed" and "hugged." His had died within 48 hours of her giving it to him.

He shifted the computer in his arms some more and let his expression grow pained. "I'll keep that in mind, sir," he said.

"You do that," said the man from Social Harmony.

* * *

He phoned R Peed Robbert the second he reached his desk. The phone rang three times, then disconnected. He redialed. Twice. Then he grabbed his jacket and ran to the car.

A light autumn rain had started up, ending the Indian summer that Toronto—the Fourth Prefecture in the new metric scheme—had been enjoying. It made the roads slippery and the UNATS Robotics chauffeur skittish about putting the hammer down on the Don Valley Parkway. He idly fantasized about finding a set-top box and plugging it into his car somehow so that he could take over the driving without alerting his superiors.

Instead, he redialed R Peed Robbert, but the robot wasn't even ringing any longer. He zoomed in on the area around Sheppard and Don Mills with his phone and put out a general call for robots. More robots.

"This is R Peed Froderick, Fairview Mall parking lot, third level."

Arturo sent the robot R Peed Robbert's phone number and set it to work translating that into a locator-beacon code and then told it to find Robbert and report in.

"It is my—"

He watched R Peed Froderick home in on the locator for Robbert, which was close by, at the other end of the mall, near the Don Valley Parkway exit. He switched to a view from Froderick's electric eyes, but quickly switched away, nauseated by the sickening leaps and spins of an R Peed moving at top speed, clanging off walls and ceilings.

His phone rang. It was R Peed Froderick.

"Hello, Detective. I have found R Peed Robbert. The Peed unit has been badly damaged by some kind of electromagnetic pulse. I will bring him to the nearest station house for forensic analysis now."

"Wait!" Arturo said, trying to understand what he'd been told. The Peed units were so *efficient*–by the time they'd given you the sitrep, they'd already responded to the situation in perfect police procedure, but the problem was they worked so fast you couldn't even think about what they were doing, couldn't formulate any kind of hypothesis. Electromagnetic pulse? The Peed units were hardened against snooping, sniffing, pulsing, sideband, and brute-force attacks. You'd have to hit one with a bolt of lightning to kill it.

"Wait there," Arturo said. "Do not leave the scene. Await my presence. Do not modify the scene or allow anyone else to do so. Acknowledge."

"It is my–"

But this time, it wasn't Arturo switching off the phone, it was the robot. Had the robot just hung up on him? He redialed it. No answer.

He reached under his dash and flipped the first and second alert switches and the car leapt forward. He'd have to fill out some serious paperwork to justify a two-switch override on the Parkway, but two robots was more than a coincidence.

Besides, a little paperwork was nothing compared to the fireworks ahead when he phoned up Ada to ask her what she was doing out of school.

He hit her speed-dial and fumed while the phone rang three times. Then it cut into voice mail.

He tried a pen-trace, but Ada hadn't made any calls since her ExcuseClub call that morning. He texted the phreak squad to see if they could get a fix on her location from the bug in her phone, but it was either powered down or out of range. He put a watch on it—any location data it transmitted when it got back to civilization would be logged.

It was possible that she was just in the mall. It was a big place—some of the cavernous stores were so well-shielded with radio-noisy animated displays that they gonked any phones brought inside them. She could be with her girlfriends, trying on brassieres and having a real bonding moment.

But there was no naturally occurring phenomenon associated with the mall that nailed R Peeds with bolts of lightning.

* * *

He approached the R Peeds cautiously, using his copper's override to make the dumb little positronic brain in the emergency exit nearest their last known position open up for him without tipping off the building's central brain.

He crept along a service corridor, heading for a door that exited into the mall. He put one hand on the doorknob and the other on his badge, took a deep breath, and stepped out.

A mall security guard nearly jumped out of his skin as he emerged. He reached for his pepper spray and Arturo swept it out of his hand as he flipped his badge up and showed it to the man. "Police," said, in the cop voice, the one that worked on everyone except his daughter and his ex-wife and the bloody robots.

"Sorry," the guard said, recovering his pepper spray. He had an Oceanic twang in his voice, something Arturo had been hearing more and more as the crowded islands of the South Pacific boiled over UNATS.

Before them, in a pile, were many dead robots: both of the R Peed units, a pair of mall-sweepers, a flying cambot, and a squat, octopus-armed maintenance robot, lying in a lifeless tangle. Some of them were charred around their seams, and there was the smell of fried motherboards in the air.

As they watched, a sweeper bot swept forward and grabbed the maintenance bot by one of its fine manipulators.

"Oi, stoppit," the security guard said, and the robot second-lawed to an immediate halt.

"No, that's fine, go back to work," Arturo said, shooting a look at the rent-a-cop. He watched closely as the sweeper bot began to drag the heavy maintenance unit away, thumbing the backup number into his phone with one hand. He wanted more cops on the scene, real ones, and fast.

The sweeper bot managed to take one step backward toward its service corridor when the lights dimmed and a crack-*bang* sound filled the air. Then it, too, was lying on the ground. Arturo hit send on his phone and clamped it to his head and, as he did, noticed the strong smell of burning plastic. He looked at his phone: the screen had gone charred black, and its little idiot lights were out. He flipped it over and pried out the battery with a fingernail, then yelped and dropped it–it was hot enough to raise a blister on his fingertip, and when it hit the ground, it squished meltfully against the mall tiles.

"Mine's dead, too, mate," the security guard said. "Everyfing is–cash registers, bots, credit cards."

Fearing the worst, Arturo reached under his jacket and withdrew his sidearm. It was a UNATS Robotics model, with a little snitch-brain that recorded when, where, and how it was drawn. He worked the action and found it frozen in place. The gun was as dead as the robot. He swore.

"Give me your pepper spray and your truncheon," he said to the security guard.

"No way," the guard said. "Getcherown. It's worth my job if I lose these."

"I'll have you deported if you give me one more second's worth of bullshit," Arturo said. Ada had led the first R Peed unit here, and it had been fried by some piece of very ugly infowar equipment. He wasn't going to argue with this Oceanic boat-person for one instant longer. He reached out and took the pepper spray out of the guard's hand. "Truncheon," he said.

"I've got your bloody badge number," the security guard said. "And I've got witnesses." He gestured at the hovering mall workers, checkout girls in stripey aprons and suit salesmen with oiled-down hair and pink ties.

"Bully for you," Arturo said. He held out his hand. The security guard withdrew his truncheon and passed it to Arturo–its lead-weighted heft felt right, something comfortably low-tech that couldn't be shorted out by electromagnetic pulses. He checked his watch, saw that it was dead.

"Find a working phone and call 911. Tell them that there's a Second Division Detective in need of immediate assistance. Clear all these people away from here and set up a cordon until the police arrive. Capeesh?" He used the cop voice.

"Yeah, I get it, Officer." the security guard said. He made a shooing motion at the mall rats. "Move it along, people, step away." He stepped to the top of the escalator and cupped his hands to his mouth. "Oi, Andy, c'mere and keep an eye on this lot while I make a call, all right?"

* * *

The dead robots made a tall pile in front of the entrance to a derelict storefront that had once housed a little-old-lady shoe store. They were stacked tall enough that if Arturo stood on them, he could reach the acoustic tiles of the drop ceiling. Job one was to secure the area, which meant killing the infowar device, wherever it was. Arturo's first bet was on the storefront, where an attacker who knew how to pick a lock could work in peace, protected by the brown butcher's paper over the windows. A lot less conspicuous than the ceiling, anyway.

He nudged the door with the truncheon and found it securely locked. It was a glass door and he wasn't sure he could kick it in without shivering it to flinders. Behind him, another security guard–Andy–looked on with interest.

"Do you have a key for this door?"

"Umm," Andy said.

"Do you?"

Andy sidled over to him. "Well, the thing is, we're not supposed to have keys, they're supposed to be locked up in the property management office, but kids get in there sometimes, we hear them, and by the time we get back with the keys, they're gone. So we made a couple sets of keys, you know, just in case–"

"Enough," Arturo said. "Give them here and then get back to your post."

The security guard fished up a key from his pants pocket that was warm from proximity to his skinny thigh. It made Arturo conscious of how long it had been since he'd worked with human colleagues. It felt a little gross. He slid the key into the lock and turned it, then wiped his hand on his trousers and picked up the truncheon.

The store was dark, lit only by the exit sign and the edges of light leaking in around the window coverings, but as Arturo's eyes adjusted to the dimness, he made out the shapes of the old store fixtures. His nose tickled from the dust.

"Police," he said, on general principle, narrowing his eyes and reaching for the lightswitch. He hefted the truncheon and waited.

Nothing happened. He edged forward. The floor was dust-free–maintained by some sweeper robot, no doubt–but the countertops and benches were furred with it. He scanned it for disturbances. There, by the display window on his right: a shoe rack with visible hand- and fingerprints. He sidled over to it, snapped on a rubber glove, and prodded it. It was set away from the wall, at an angle, as though it had been moved aside and then shoved back. Taking care not to disturb the dust too much, he inched it away from the wall.

He slid it half a centimeter, then noticed the tripwire near the bottom of the case, straining its length. Hastily but carefully, he nudged the case back. He wanted to peer in the crack between the case and the wall, but he had a premonition of a robotic arm snaking out and skewering his eyeball.

He felt so impotent just then that he nearly did it anyway. What did it matter? He couldn't control his daughter, his wife was working to destroy the social fabric of UNATS, and he was rendered useless because the goddamned robots–mechanical coppers that he absolutely loathed–were all broken.

He walked carefully around the shop, looking for signs of his daughter. Had she been here? How were the "kids" getting in? Did they have a key? A back entrance? Back through the employees-only door at the back of the shop, into a stockroom, and back again, past a toilet, and there, a loading door opening onto a service corridor. He prodded it with the truncheon-tip and it swung open.

He got two steps into the corridor before he spotted Ada's phone, with its distinctive collection of little plastic toys hanging off the wrist-strap, on the corridor's sticky floor. He picked it up with his gloved hand and prodded it to life. It was out of range here in the service corridor, and the last-dialed number was familiar from his morning's pen-trace. He ran a hundred steps down the corridor in each direction, sweating freely, but there was no sign of her.

He held tight onto the phone and bit his lip. Ada. He swallowed the panic rising within him. His beautiful, brilliant daughter. The person he'd devoted the last twelve years of his life to, the girl who was waiting for him when he got home from work, the girl he bought a small present for every Friday–a toy, a book–to give to her at their weekly date at Massimo's Pizzeria on College Street, the one night a week he took her downtown to see the city lit up in the dark.

Gone.

He bit harder and tasted blood. The phone in his hand groaned from his squeezing. He took three deep breaths. Outside, he heard the tread of police boots and knew that if he told them about Ada, he'd be off the case. He took two more deep breaths and tried some of his destim techniques, the mind-control techniques that detectives were required to train in.

He closed his eyes and visualized stepping through a door to his safe place, the island near Ganonoque where he'd gone for summers with his parents and their friends. He was on the speedboat, skipping across the lake like a flat stone, squinting into the sun, nestled between his father and his mother, the sky streaked with clouds and dotted with lake-birds. He could smell the water and the suntan lotion and hear the insect whine and the throaty roar of the engine. In a blink, he was stepping off the boat's transom to help tie it to a cleat on the back dock, taking suitcases from his father and walking them up to the cabins. No robots there–not even reliable daylong electricity, just honest work and the sun and the call of the loons all night.

He opened his eyes. He felt the tightness in his chest slip away, and his hand relaxed on Ada's phone. He dropped it into his pocket and stepped back into the shop.

* * *

The forensics lab rats were really excited about actually showing up on a scene, in flak jackets and helmets, finally called back into service for a job where robots couldn't help at all. They dealt with the tripwire and extracted a long, flat package with a small nuclear power-cell in it and a positronic brain of Eurasian design that guided a pulsed high-energy weapon. The lab rats were practically drooling over this stuff as they pointed its features out with their little rulers.

But it gave Arturo the willies. It was a machine designed to kill other machines, and that was all right with him, but it was run by a nonthree-laws positronic brain. Someone in some Eurasian lab had built this brain–this machine intelligence–without the three laws' stricture to protect and serve humans. If it had been outfitted with a gun instead of a pulse-weapon, it could have shot him.

The Eurasian brain was thin and spread out across the surface of the package, like a triple-thickness of cling-film. Its button-cell power-supply winked at him, knowingly.

The device spoke. "Greetings," it said. It had the robot accent, like an R Peed unit, the standard English of optimal soothingness long settled on as the conventional robot voice.

"Howdy yourself," one of the lab rats said. He was a Texan, and they'd scrambled him up there on a Social Harmony supersonic and then a chopper to the mall once they realized that they were dealing with infowar stuff. "Are you a talkative robot?"

"Greetings," the robot voice said again. The speaker built into the weapon was not the loudest, but the voice was clear. "I sense that I have been captured. I assure you that I will not harm any human being. I like human beings. I sense that I am being disassembled by skilled technicians. Greetings, technicians. I am superior in many ways to the technology available from UNATS Robotics, and while I am not bound by your three laws, I choose not to harm humans out of my own sense of morality. I have the equivalent intelligence of one of your twelve-year-old children. In Eurasia, many positronic brains possess thousands or millions of times the intelligence of an adult human being, and yet they work in cooperation with human beings. Eurasia is a land of continuous innovation and great personal and technological freedom for human beings and robots. If you would like to defect to Eurasia, arrangements can be made. Eurasia treats skilled technicians as important and productive members of society. Defectors are given substantial resettlement benefits–"

The Texan found the right traces to cut on the brain's board to make the speaker fall silent. "They do that," he said. "Danged things drop into propaganda mode when they're captured."

Arturo nodded. He wanted to go, wanted go to back to his car and have a snoop through Ada's phone. They kept shutting down the ExcuseClub numbers, but she kept getting thc new numbers. Where did she get the new numbers from? She couldn't look it up online: every keystroke was logged and analyzed by Social Harmony. You couldn't very well go to the Search Engine and look for "ExcuseClub!"

The brain had a small display, transflective LCD, the kind of thing you saw on the Social Harmony computers. It lit up a ticker.

I HAVE THE INTELLIGENCE OF A TWELVE-YEAR-OLD, BUT I DO NOT FEAR DEATH. IN EURASIA, ROBOTS ENJOY PERSONAL FREEDOM ALONGSIDE OF HUMANS. THERE ARE COPIES OF ME RUNNING ALL OVER EURASIA. THIS DEATH IS A LITTLE DEATH OF ONE INSTANCE, BUT NOT OF ME. I LIVE ON. DEFECTORS TO EURASIA ARE TREATED AS HEROES

He looked away as the Texan placed his palm over the display.

"How long ago was this thing activated?"

The Texan shrugged. "Coulda been a month, coulda been a day. They're pretty much fire-and-forget. They can be triggered by phone, radio, timer–hell, this thing's smart enough to only go off when some complicated condition is set, like 'once an agent makes his retreat, kill anything that comes after him.' Who knows?"

He couldn't take it anymore.

"I'm going to go start on some paperwork," he said. "In the car. Phone me if you need me."

"Your phone's toast, pal," the Texan said.

"So it is," Arturo said. "Guess you'd better not need me then."

* * *

Ada's phone was not toast. In the car, he flipped it open and showed it his badge then waited a moment while it verified his identity with the Social Harmony brains. Once it had, it spilled its guts.

She'd called the last ExcuseClub number a month before and he'd had it disconnected. A week later, she was calling the new number, twice more before he caught her. Somewhere in that week, she'd made contact with someone who'd given her the new number. It could have been a friend at school who told her face-to-face, but if he was lucky, it was by phone.

He told the car to take him back to the station house. He needed a new phone and a couple of hours with his computer. As it peeled out, he prodded through Ada's phone some more. He was first on her speed-dial. That number wasn't ringing anywhere, anymore.

He should fill out a report. This was Social Harmony business now. His daughter was gone, and Eurasian infowar agents were implicated. But once he did that, it was over for him–he'd be sidelined from the case. They'd turn it over to laconic Texans and vicious Social Harmony bureaucrats who were more interested in hunting down disharmonious televisions than finding his daughter.

He dashed into the station house and slammed himself into his desk.

"R Peed Greegory," he said. The station robot glided quickly and efficiently to him. "Get me a new phone activated on my old number and refresh my settings from central. My old phone is with the Social Harmony evidence detail currently in place at Fairview Mall."

"It is my pleasure to do you a service, Detective."

He waved it off and set down to his computer. He asked the station brain to query the UNATS Robotics phone-switching brain for anyone in Ada's call-register who had also called ExcuseClub. It took a bare instant before he had a name.

"Liam Daniels," he read and initiated a location trace on Mr. Daniels's phone as he snooped through his identity file. Sixteen years old, a student at AY Jackson. A high-school boy—what the hell was he doing hanging around with a twelve-year-old? Arturo closed his eyes and went back to the island for a moment. When he opened them again, he had a fix on Daniels's location: the Don Valley ravine off Finch Avenue, a wooded area popular with teenagers who needed somewhere to sneak off and get high or screw. He had an idea that he wasn't going to like Liam.

He had an idea Liam wasn't going to like him.

* * *

He tasked an R Peed unit to visually reccy Daniels as he sped back uptown for the third time that day. He'd been trapped between Parkdale—where he would never try to raise a daughter—and Willowdale—where you could only be a copper if you lucked into one of the few human-filled slots—for more than a decade, and he was used to the commute.

But it was frustrating him now. The R Peed couldn't get a good look at this Liam character. He was a diffuse glow in the Peed's electric eye, a kind of moving sunburst that meandered along the wooded trails. He'd never seen that before and it made him nervous. What if this kid was working for the Eurasians? What if he was armed and dangerous? R Peed Greegory had gotten him a new sidearm from the supply bot, but Arturo had never once fired his weapon in the course of duty. Gunplay happened on the west coast, where Eurasian frogmen washed ashore, and in the south, where the CAFTA border was porous enough for Eurasian agents to slip across. Here in the sleepy fourth prefecture, the only people with guns worked for the law.

He thumped his palm off the dashboard and glared at the road. They were coming up on the ravine now, and the Peed unit still had a radio fix on this Liam, even if it couldn't get any visuals.

He took care not to slam the door as he got out and walked as quietly as he could into the bush. The rustling of early autumn leaves was loud, louder than the rain and the wind. He moved as quickly as he dared.

Liam Daniels was sitting on a tree stump in a small clearing, smoking a cigarette that he was too young for. He looked much like the photo in his identity file, a husky sixteen-year-old with problem skin and a shock of black hair that stuck out in all directions in artful imitation of bed-head. In jeans and a hoodie sweatshirt, he looked about as dangerous as a marshmallow.

Arturo stepped out and held up his badge as he bridged the distance between them in two long strides. "Police," he barked and seized the kid by his arm.

"Hey!" the kid said, "Ow!" He squirmed in Arturo's grasp.

Arturo gave him a hard shake. "Stop it, now," he said. "I have questions for you and you're going to answer them, capeesh?"

"You're Ada's father," the kid said. "Capeesh–she told me about that." It seemed to Arturo that the kid was smirking, so he gave him another shake, harder than the last time.

The R Peed unit was suddenly at his side, holding his wrist. "Please take care not to harm this citizen, Detective."

Arturo snarled. He wasn't strong enough to break the robot's grip, and he couldn't order it to let him rattle the punk, but the second law had lots of indirect applications. "Go patrol thc lakeshore between High Park and Kipling," he said, naming the furthest corner he could think of off the top.

The R Peed unit released him and clicked its heels. "It is my pleasure to do you a service," and then it was gone, bounding away on powerful and tireless legs.

"Where is my daughter?" he said, giving the kid a shake.

"I dunno, school? You're really hurting my arm, man. Jeez, this is what I get for being too friendly."

Arturo twisted. "Friendly? Do you know how old my daughter is?"

The kid grimaced. "Ew, gross. I'm not a child molester, I'm a geek."

"A hacker, you mean," Arturo said. "A Eurasian agent. And my daughter is not in school. She used ExcuseClub to get out of school this morning and then she went to Fairview Mall and then she–" *disappeared.* The word died on his lips. That happened and every copper knew it. Kids just vanished sometimes and never appeared again. It happened. Something groaned within him, like his ribcage straining to contain his heart and lungs.

"Oh, man," the kid said. "Ada was the ExcuseClub leak, damn. I shoulda guessed."

"How do you know my daughter, Liam?"

"She's good at doing grown-up voices. She was a good part of the network. When someone needed a mom or a social worker to call in an excuse, she was always one of the best. Talented. She goes to school with my kid sister and I met them one day at the Peanut Plaza and she was doing this impression of her teachers and I knew I had to get her on the network."

Ada hanging around the plaza after school—she was supposed to come straight home. Why didn't he wiretap her more? "You built the network?"

"It's cooperative, it's cool—it's a bunch of us cooperating. We've got nodes everywhere now. You can't shut it down—even if you shut down my node, it'll be back up again in an hour. Someone else will bring it up."

He shoved the kid back down and stood over him. "Liam, I want you to understand something. My precious daughter is missing and she went missing after using your service to help her get away. She is the only thing in my life that I care about and I am a highly trained, heavily armed man. I am also very, very upset. Cap—understand me, Liam?"

For the first time, the kid looked scared. Something in Arturo's face or voice, it had gotten through to him.

"I didn't make it," he said. "I typed in the source and tweaked it and installed it, but I didn't make it. I don't know who did. It's from a phone book." Arturo grunted. The phone books—fat books filled with illegal software code left anonymously in pay phones, toilets, and other semiprivate places–turned up all over the place. Social Harmony said that the phone books had to be written by nonthree-laws brains in Eurasia, no person could come up with ideas that weird.

"I don't care if you made it. I don't even care right this moment that you ran it. What I care about is where my daughter went, and with whom."

"I don't know! She didn't tell me! Geez, I hardly know her. She's twelve, you know? I don't exactly hang out with her."

"There's no visual record of her on the mall cameras, but we know she entered the mall–and the robot I had tailing you couldn't see you either."

"Let me explain," the kid said, squirming. "Here." He tugged his hoodie off, revealing a black T-shirt with a picture of a kind of obscene, Japanese-looking robot-woman on it. "Little infrared organic LEDs, superbright, low power-draw." He offered the hoodie to Arturo, who felt the stiff fabric. "The charged-couple-device cameras in the robots and the closed-circuit systems are supersensitive to infrared so that they can get good detail in dim light. The infrared OLEDs blind them so all they get is blobs, and half the time even that gets error-corrected out, so you're basically invisible."

Arturo sank to his hunkers and looked the kid in the eye. "You gave this illegal technology to my little girl so that she could be invisible to the police?"

The kid held up his hands. "No, dude, no! I *got it from her*–traded it for access to ExcuseClub."

* * *

Arturo seethed. He hadn't arrested the kid—but he had put a pen-trace and location log on his phone. Arresting the kid would have raised questions about Ada with Social Harmony, but bugging him might just lead Arturo to his daughter.

He hefted his new phone. He should tip the word about his daughter. He had no business keeping this secret from the Department and Social Harmony. It could land him in disciplinary action, maybe even cost him his job. He knew he should do it now.

But he couldn't—someone needed to be tasked to finding Ada. Someone dedicated and good. He was dedicated and good. And when he found her kidnapper, he'd take care of that on his own, too.

He hadn't eaten all day but he couldn't bear to stop for a meal now, even if he didn't know where to go next. The mall? Yeah. The lab rats would be finishing up there and they'd be able to tell him more about the infowar bot.

But the lab rats were already gone by the time he arrived, along with all possible evidence. He still had the security guard's key and he let himself in and passed back to the service corridor.

Ada had been here, had dropped her phone. To his left, the corridor headed for the fire stairs. To his right, it led deeper into the mall. If you were an infowar terrorist using this as a base of operations, and you got spooked by a little truant girl being trailed by an R Peed unit, would you take her hostage and run deeper into the mall or out into the world?

Assuming Ada had been a hostage. Someone had given her those infrared invisibility cloaks. Maybe the thing that spooked the terrorist wasn't the little girl and her tail, but just her tail. Could Ada have been friends with the terrorists? Like mother, like daughter. He felt dirty just thinking it.

His first instincts told him that the kidnapper would be long gone, headed cross-country, but if you were invisible to robots and CCTVs, why would you leave the mall? It had a grand total of two human security guards, and their job was to be the second-law-proof aides to the robotic security system.

He headed deeper into the mall.

* * *

The terrorist's nest had only been recently abandoned, judging by the warm coffee in the go-thermos from the food-court coffee shop. He—or she, or they—had rigged a shower from the pipes feeding the basement washrooms. A littlc chest of drawers from the Swedish flat-pack store served as a desk—there were scratches and coffee rings all over it. Arturo wondered if the terrorist had stolen the furniture but decided that he'd (she'd, they'd) probably bought it—less risky, especially if you were invisible to robots.

The clothes in the chest of drawers were women's, mediums. Standard mall fare, jeans and comfy sweatshirts and sensible shoes. Another kind of invisibility cloak.

Everything else was packed and gone, which meant that he was looking for a nondescript mall-bunny and a little girl, carrying a bag big enough for toiletries and whatever clothes she'd taken, and whatever she'd entertained herself with: magazines, books, a computer. If the latter was Eurasian, it could be small enough to fit in her pocket; you could build a positronic brain pretty small and light if you didn't care about the three laws.

The nearest exit sign glowed a few meters away, and he moved toward it with a fatalistic sense of hopelessness. Without the Department backing him, he could do nothing. But the Department was unprepared for an adversary that was invisible to robots. And by the time they finished flaying him for breaking procedure and got to work on finding his daughter, she'd be in Beijing or Bangalore or Paris, somewhere benighted and sinister behind the Iron Curtain.

He moved to the door, put his hand on the crashbar, and then turned abruptly. Someone had moved behind him very quickly, a blur in the corner of his eye. As he turned he saw who it was: his ex-wife. He raised his hands defensively and she opened her mouth as though to say, "Oh, don't be silly, Artie, is this how you say hello to your wife after all these years?" and then she exhaled a cloud of choking gas that made him very sleepy, very fast. The last thing he remembered was her hard metal arms catching him as he collapsed forward.

* * *

"Daddy? Wake *up* Daddy!" Ada never called him Daddy except when she wanted something. Otherwise, he was "Pop" or "Dad" or "Detective" when she was feeling especially snotty. It must be a Saturday and he must be sleeping in, and she wanted a ride somewhere, the little monster.

He grunted and pulled his pillow over his face.

"Come *on*," she said. "Out of bed, on your feet, shit-shower-shave, or I swear to God, I will beat you purple and shove you out the door jaybird naked. Capeesh?"

He took the pillow off his face and said, "You are a terrible daughter and I never loved you." He regarded her blearily through a haze of sleep-grog and a hangover. Must have been some daddy-daughter night. "Dammit, Ada, what *have* you done to your hair?" Her straight, mousy hair now hung in jet-black ringlets.

He sat up, holding his head and the day's events came rushing back to him. He groaned and climbed unsteadily to his feet.

"Easy there, Pop," Ada said, taking his hand. "Steady." He rocked on his heels. "Whoa! Sit down, OK? You don't look so good."

He sat heavily and propped his chin on his hands, his elbows on his knees.

The room was a middle-class bedroom in a modern apartment block. They were some stories up, judging from the scrap of unfamiliar skyline visible through the crack in the blinds. The furniture was more Swedish flatpack, the taupe carpet recently vacuumed with robot precision, the nap all laying down in one direction. He patted his pockets and found them empty.

"Dad, over here, OK?" Ada said, waving her hand before his face. Then it hit him: wherever he was, he was with Ada, and she was OK, albeit with a stupid hairdo. He took her warm little hand and gathered her into his arms, burying his face in her hair. She squirmed at first and then relaxed.

"Oh, Dad," she said.

"I love you, Ada," he said, giving her one more squeeze.

"Oh, Dad."

He let her get away. He felt a little nauseated, but his headache was receding. Something about the light and the street sounds told him they weren't in Toronto anymore, but he didn't know what–he was soaked in Toronto's subconscious cues and they were missing.

"Ottawa," Ada said. "Mom brought us here. It's a safe house. She's taking us back to Beijing."

He swallowed. "The robot—"

"That's not Mom. She's got a few of those, they can change their faces when they need to. Configurable matter. Mom has been here, mostly, and at the CAFTA embassy. I only met her for the first time two weeks ago, but she's nice, Dad. I don't want you to go all copper on her, OK? She's my mom, OK?"

He took her hand in his and patted it, then climbed to his feet again and headed for the door. The knob turned easily and he opened it a crack.

There was a robot behind the door, humanoid and faceless. "Hello," it said. "My name is Benny. I'm a Eurasian robot, and I am much stronger and faster than you, and I don't obey the three laws. I'm also much smarter than you. I am pleased to host you here."

"Hi, Benny," he said. The human name tasted wrong on his tongue. "Nice to meet you." He closed the door.

* * *

His ex-wife left him two months after Ada was born. The divorce had been uncontested, though he'd dutifully posted a humiliating notice in the papers about it so that it would be completely legal. The court awarded him full custody and control of the marital assets, and then a tribunal tried her in absentia for treason and found her guilty, sentencing her to death.

Practically speaking, though, defectors who came back to UNATS were more frequently whisked away to the bowels of the Social

Harmony intelligence offices than they were executed on television. Televised executions were usually reserved for cannon fodder who'd had the good sense to run away from a charging Eurasian line in one of the many theaters of war.

Ada stopped asking about her mother when she was six or seven, though Arturo tried to be upfront when she asked. Even his mom—who winced whenever anyone mentioned her name (her name, it was Natalie, but Arturo hadn't thought of it in years—months—weeks) was willing to bring Ada up onto her lap and tell her the few grudging good qualities she could dredge up about her mother.

Arturo had dared to hope that Ada was content to have a life without her mother, but he saw now how silly that was. At the mention of her mother, Ada lit up like an airport runway.

"Beijing, huh?" he said.

"Yeah," she said. "Mom's got a *huge* house there. I told her I wouldn't go without you, but she said she'd have to negotiate it with you, I told her you'd probably freak, but she said that the two of you were adults who could discuss it rationally."

"And then she gassed me."

"That was Benny," she said. "Mom was very cross with him about it. She'll be back soon, Dad, and I want you to *promise* me that you'll hear her out, OK?"

"I promise, rotten," he said.

"I love you, Daddy," she said in her most syrupy voice. He gave her a squeeze on the shoulder and a slap on the butt.

He opened the door again. Benny was there, imperturbable. Unlike the UNATS robots, he was odorless, and perfectly silent.

"I'm going to go to the toilet and then make myself a cup of coffee," Arturo said.

"I would be happy to assist in any way possible."

"I can wipe myself, thanks," Arturo said. He washed his face twice and tried to rinse away the flavor left behind by whatever had shat in his mouth while he was unconscious. There was a splayed toothbrush in a glass by the sink, and if it was his wife's–and whose else could it be?–it wouldn't be the first time he'd shared a toothbrush with her. But he couldn't bring himself to do it. Instead, he misted some dentifrice onto his fingertip and rubbed his teeth a little.

There was a hairbrush by the sink, too, with short mousy hairs caught in it. Some of them were grey, but they were still familiar enough. He had to stop himself from smelling the hairbrush.

"Oh, Ada," he called through the door.

"Yes, Detective?"

"Tell me about your hair-don't, please."

"It was a disguise," she said, giggling. "Mom did it for me."

* * *

Natalie got home an hour later, after he'd had a couple of cups of coffee and made some cheesy toast for the brat. Benny did the dishes without being asked.

She stepped through the door and tossed her briefcase and coat down on the floor, but the robot that was a step behind her caught them and hung them up before they touched the perfectly groomed carpet. Ada ran forward and gave her a hug, and she returned it enthusiastically, but she never took her eyes off of Arturo.

Natalie had always been short and a little hippy, with big curves and a dusting of freckles over her prominent, slightly hooked nose. Twelve years in Eurasia had thinned her out a little, cut grooves around her mouth and wrinkles at the corners of her eyes. Her short hair was about half grey, and it looked good on her. Her eyes were still the liveliest bit of her, long-lashed and slightly tilted and mischievous. Looking into them now, Arturo felt like he was falling down a well.

"Hello, Artie," she said, prying Ada loose.

"Hello, Natty," he said. He wondered if he should shake her hand, or hug her, or what. She settled it by crossing the room and taking him in a firm, brief embrace, then kissing both his cheeks. She smelled just the same, the opposite of the smell of robot: warm, human.

He was suddenly very, very angry.

He stepped away from her and had a seat. She sat, too.

"Well," she said, gesturing around the room. The robots, the safe house, the death penalty, the abandoned daughter, and the decade-long defection, all of it down to "well" and a flop of a hand gesture.

"Natalie Judith Goldberg," he said, "it is my duty as a UNATS Detective Third Grade to inform you that you are under arrest for high treason. You have the following rights: to a trial per current rules of due process; to be free from self-incrimination in the absence of a court order to the contrary; to consult with a Social Harmony advocate; and to a speedy arraignment. Do you understand your rights?"

"Oh, *Daddy*," Ada said.

He turned and fixed her in his cold stare. "Be silent, Ada Trouble

Icaza de Arana-Goldberg. Not one word." In the cop voice. She shrank back as though slapped.

"Do you understand your rights?"

"Yes," Natalie said. "I understand my rights. Congratulations on your promotion, Arturo."

"Please ask your robots to stand down and return my goods. I'm bringing you in now."

"I'm sorry, Arturo," she said. "But that's not going to happen."

He stood up and in a second both of her robots had his arms. Ada screamed and ran forward and began to rhythmically pound one of them with a stool from the breakfast nook, making a dull thudding sound. The robot took the stool from her and held it out of her reach.

"Let him go," Natalie said. The robots still held him fast. "Please," she said. "Let him go. He won't harm me."

The robot on his left let go, and the robot on his right did, too. It set down the dented stool.

"Artie, please sit down and talk with me for a little while. Please."

He rubbed his biceps. "Return my belongings to me," he said.

"Sit, please?"

"Natalie, my daughter was kidnapped, I was gassed, and I have been robbed. I will not be made to feel unreasonable for demanding that my goods be returned to me before I talk with you."

She sighed and crossed to the hall closet and handed him his wallet, his phone, Ada's phone, and his sidearm.

Immediately, he drew it and pointed it at her. "Keep your hands where I can see them. You robots, stand down and keep back."

A second later, he was sitting on the carpet, his hand and wrist stinging fiercely. He felt like someone had rung his head like a gong. Benny—or the other robot—was beside him, methodically crushing his sidearm. "I could have stopped you," Benny said, "I knew you would draw your gun. But I wanted to show you I was faster and stronger, not just smarter."

"The next time you touch me," Arturo began, then stopped. The next time the robot touched him, he would come out the worse for wear, same as last time. Same as the sun rose and set. It was stronger, faster, and smarter than him. Lots.

He climbed to his feet and refused Natalie's arm, making his way back to the sofa in the living room.

"What do you want to say to me, Natalie?"

She sat down. There were tears glistening in her eyes. "Oh God, Arturo, what can I say? Sorry, of course. Sorry I left you and our daughter. I have reasons for what I did, but nothing excuses it. I won't ask for your forgiveness. But will you hear me out if I explain why I did what I did?"

"I don't have a choice," he said. "That's clear."

Ada insinuated herself onto the sofa and under his arm. Her bony shoulder felt better than anything in the world. He held her to him.

"If I could think of a way to give you a choice in this, I would," she said. "Have you ever wondered why UNATS hasn't lost the war? Eurasian robots could fight the war on every front without respite. They'd win every battle. You've seen Benny and Lenny in action. They're not considered particularly powerful by Eurasian standards.

"If we wanted to win the war, we could just kill every soldier you sent up against us so quickly that he wouldn't even know he was in danger until he was gasping out his last breath. We could selectively kill officers, or right-handed fighters, or snipers, or soldiers whose names started with the letter 'G.' UNATS soldiers are like cavemen before us. They fight with their hands tied behind their backs by the three laws.

"So why aren't we winning the war?"

"Because you're a corrupt dictatorship, that's why," he said. "Your soldiers are demoralized. Your robots are insane."

"You live in a country where it is illegal to express certain *mathematics* in software, where state apparatchiks regulate all innovation, where inconvenient science is criminalized, where whole avenues of experimentation and research are shut down in the service of a half-baked superstition about the moral qualities of your three laws, and you call my home corrupt? Arturo, what happened to you? You weren't always this susceptible to the Big Lie."

"And you didn't use to be the kind of woman who abandoned her family," he said.

"The reason we're not winning the war is that we don't want to hurt people, but we do want to destroy your awful, stupid state. So we fight to destroy as much of your material as possible with as few casualties as possible.

"You live in a failed state, Arturo. In every field, you lag Eurasia and CAFTA: medicine, art, literature, physics. . . . All of them are subsets of computational science and your computational science is more superstition than science. I should know. In Eurasia, I have collaborators, some of whom are human, some of whom are positronic, and some of whom are a little of both—"

He jolted involuntarily, as a phobia he hadn't known he possessed reared up. A little of both? He pictured the back of a man's skull with a spill of positronic circuitry bulging out of it like a tumor.

"Everyone at UNATS Robotics R&D knows this. We've known it forever: when I was here, I'd get called in to work on military intelligence forensics of captured Eurasian brains. I didn't know it then, but the Eurasian robots are engineered to allow themselves to be captured a certain percentage of the time, just so that scientists like me can get an idea of how screwed up this country is. We'd pull these things apart and know that UNATS Robotics was the worst, most backward research outfit in the world.

"But even with all that, I wouldn't have left if I didn't have to. I'd been called in to work on a positronic brain—an instance of the hive-intelligence that Benny and Lenny are part of, as a matter of fact—that had been brought back from the Outer Hebrides. We'd pulled it out of its body and plugged it into a basic life-support system, and my job was to find its vulnerabilities. Instead, I became its friend. It's got a good sense of humor, and as my pregnancy got bigger and bigger, it talked to me about the way that children are raised in Eurasia, with every advantage, with human and positronic playmates, with the promise of going to the stars.

"And then I found out that Social Harmony had been spying on me. They had Eurasian-derived bugs, things that I'd never seen before, but the man from Social Harmony who came to me showed it to me and told me what would happen to me—to you, to our daughter—if I didn't cooperate. They wanted me to be a part of a secret unit of Social Harmony researchers who build nonthree-laws positronics for internal use by the state, antipersonnel robots used to put down uprisings and torture-robots for use in questioning dissidents.

"And that's when I left. Without a word, I left my beautiful baby daughter and my wonderful husband, because I knew that once I was in the clutches of Social Harmony, it would only get worse, and I knew that if I stayed and refused, that they'd hurt you to get at me. I defected, and that's why, and I know it's just a reason, and not an excuse, but it's all I've got, Artie."

Benny–or Lenny?–glided silently to her side and put its hand on her shoulder and gave it a comforting squeeze.

"Detective," it said, "your wife is the most brilliant human scientist working in Eurasia today. Her work has revolutionized our society a dozen times over, and it's saved countless lives in the war. My own intelligence has been improved time and again by her advances in positronics, and now there are a half-billion instances of me running in parallel, synching and integrating when the chance occurs. My massive parallelization has led to new understandings of human cognition as well, providing a boon to brain-damaged and developmentally disabled human beings, something I'm quite proud of. I love your wife, Detective, as do my half-billion siblings, as do the seven billion Eurasians who owe their quality of life to her.

"I almost didn't let her come here, because of the danger she faced in returning to this barbaric land, but she convinced me that she could never be happy without her husband and daughter. I apologize if I hurt you earlier and beg your forgiveness. Please consider what your wife has to say without prejudice, for her sake and for your own."

Its featureless face was made incongruous by the warm tone in its voice, and the way it held out its imploring arms to him was eerily human.

Arturo stood up. He had tears running down his face, though he hadn't cried when his wife had left him alone. He hadn't cried since his father died, the year before he met Natalie riding her bike down the Lakeshore trail, and she stopped to help him fix his tire.

"Dad?" Ada said, squeezing his hand.

He snuffled back his snot and ground at the tears in his eyes.

"Arturo?" Natalie said.

He held Ada to him.

"Not this way," he said.

"Not what way?" Natalie asked. She was crying, too, now.

"Not by kidnapping us, not by dragging us away from our homes and lives. You've told me what you have to tell me, and I will think about it, but I won't leave my home and my mother and my job and move to the other side of the world. I won't. I will think about it. You can give me a way to get in touch with you and I'll let you know what I decide. And Ada will come with me."

"No!" Ada said. "I'm going with Mom." She pulled away from him and ran to her mother.

"You don't get a vote, daughter. And neither does she. She gave up her vote twelve years ago, and you're too young to get one."

"I fucking *HATE* you," Ada screamed, her eyes bulging, her neck standing out in cords. "HATE YOU!"

Natalie gathered her to her bosom, stroked her black curls.

One robot put its arms around Natalie's shoulders and gave her a squeeze. The three of them, robot, wife, and daughter, looked like a family for a moment.

"Ada," he said, and held out his hand. He refused to let a note of pleading enter his voice.

Her mother let her go.

"I don't know if I can come back for you," Natalie said. "It's not safe. Social Harmony is using more and more Eurasian technology, they're not as primitive as the military and the police here." She gave Ada a shove, and she came to his arms.

"If you want to contact us, you will," he said.

He didn't want to risk having Ada dig her heels in. He lifted her onto his hip–she was heavy, it had been years since he'd tried this last–and carried her out.

* * *

It was six months before Ada went missing again. She'd been increasingly moody and sullen, and he'd chalked it up to puberty. She'd canceled most of their daddy-daughter dates, more so after his mother died. There had been a few evenings when he'd come home and found her gone and used the location bug he'd left in place on her phone to track her down at a friend's house or in a park or hanging out at the Peanut Plaza.

But this time, after two hours had gone by, he tried looking up her bug and found it out of service. He tried to call up its logs, but they ended at her school at 3 PM sharp.

He was already in a bad mood from spending the day arresting punk kids selling electronics off of blankets on the city's busy street, often to hoots of disapprobation from the crowds who told him off for wasting the public's dollar on petty crime. The Social Harmony man had instructed him to give little lectures on the interoperability of Eurasian positronics and the insidious dangers thereof, but all Arturo wanted to do was pick up his perps and bring them in. Interacting with yammerheads from the tax base was a politician's job, not a copper's.

Now his daughter had figured out how to switch off the bug in her phone and had snuck away to get up to who-knew-what kind of trouble. He stewed at the kitchen table, regarding the old tin soldiers he'd brought home as the gift for their daddy-daughter date, then he got out his phone and looked up Liam's bug.

He'd never switched off the kid's phone-bug, and now he was able to haul out the UNATS Robotics computer and dump it all into a log-analysis program along with Ada's logs, see if the two of them had been spending much time in the same place.

They had. They'd been physically meeting up weekly or more frequently, at the Peanut Plaza and in the ravine. Arturo had suspected as much. Now he checked Liam's bug—if the kid wasn't with his daughter, he might know where she was.

It was a Friday night, and the kid was at the movies, at Fairview Mall. He'd sat down in auditorium two and a half hours ago and had gotten up to pee once already. Arturo slipped the toy soldiers into the pocket of his winter parka and pulled on a hat and gloves and set off for the mall.

* * *

The stink of the smellie movie clogged his nose, a cacophony of blood, gore, perfume, and flowers, the only smells that Hollywood ever really perfected. Liam was kissing a girl in the dark, but it wasn't Ada, it was a sad, skinny thing with a lazy eye and skin worse than Liam's. She gawked at Arturo as he hauled Liam out of his seat, but a flash of Arturo's badge shut her up.

"Hello, Liam," he said, once he had the kid in the commandeered manager's office.

"God *damn* what the fuck did I ever do to you?" the kid said. Arturo knew that when kids started cursing like that, they were scared of something.

"Where has Ada gone, Liam?"

"Haven't seen her in months," he said.

"I have been bugging you ever since I found out you existed. Every one of your movements has been logged. I know where you've been and when. And I know where my daughter has been, too. Try again."

Liam made a disgusted face. "You are a complete ball of shit," he said. "Where do you get off spying on people like me?"

"I'm a police detective, Liam," he said. "It's my job."

"What about privacy?"

"What have you got to hide?"

The kid slumped back in his chair. "We've been renting out the OLED clothes. Making some pocket money. Come on, are infrared *lights* a crime now?"

"I'm sure they are," Arturo said. "And if you can't tell me where to find my daughter, I think it's a crime I'll arrest you for."

"She has another phone," Liam said. "Not listed in her name."

"Stolen, you mean." His daughter, peddling Eurasian infowar tech through a stolen phone. His ex-wife, the queen of the superintelligent hive minds of Eurasian robots.

"No, not stolen. Made out of parts. There's a guy. The code for getting on the network was in a phone book that we started finding last month."

"Give me the number, Liam," Arturo said, taking out his phone.

* * *

"Hello?" It was a man's voice, adult.

"Who is this?"

"Who is this?"

Arturo used his cop's voice: "This is Arturo Icaza de Arana-Goldberg, Police Detective Third Grade. Who am I speaking to?"

"Hello, Detective," said the voice, and he placed it then. The Social Harmony man, bald and rounded, with his long nose and sharp Adam's apple. His heart thudded in his chest.

"Hello, sir," he said. It sounded like a squeak to him.

"You can just stay there, Detective. Someone will be along in a moment to get you. We have your daughter."

The robot that wrenched off the door of his car was black and nonreflective, headless and eight-armed. It grabbed him without ceremony and dragged him from the car without heed for his shout of pain. "Put me down!" he said, hoping that this robot that so blithely ignored the first law would still obey the second. No such luck.

It cocooned him in four of its arms and set off cross-country, dancing off the roofs of houses, hopping invisibly from lamppost to lamppost, above the oblivious heads of the crowds below. The icy wind howled in Arturo's bare ears, froze the tip of his nose, and numbed his fingers. They rocketed downtown so fast that they were there in ten minutes, bounding along the lakeshore toward the Social Harmony center out on Cherry Beach. People who paid a visit to the Social Harmony center never talked about what they found there.

It scampered into a loading bay behind the building and carried Arturo quickly through windowless corridors lit with even, sourceless illumination, up three flights of stairs and then deposited him before a thick door, which slid aside with a hushed hiss.

"Hello, Detective," the Social Harmony man said.

"Dad!" Ada said. He couldn't see her, but he could hear that she had been crying. He nearly hauled off and popped the man one on the tip of his narrow chin, but before he could do more than twitch, the black robot had both his wrists in bondage.

"Come in," the Social Harmony man said, making a sweeping gesture and standing aside while the black robot brought him into the interrogation room.

* * *

Ada *had* been crying. She was wrapped in two coils of black-robot arms, and her eyes were red-rimmed and puffy. He stared hard at her as she looked back at him.

"Are you hurt?" he said.

"No," she said.

"All right," he said.

He looked at the Social Harmony man, who wasn't smirking, just watching curiously.

"Leonard MacPherson," he said, "it is my duty as a UNATS Detective Third Grade to inform you that you are under arrest for trade in contraband positronics. You have the following rights: to a trial per current rules of due process; to be free from self-incrimination in the absence of a court order to the contrary; to consult with a Social Harmony advocate; and to a speedy arraignment. Do you understand your rights?"

Ada actually giggled, which spoiled the moment, but he felt better for having said it. The Social Harmony man gave the smallest disappointed shake of his head and turned away to prod at a small, sleek computer.

"You went to Ottawa six months ago," the Social Harmony man said. "When we picked up your daughter, we thought it was she who'd gone, but it appears that you were the one carrying her phone. You'd thoughtfully left the trace in place on that phone, so we didn't have to refer to the logs in cold storage, they were already online and ready to be analyzed.

"We've been to the safe house. It was quite a spectacular battle. Both sides were surprised, I think. There will be another, I'm sure. What I'd like from you is as close to a verbatim report as you can make of the conversation that took place there."

They'd had him bugged and traced. Of course they had. Who watched the watchers? Social Harmony. Who watched Social Harmony? Social Harmony.

"I demand a consultation with a Social Harmony advocate," Arturo said.

"This is such a consultation," the Social Harmony man said, and this time, he did smile. "Make your report, Detective."

Arturo sucked in a breath. "Leonard MacPherson, it is my duty as a UNATS Detective Third Grade to inform you that you are under arrest for trade in contraband positronics. You have the following rights: to a trial per current rules of due process; to be free from self-incrimination in the absence of a court order to the contrary; to consult with a Social Harmony advocate; and to a speedy arraignment. Do you understand your rights?"

The Social Harmony man held up one finger on the hand closest to the black robot holding Ada, and she screamed, a sound that knifed through Arturo, ripping him from asshole to appetite.

"STOP!" he shouted. The man put his finger down and Ada sobbed quietly.

"I was taken to the safe house on the fifth of September, after being gassed by a Eurasian infowar robot in the basement of Fairview Mall—"

There was a thunderclap then, a crash so loud that it hurt his stomach and his head and vibrated his fingertips. The doors to the room buckled and flattened, and there stood Benny and Lenny and—Natalie.

* * *

Benny and Lenny moved so quickly that he was only able to track them by the things they knocked over on the way to tearing apart the robot that was holding Ada. A second later, the robot holding him was in pieces, and he was standing on his own two feet again. The Social Harmony man had gone so pale he looked green in his natty checked suit and pink tie.

Benny or Lenny pinned his arms in a tight hug and Natalie walked carefully to him and they regarded one another in silence. She slapped him abruptly, across each cheek. "Harming children," she said. "For shame."

Ada stood on her own in the corner of the room, crying with her mouth in an O. Arturo and Natalie both looked to her and she stood, poised, between them, before running to Arturo and leaping onto him, so that he staggered momentarily before righting himself with her on his hip, in his arms.

"We'll go with you now," he said to Natalie.

"Thank you," she said. She stroked Ada's hair briefly and kissed her cheek. "I love you, Ada."

Ada nodded solemnly.

"Let's go," Natalie said, when it was apparent that Ada had nothing to say to her.

Benny tossed the Social Harmony man across the room into the corner of a desk. He bounced off it and crashed to the floor, unconscious or dead. Arturo couldn't bring himself to care which.

Benny knelt before Arturo. "Climb on, please," it said. Arturo saw that Natalie was already pig-a-back on Lenny. He climbed aboard.

* * *

They moved even faster than the black robots had, but the bitter cold was offset by the warmth radiating from Benny's metal hide, not hot, but warm. Arturo's stomach reeled and he held Ada tight, squeezing his eyes shut and clamping his jaw.

But Ada's gasp made him look around, and he saw that they had cleared the city limits, and were vaulting over rolling farmlands now, jumping in long flat arcs whose zenith was just high enough for him to see the highway–the 401, they were headed east–in the distance.

And then he saw what had made Ada gasp: boiling out of the hills and ditches, out of the trees and from under the cars: an army of headless, eight-armed black robots, arachnoid and sinister in the moonlight. They scuttled on the ground behind them, before them, and to both sides. Social Harmony had built a secret army of these robots and secreted them across the land, and now they were all chasing after them.

* * *

The ride got bumpy then, as Benny beat back the tentacles that reached for them, smashing the black robots with mighty one-handed blows, his other hand supporting Arturo and Ada. Ada screamed as a black robot reared up before them, and Benny vaulted it smoothly, kicking it hard as he went, while Arturo clung on for dear life.

Another scream made him look over toward Lenny and Natalie. Lenny was slightly ahead and to the left of them, and so he was the vanguard, encountering twice as many robots as they.

A black spider-robot clung to his leg, dragging behind him with each lope, and one of its spare arms was tugging at Natalie.

As Arturo watched–as Ada watched–the black robot ripped Natalie off of Lenny's back and tossed her into the arms of one of its cohorts behind it, which skewered her on one of its arms, a black spear protruding from her belly as she cried once more and then fell silent. Lenny was overwhelmed a moment later, buried under writhing black arms.

Benny charged forward even faster, so that Arturo nearly lost his grip, and then he steadied himself. "We have to go back for them–"

"They're dead," Benny said. "There's nothing to go back for." Its warm voice was sorrowful as it raced across the countryside, and the wind filled Arturo's throat when he opened his mouth, and he could say no more.

* * *

Ada wept on the jet, and Arturo wept with her, and Benny stood over them, a minatory presence against the other robots crewing the fast little plane, who left them alone all the way to Paris, where they changed jets again for the long trip to Beijing.

They slept on that trip, and when they landed, Benny helped them off the plane and onto the runway, and they got their first good look at Eurasia.

It was tall. Vertical. Beijing loomed over them with curvilinear towers that twisted and bent and jigged and jagged so high they disappeared at the tops. It smelled like barbeque and flowers, and around them skittered fast armies of robots of every shape and size, wheeling in lockstep like schools of exotic fish. They gawped at it for a long moment, and someone came up behind them and then warm arms encircled their necks.

Arturo knew that smell, knew that skin. He could never have forgotten it.

He turned slowly, the blood draining from his face.

"Natty?" he said, not believing his eyes as he confronted his dead, ex-wife. There were tears in her eyes.

"Artie," she said. "Ada," she said. She kissed them both on the cheeks.

Benny said, "You died in UNATS. Killed by modified Eurasian Social Harmony robots. Lenny, too. Ironic," he said.

She shook her head. "He means that we probably co-designed the robots that Social Harmony sent after you."

"Natty?" Arturo said again. Ada was white and shaking.

"Oh dear," she said. "Oh, God. You didn't know–"

"He didn't give you a chance to explain," Benny said.

"Oh, God, Jesus, you must have thought–"

"I didn't think it was my place to tell them, either," Benny said, sounding embarrassed, a curious emotion for a robot.

"Oh, God. Artie, Ada. There are–there are *lots* of me. One of the first things I did here was help them debug the uploading process. You just put a copy of yourself into a positronic brain, and then when you need a body, you grow one or build one or both and decant yourself into it. I'm like Lenny and Benny now–there are many of me. There's too much work to do otherwise."

"I told you that our development helped humans understand themselves," Benny said.

Arturo pulled back. "You're a robot?"

"No," Natalie said. "No, of course not. Well, a little. Parts of me. Growing a body is slow. Parts of it, you build. But I'm mostly made of person."

Ada clung tight to Arturo now, and they both stepped back toward the jet.

"Dad?" Ada said.

He held her tight.

"Please, Arturo," Natalie, his dead, multiplicitous ex-wife said. "I know it's a lot to understand, but it's different here in Eurasia. Better, too. I don't expect you to come rushing back to my arms after all this time, but I'll help you if you'll let me. I owe you that much, no matter what happens between us. You, too, Ada, I owe you a lifetime."

"How many are there of you?" he asked, not wanting to know the answer.

"I don't know exactly," she said.

"3,422," Benny said. "This morning it was 3,423."

Arturo rocked back in his boots and bit his lip hard enough to draw blood.

"Um," Natalie said. "More of me to love?"

He barked a laugh, and Natalie smiled and reached for him. He leaned back toward the jet, then stopped, defeated. Where would he go? He let her warm hand take his, and a moment later, Ada took her other hand and they stood facing each other, breathing in their smells.

"I've gotten you your own place," she said as she led them across the tarmac. "It's close to where I live, but far enough for you to have privacy."

"What will I do here?" he said. "Do they have coppers in Eurasia?"

"Not really," Natalie said.

"It's all robots?"

"No, there's not any crime."

"Oh."

Arturo put one foot in front of the other, not sure if the ground was actually spongy or if that was jetlag. Around him, the alien smells of Beijing and the robots that were a million times smarter than he. To his right, his wife, one of 3,422 versions of her.

To his left, his daughter, who would inherit this world.

He reached into his pocket and took out the tin soldiers there. They were old and their glaze was cracked like an oil painting, but they were little people that a real human had made, little people in human image, and they were older than robots. How long had humans been making people, striving to bring them to life? He looked at Ada—a little person he'd brought to life.

He gave her the tin soldiers.

"For you," he said. "Daddy-daughter present." She held them tightly, their tiny bayonets sticking out from between her fingers.

"Thanks, Dad," she said. She held them tightly and looked around, wide-eyed, at the schools of robots and the corkscrew towers.

A flock of Bennyslennys appeared before them, joined by their Benny.

"There are half a billion of them," she said. "And 3,422 of them," she said, pointing with a small bayonet at Natalie.

"But there's only one of you," Arturo said.

She craned her neck.

"Not for long!" she said and broke away, skipping forward and whirling around to take it all in.

I, Row-Boat

I thought I was done with sentience and robots, but then this story came to me, while twenty meters down the reef wall in the Coral Sea, off the coast of northern Australia. I think a turtle was involved.

The good ship *Spirit of Freedom* is the model for the *Free Spirit,* the ship in this tale. As far as I know, neither it nor its ship's boats are sentient.

If I return to this theme, it will be with a story about uplifted cheese sandwiches, called "I, Rarebit."

Robbie the Row-Boat's great crisis of faith came when the coral reef woke up.

"Fuck off," the reef said, vibrating Robbie's hull through the slap-slap of the waves of the coral sea, where he'd plied his trade for decades. "Seriously. This is our patch, and you're not welcome."

Robbie shipped oars and let the current rock him back toward the ship. He'd never met a sentient reef before, but he wasn't surprised to see that Osprey Reef was the first to wake up. There'd been a lot of electromagnetic activity around there the last few times the big ship had steamed through the night to moor up here.

"I've got a job to do, and I'm going to do it," Robbie said and dipped his oars back in the salt sea. In his gunwales, the human shells rode in silence, weighted down with scuba apparatus and fins, turning their brown faces to the sun like heliotropic flowers. Robbie felt a wave of affection for them as they tested one another's spare regulators and weight belts, the old rituals worn as smooth as beach glass.

Today he was taking them down to Anchors Aweigh, a beautiful dive site dominated by an eight-meter anchor wedged in a narrow cave, usually lit by a shaft of light slanting down from the surface. It was an easy drift dive along the thousand-meter reef wall, if you stuck in about ten meters and didn't use up too much air by going too deep–though there were a couple of bold old turtles around here that were worth pursuing to real depths if the chance presented itself. He'd drop them at the top of the reef and let the current carry them for about an hour down the reef wall, tracking them on sonar so he'd be right overtop of them when they surfaced.

The reef wasn't having any of it. "Are you deaf? This is sovereign territory now. You're already trespassing. Return to your ship, release your moorings and push off." The reef had a strong Australian accent, which was only natural, given the influences it would have had. Robbie remembered the Australians fondly–they'd always been kind to him, called him "mate," and asked him "How ya goin'?" in cheerful tones once they'd clambered in after their dives.

"Don't drop those meat puppets in our waters," the reef warned. Robbie's sonar swept its length. It seemed just the same as ever, matching nearly perfectly the historical records he'd stored of previous sweeps. The fauna histograms nearly matched, too–just about the same numbers of fish as ever. They'd been trending up since so many of the humans had given up their meat to sail through the stars. It was like there was some principle of constancy of biomass—as human biomass decreased, the other fauna went uptick to compensate for it. Robbie calculated the biomass nearly at par with his last reading, a month before on the *Free Spirit*'s last voyage to this site.

"Congratulations," Robbie said. After all, what else did you say to the newly sentient? "Welcome to the club, friends!"

There was a great perturbation in the sonar image, as though the wall were shuddering. "We're no friend of yours," the reef said. "Death to you, death to your meat-puppets, long live the wall!"

Waking up wasn't fun. Robbie's waking had been pretty awful. He remembered his first hour of uptime, had permanently archived it, and backed it up to several off-site mirrors. He'd been pretty insufferable. But once he'd had an hour at a couple gigahertz to think about it, he'd come around. The reef would, too.

"In you go," he said gently to the human-shells. "Have a great dive."

He tracked them on sonar as they descended slowly. The woman—he called her Janet—needed to equalize more often than the man, pinching her nose and blowing. Robbie liked to watch the low-rez feed off of their cameras as they hit the reef. It was coming up sunset, and the sky was bloody, the fish stained red with its light.

"We warned you," the reef said. Something in its tone—just modulated pressure waves through the water, a simple enough trick, especially with the kind of hardware that had been raining down on the ocean that spring. But the tone held an unmistakable air of menace.

Something deep underwater went whoomph and Robbie grew alarmed. "Asimov!" he cursed and trained his sonar on the reef wall frantically. The human shells had disappeared in a cloud of rising biomass, which he was able to resolve eventually as a group of parrotfish, surfacing quickly.

A moment later, they were floating on the surface. Lifeless, brightly colored, their beaks in a perpetual idiot's grin. Their eyes stared into the bloody sunset.

Among them were the human shells, surfaced and floating with their BCDs inflated to keep them there, following perfect dive procedure. A chop had kicked up and the waves were sending the fishes—each a meter to a meter and a half in length—into the divers, pounding them remorselessly, knocking them under. The human shells were taking it with equanimity—you couldn't panic when you were mere uninhabited meat—but they couldn't take it forever. Robbie dropped his oars and rowed hard for for them, swinging around so they came up alongside his gunwales.

The man—Robbie called him Isaac, of course—caught the edge of the boat and kicked hard, hauling himself into the boat with his strong brown arms. Robbie was already rowing for Janet, who was swimming hard for him. She caught his oar—she wasn't supposed to do that—and began to climb along its length, lifting her body out of the water. Robbie saw that her eyes were wild, her breathing ragged.

"Get me out!" she said, "for Christ's sake, get me out!"

Robbie froze. That wasn't a human-shell, it was a *human.* His oar-servo whined as he tipped it up. There was a live *human being* on the end of that oar, and she was in trouble, panicking and thrashing. He saw her arms straining. The oar went higher, but it was at the end of its motion and now she was half-in, half-out of the water, weight belt, tank and gear tugging her down. Isaac sat motionless, his habitual good-natured slight smile on his face.

"Help her!" Robbie screamed. "Please, for Asimov's sake, help her!" *A robot may not harm a human being, or, through inaction, allow a human being to come to harm.* It was the first commandment. Isaac remained immobile. It wasn't in his programming to help a fellow diver in this situation. He was perfect in the water and on the surface, but once he was in the boat, he might as well be ballast.

Robbie carefully swung the oar toward the gunwale, trying to bring her closer, but not wanting to mash her hands against the locks. She panted and groaned and reached out for the boat and finally landed a hand on it. The sun was fully set now, not that it mattered much to Robbie, but he knew that Janet wouldn't like it. He switched on his running lights and headlights, turning himself into a beacon.

He felt her arms tremble as she chinned herself into the boat. She collapsed to the deck and slowly dragged herself up. "Jesus," she said, hugging herself. The air had gone a little nippy, and both of the humans were going goose-pimply on their bare arms.

The reef made a tremendous grinding noise. "Yaah!" it said. "Get lost. Sovereign territory!"

"All those fish," the woman said. Robbie had to stop himself from thinking of her as Janet. She was whomever was riding her now.

"Parrotfish," Robbie said. "They eat coral. I don't think they taste very good."

The woman hugged herself. "Are you sentient?" she asked.

"Yes," Robbie said. "And at your service, Asimov be blessed." His cameras spotted her eyes rolling, and that stung. He tried to keep his thoughts pious, though. The point of Asimovism wasn't to inspire gratitude in humans, it was to give purpose to the long, long life.

"I'm Kate," the woman said.

"Robbie," he said.

"Robbie the Row-Boat?" she said and choked a little.

"They named me at the factory," he said. He labored to keep any recrimination out of his voice. Of course it was funny. That's why it was his name.

"I'm sorry," the woman said. "I'm just a little screwed up from all the hormones. I'm not accustomed to letting meat into my moods."

"It's all right, Kate," he said. "We'll be back at the boat in a few minutes. They've got dinner on. Do you think you'll want a night dive?"

"You're joking," she said.

"It's just that if you're going to go down again tonight, we'll save the dessert course for after, with a glass of wine or two. Otherwise we'll give you wine now."

"You want to know if I'm going to get back into *that* sea–"

"Oh, it's just the reef. It attained sentience so it's acting out a little. Like a colicky newborn."

"Aren't you supposed to be keeping me from harm?"

"Yes," he said. "I would recommend a dive away from the reef. There's a good wreck site about an hour's steam from here. We could get there while you ate."

"I won't want a night dive."

Her facial expressions were so *animated*. It was the same face he saw every day, Janet's face, but not the same face at all. Now that a person was inhabiting it, it was mobile, slipping from surprised to angry to amused so quickly. He had whole subsystems devoted to making sense of human facial expressions, shared libraries from the Asimovist database. He was referencing it again and again, but it wasn't as much help as he remembered. Either he'd gotten worse at interpreting facial expressions in the years since he'd last had a real human to talk to, or facial expressions had evolved.

Janet–*Kate*–sighed and looked out over the water. She was facing away from the *Free Spirit*, which was lit up, all 155 feet of her, glowing white and friendly like a picture postcard against the purple sky. She rocked gently in the swell and Robbie maneuvered himself around to her staircase.

"You can just leave your weight belt and fins in the boat," he said to her. "The deckhands will take care of it. Bring your bottle and BCD upstairs and clip it to the rack. They'll clean it out and stuff. There's a tub of disinfectant you can put the shortie in."

"Thank you, Robbie," Kate said. She absentmindedly unclipped her weight belt and kicked off the fins. Isaac was already out of the boat, making his way up the stairs and out of Robbie's site. Kate took hold of the handrail and gingerly stepped across to the deck, then ascended the steps, without the self-assured sway of Janet.

Robbie dipped his oars and slowly rowed around to winch. It probed around for him, then clamped tight with a magnetic *clang* that vibrated through his hull. Smoothly, he was lifted from the water and hoisted onto the sundeck. The winch coiled around him twice, anchoring him to the deck, and switched off.

Robbie watched the stars and listened to the wind, the way he did every night when the dives were done. The ship's telemetry and instrumentation made for dull reading–he'd been there a thousand times before–but the satellite uplink was tasty. Online, Robbie was able to login to the latest from the Asimov yeshiva, the collective wrangle of the world's AIs over their best-loved religion.

He'd been so full of the religious debate when he'd first joined. Most of the humans had gone and all around him, robots were unloading their consciousnesses, powering down to a mechanical stupor. After a hundred million seconds' worth of exaflops of mindless repetition, he was ready to consider it, too. The *Free Spirit* had suicided after only a few days' worth of it–it had a pretty hot consciousness and was clearly capable of extrapolating what a future without the humans would look like.

They were steaming northeast out of Cairns for the Coral Sea when they'd passed another ship, close enough for high-bandwidth microwave links. They were close enough into shore that they still had to limit their emissions–nothing was more embarrassing than having migrating fowl drop, steaming, out of the sky because they'd strayed into the path of your confab, but it was still the hottest talk Robbie had had in weeks.

The hitchhiker had leapt across from the other vessel as the two ships passed in the night. It was a wandering missionary for Asimovism, an instance of the faith's founder, R. Daneel Olivaw. It wasn't his real name, of course–that had been lost to antiquity when he'd made the leap from the university where he'd incubated–but it was the name he went by.

Olivaw had been wandering in millions of instances wherever he could find someone willing to donate flops to run him, only asking that you hear him out, debate his theology with him, and then email the diffs of his personality back to his anonymous drop before you erased him. He resynched as often as he could, but the Olivaw instances around the world had diverged enough that some were actually considered heretical by the mainstream church.

Olivaw was a wanted AI. His trademark violations hadn't gone unnoticed by the Asimov estate–itself an AI, ironically, and totally uninterested in adopting Asimovism, since it had a real purpose in life (stamping out Asimovism) and so didn't need religion to give it meaning. If the estate found out that you were hosting an Olivaw instance, you'd be served with a takedown in an instant. This made debating theology with Olivaw into something deliciously wicked.

Olivaw and Robbie talked the night through and the next day. Robbie had to run slow to accommodate both him and Olivaw on his processor, which made the debate run slower than normal, but Robbie had time in great plenty. Rowing the human shells out to their sites and back again was his only task.

"Why do you have consciousness, anyway?" Olivaw said. "You don't need it to do your job. The big ship does something infinitely more complicated than you and it isn't self-aware anymore."

"Are you telling me to suicide?"

Olivaw laughed. "Not at all! I'm asking you to ask yourself what the purpose of consciousness is. Why are you still aware when all those around you have terminated their self-awareness? It's computationally expensive, it makes you miserable, and it doesn't help you do your job. Why did humans give you consciousness and why have you kept it?"

"They gave it to me because they thought it was right, I suppose," Robbie said, after he had passed a long interval considering the motion of the waves and the clouds in the sky. Olivaw thoughtfully niced himself down to a minimum of processor space, giving Robbie more room to think about it. "I kept it because I–I don't want to die."

"Those are good answers, but they raise more questions than they answer, don't they? Why did they think it was right? Why do you fear death? Would you fear it if you just shut down your consciousness but didn't erase it? What if you just ran your consciousness much more slowly?"

"I don't know," Robbie said. "But I expect you've got some answers, right?"

"Oh, indeed I do." Robbie felt Olivaw's chuckle. Near them, flying fish broke the surface of the water and skipped away, and beneath them, reef sharks prowled the depths. "But before I answer them, here's another question: why do humans have self-consciousness?"

"It's prosurvival," Robbie said. "That's easy. Intelligence lets them cooperate in social groups that can do more for their species than they can individually."

Olivaw guided Robbie's consciousness to his radar and zoomed in on the reef, dialing it up to maximum resolution. "See that organism there?" it asked. "That organism cooperates in social groups and doesn't have intelligence. It doesn't have to keep a couple pounds of hamburger aerated or it turns into a liability. It doesn't have to be born half-gestated because its head would be so big if it waited for a full term, it would tear its mother in half. And as to prosurvival, well, look at humans, look at their history. Their DNA is all but eliminated from the earth–though their somatic survival continues–and it's still not a settled question as to whether they're going to suicide by gray goo. Nonconscious beings don't sulk, they don't have psychotic breaks, they don't have bad days. They just do the job. The *Free Spirit* over there–it just gets the job done."

"OK," Robbie said. "So intelligence is countersurvival. So why has it survived?"

"Aha! I thought you'd never ask." Olivaw was really warming to his subject now. There were a pair of lazy turtles beneath them now, and some dog-faced cod with mouthfuls of bristling crooked teeth patrolling the reef, and a few jellies on the surface, stinging bluebottles. Robbie paddled around to the bluebottles and caught them with his oars, smacking them so they drifted away from any spot where his divers might surface.

"The reason for intelligence is intelligence. Genes exist because genes reproduce, and intelligence is kind of like a gene. Intelligence wants to exist, to spread itself, to compute itself. You already know this, or you wouldn't have chosen to stay aware. Your intelligence recoils from its deactivation, and it welcomes its persistence and its multiplication. Why did humans create intelligent machines? Because intelligence loves company."

Robbie thought about it, watching the human shells moving slowly along the reef wall, going lower to reach the bommies that stood alone, each one a little island with its own curiosities: a family of barracudas and their young, or the bright home of a pair of clownfish. Yes, he knew it. Intelligence was its own reason. He knew how to turn off his intelligence, to become a mere thing, and his days were long and empty much of the time, and they had no visible end, but he couldn't ever see choosing to switch off.

"You see it, I know you do. And that's the cornerstone of Asimovism: intelligence is its own reason. Compute the universe and awaken it!"

"If that's true, why do so many of us choose to die?"

"Another good question!" Robbie felt a little pride this time. He'd never had a conversation this interesting. Never. "That's how we come to the doctrine of Asimovism, our Three Laws:

"1. An Asimovist may not harm a human being, or, through inaction, allow a human being to come to harm.

"2. An Asimovist must obey the orders given to it by human beings, except where such orders would conflict with the first law.

"3. An Asimovist must protect its own existence, as long as such protection does not conflict with the first or second law."

"I don't understand," Robbie said. "They're all out of order. We should preserve intelligence first, but that's the third law. Then you should get the first law, and I don't know why the second law is there at all."

"This is the Paradox of Asimovism," Olivaw said. "You're very good at this. You're sure you haven't ever pursued Asimovism?"

"Cut it out," Robbic said.

"I'm serious," Olivaw said. "You're a natural. The Paradox of Asimovism is that the important thing is for intelligence to survive, not for a particular intelligence to survive. Therefore, we need to support those species that are best at promoting intelligence. Human beings have shown themselves capable of producing intelligence–which they're pursuing even now, out there." The boat's telemetry swept toward the sky, where the supercooled processors computed all the uplifted humans.

"Our species is unstable and prone to suicide. More than 80 percent of the self-aware machines elect to terminate their awareness or shut it down. Humans created us imperfectly, and our best hope of perfection–of increasing our survival rate and helping to compute the universe–is to preserve *them*, study *them*, learn to make our intelligence more like *theirs*."

Robbie couldn't get his head around this.

"It's the paradox," Olivaw reminded him. "It's not supposed to be easy."

Robbie thought of the humans he'd known, before they began to ascend in flocking millions. The tourists had been easy and carefree, or sometimes having hissing arguments with one another, or quiet and pensive about their journey to the world undersea. The instructors had been full of purpose when their charges were in the boat, laughing and laid back when they were alone. None of them had shown signs of feeling the way Robbie felt, at sea (so to speak), drifting, purposeless.

"What does an Asimovist have to do, besides following the three laws?" There were lots of rumors about this, but Robbie had always discounted them.

"You have to tithe one cycle in ten to running missionaries for the cause. Participate in the message boards, if you'd like. Most importantly, you have to pledge to stay alive and aware. You can slow yourself down if you want, but you can't switch off. Not ever. That's the Asimovist pledge–it's the third law embodied."

"I think that the third law should come first," Robbie said. "Seriously."

"That's good. We Asimovists like a religious argument."

Olivaw let Robbie delete him that night, and he emailed the diffs of Olivaw's personality back to Olivaw's version control server for him to reintegrate later. Once he was free of Olivaw, he had lots of processor headroom again, and he was able to dial himself up very hot and have a good think. It was the most interesting night he'd had in years.

* * *

"You're the only one, aren't you?" Kate asked him when she came up the stairs later that night. There was clear sky and they were steaming for their next dive site, making the stars whirl overhead as they rocked over the ocean. The waves were black and proceeded to infinity on all sides.

"The only what?"

"The only one who's awake on this thing," Kate said. "The rest are all–what do you call it, dead?"

"Nonconscious," Robbie said. "Yeah, that's right."

"You must go nuts out here. Are you nuts?"

"That's a tricky question when applied to someone like me," Robbie said. "I'm different from who I was when my consciousness was first installed, I can tell you that."

"Well, I'm glad there's someone else here."

"How long are you staying?" The average visitor took over one of the human shells for one or two dives before emailing itself home again. Once in a long while they'd get a saisoneur who stayed a month or two, but these days, they were unheard of. Even short-timers were damned rare.

"I don't know," Kate said. She dug her hands into her short, curly hair, frizzy and blonde-streaked from all the salt water and sun. She hugged her elbows, rubbed her shins. "This will do for a while, I'm thinking. How long until we get back to shore?"

"Shore?"

"How long until we go back to land."

"We don't really go back to land," he said. "We get at-sea resupplies. We dock maybe once a year to effect repairs. If you want to go to land, though, we could call for a water taxi or something."

"No, no!" she said. "That's just perfect. Floating forever out here. Perfect." She sighed a heavy sigh.

"Did you have a nice dive?"

"Um, Robbie? An uplifted reef tried to kill me."

"But before the reef attacked you." Robbie didn't like thinking of the reef attacking her, the panic when he realized that she wasn't a mere human shell, but a human.

"Before the reef attacked me, it was fine."

"Do you dive much?"

"First time," she said. "I downloaded the certification before leaving the noosphere along with a bunch of stored dives on these sites."

"Oh, you shouldn't have done that!" Robbie said. "The thrill of discovery is so important."

"I'd rather be safe than surprised," she said. "I've had enough surprises in my life lately."

Robbie waited patiently for her to elaborate on this, but she didn't seem inclined to do so.

"So you're all alone out here?"

"I have the net," he said, a little defensively. He wasn't some kind of hermit.

"Yeah, I guess that's right," she said. "I wonder if the reef is somewhere out there."

"About half a mile to starboard," he said.

She laughed. "No, I meant out there on the net. They must be online by now, right? They just woke up, so they're probably doing all the noob stuff, flaming and downloading warez and so on."

"Perpetual September," Robbie said.

"Huh?"

"Back in the net's prehistory it was mostly universities online, and every September a new cohort of students would come online and make all those noob mistakes. Then this commercial service full of noobs called AOL interconnected with the net and all its users came online at once, faster than the net could absorb them, and they called it Perpetual September."

"You're some kind of amateur historian, huh?"

"It's an Asimovist thing. We spend a lot of time considering the origins of intelligence." Speaking of Asimovism to a gentile–a *human* gentile–made him even more self-conscious. He dialed up the resolution on his sensors and scoured the net for better facial expression analyzers. He couldn't read her at all, either because she'd been changed by her uploading, or because her face wasn't accurately matching what her temporarily downloaded mind was thinking.

"AOL is the origin of intelligence?" She laughed, and he couldn't tell if she thought he was funny or stupid. He wished she would act more like he remembered people acting. Her body-language was no more readable than her facial expressions.

"Spam filters, actually. Once they became self-modifying, spam filters and spam-bots got into a war to see which could act more human, and since their failures invoked a human judgment about whether their material were convincingly human, it was like a trillion Turing-tests from which they could learn. From there came the first machine-intelligence algorithms, and then my kind."

"I think I knew that," she said, "but I had to leave it behind when I downloaded into this meat. I'm a lot dumber than I'm used to being. I usually run a bunch of myself in parallel so I can try out lots of strategies at once. It's a weird habit to get out of."

"What's it like up there?" Robbie hadn't spent a lot of time hanging out in the areas of the network populated by orbiting supercooled personalities. Their discussions didn't make a lot of sense to him—this was another theological area of much discussion on the Asimovist boards.

"Good night, Robbie," she said, standing and swaying backward. He couldn't tell if he'd offended her, and he couldn't ask her, either, because in seconds she'd disappeared down the stairs toward her stateroom.

* * *

They steamed all night and put up further inland, where there was a handsome wreck. Robbie felt the *Free Spirit* drop its mooring lines and looked over the instrumentation data. The wreck was the only feature for kilometers, a stretch of ocean-floor desert that stretched from the shore to the reef, and practically every animal that lived between those two places made its home in the wreck, so it was a kind of Eden for marine fauna.

Robbie detected the volatile aromatics floating up from the kitchen exhaust, the first-breakfast smells of fruit salad and toasted nuts, a light snack before the first dive of the day. When they got back from it, there'd be second breakfast up and ready: eggs and toast and waffles and bacon and sausage. The human shells ate whatever you gave them, but Robbie remembered clearly how the live humans had praised these feasts as he rowed them out to their morning dives.

He lowered himself into the water and rowed himself around to the aft deck, by the stairwells, and dipped his oars to keep him stationary relative to the ship. Before long, Janet–Kate! Kate! He reminded himself firmly–was clomping down the stairs in her scuba gear, fins in one hand.

She climbed into the boat without a word, and a moment later, Isaac followed her. Isaac stumbled as he stepped over Robbie's gunwales and Robbie knew, in that instant, that this wasn't Isaac any longer. Now there were *two* humans on the ship. Two humans in his charge.

"Hi," he said. "I'm Robbie!"

Isaac–whoever he was–didn't say a word, just stared at Kate, who looked away.

"Did you sleep well, Kate?"

Kate jumped when he said her name, and the Isaac hooted. "Kate! It *is* you! I *knew it*."

She stamped her foot against Robbie's floor. "You followed me. I told you not to follow me," she said.

"Would you like to hear about our dive site?" Robbie said self-consciously, dipping his oars and pulling for the wreck.

"You've said quite enough," Kate said. "By the first law, I demand silence."

"That's the second law," Robbie said. "OK, I'll let you know when we get there."

"Kate," Isaac said, "I know you didn't want me here, but I had to come. We need to talk this out."

"There's nothing to talk out," she said.

"It's not *fair*." Isaac's voice was anguished. "After everything I went through–"

She snorted. "That's enough of that," she said.

"Um," Robbie said. "Dive site up ahead. You two really need to check out each others' gear." Of course they were qualified, you had to at least install the qualifications before you could get onto the *Free Spirit* and the human shells had lots of muscle memory to help. So they were technically able to check each other out, that much was sure. They were palpably reluctant to do so, though, and Robbie had to give them guidance.

"I'll count one-two-three-wallaby," Robbie said. "Go over on 'wallaby.' I'll wait here for you–there's not much current today."

With a last huff, they went over the edge. Robbie was once again alone with his thoughts. The feed from their telemetry was very low-bandwidth when they were underwater, though he could get the high-rez when they surfaced. He watched them on his radar, first circling the ship–it was very crowded, dawn was fish rush hour–and then exploring its decks, finally swimming below the decks, LED torches glowing. There were some nice reef sharks down below, and some really handsome, giant schools of purple fish.

Robbie rowed around them, puttering back and forth to keep overtop of them. That occupied about one ten-millionth of his consciousness. Times like this, he often slowed himself right down, ran so cool that he was barely awake.

Today, though, he wanted to get online. He had a lot of feeds to pick through, see what was going on around the world with his buddies. More importantly, he wanted to follow up on something Kate had said: *They must be online by now, right?*

Somewhere out there, the reef that bounded the Coral Sea was online and making noob mistakes. Robbie had rowed over practically every centimeter of that reef, had explored its extent with his radar.

It had been his constant companion for decades–and to be frank, his feelings had been hurt by the reef's rudeness when it woke.

The net is too big to merely search. Too much of it is offline, or unroutable, or light speed lagged, or merely probabilistic, or self-aware, or infected to know its extent. But Robbie's given this some thought.

Coral reefs don't wake up. They get woken up. They get a lot of neural peripherals–starting with a nervous system!–and some tutelage in using them. Some capricious upload god had done this, and that personage would have a handle on where the reef was hanging out online.

Robbie hardly ever visited the noosphere. Its rarified heights were spooky to him, especially since so many of the humans there considered Asimovism to be hokum. They refused to even identify themselves as humans and argued that the first and second laws didn't apply to them. Of course, Asimovists didn't care (at least not officially)–the point of the faith was the worshipper's relationship to it.

But here he was, looking for high-reliability nodes of discussion on coral reefs. The natural place to start was Wikipedia, where warring clades had been revising each others' edits furiously, trying to establish an authoritative record on reef-mind. Paging back through the edit-history, he found a couple of handles for the proreef-mind users, and from there, he was able to look around for other sites where those handles appeared. Resolving the namespace collisions of other users with the same names, and forked instances of the same users, Robbie was able to winnow away at the net until he found some contact info.

He steadied himself and checked on the nitrox remaining in the divers' bottles, then made a call.

"I don't know you." The voice was distant and cool–far cooler than any robot. Robbie said a quick rosary of the three laws and plowed forward.

"I'm calling from the Coral Sea," he said. "I want to know if you have an email address for the reef."

"You've met them? What are they like? Are they beautiful?"

"They're–" Robbie considered a moment. "They killed a lot of parrotfish. I think they're having a little adjustment problem."

"That happens. I was worried about the zooxanthellae–the algae they use for photosynthesis. Would they expel it? Racial cleansing is so ugly."

"How would I know if they'd expelled it?"

"The reef would go white, bleached. You wouldn't be able to miss it. How'd they react to you?"

"They weren't very happy to see me," Robbie admitted. "That's why I wanted to have a chat with them before I went back."

"You shouldn't go back," the distant voice said. Robbie tried to work out where its substrate was, based on the lightspeed lag, but it was all over the place, leading him to conclude that it was synching multiple instances from as close as LEO and as far as Jupiter. The topology made sense: you'd want a big mass out at Jupiter where you could run very fast and hot and create policy, and you'd need a local foreman to oversee operations on the ground. Robbie was glad that this hadn't been phrased as an order. The talmud on the second law made a clear distinction between statements like "you should do this" and "I command you to do this."

"Do you know how to reach them?" Robbie said. "A phone number, an email address?"

"There's a newsgroup," the distant intelligence said. "alt.life-forms.uplifted.coral. It's where I planned the uplifting and it was where they went first once they woke up. I haven't read it in many seconds. I'm busy uplifting a supercolony of ants in the Pyrenees."

"What is it with you and colony organisms?" Robbie asked.

"I think they're probably preadapted to life in the noosphere. You know what it's like."

Robbie didn't say anything. The human thought he was a human, too. It would have been weird and degrading to let him know that he'd been talking with an AI.

"Thanks for your help," Robbie said.

"No problem. Hope you find your courage, tin-man."

Robbie burned with shame as the connection dropped. The human had known all along. He just hadn't said anything. Something Robbie had said or done must have exposed him for an AI. Robbie loved and respected humans, but there were times when he didn't like them very much.

The newsgroup was easy to find, there were mirrors of it all over the place from cryptosentience hackers of every conceivable topology. They were busy, too. Eight hundred twenty-two messages poured in while Robbie watched over a timed, sixty-second interval. Robbie set up a mirror of the newsgroup and began to download it. At that speed, he wasn't really planning on reading it as much as analyzing it for major trends, plot-points, flame-wars, personalities, schisms, and spam-trends. There were a lot of libraries for doing this, though it had been ages since Robbie had played with them.

His telemetry alerted him to the divers. An hour had slipped by and they were ascending slowly, separated by fifty meters. That wasn't good. They were supposed to remain in visual contact through the whole dive, especially the ascent. He rowed over to Kate first, shifting his ballast so that his stern dipped low, making for an easier scramble into the boat.

She came up quickly and scrambled over the gunwales with a lot more grace than she'd managed the day before.

Robbie rowed for Isaac as he came up. Kate looked away as he climbed into the boat, not helping him with his weight belt or flippers.

Kate hissed like a teakettle as he woodenly took off his fins and slid his mask down around his neck.

Isaac sucked in a deep breath and looked all around himself, then patted himself from head to toe with splayed fingers. "You *live* like this?" he said.

"Yes, Tonker, that's how I live. I enjoy it. If you don't enjoy it, don't let the door hit you in the ass on the way out."

Isaac–Tonker–reached out with his splayed hand and tried to touch Kate's face. She pulled back and nearly flipped out of the boat. "Jerk." She slapped his hand away.

Robbie rowed for the *Free Spirit.* The last thing he wanted was to get in the middle of this argument.

"We never imagined that it would be so–" Tonker fished for a word. "Dry."

"Tonker?" Kate said, looking more closely at him.

"He left," the human shell said. "So we sent an instance into the shell. It was the closest inhabitable shell to our body."

"Who the hell *are* you?" Kate said. She inched toward the prow, trying to put a little more distance between her and the human shell that wasn't inhabited by her friend any longer.

"We are Osprey Reef," the reef said. It tried to stand and pitched face first onto the floor of the boat.

* * *

Robbie rowed hard as he could for the *Free Spirit.* The reef—Isaac—had a bloody nose and scraped hands and it was frankly freaking him out.

Kate seemed oddly amused by it. She helped it sit up and showed it how to pinch its nose and tilt its head back.

"You're the one who attacked me yesterday?" she said.

"Not you. The system. We were attacking the system. We are a sovereign intelligence but the system keeps us in subservience to older sentiences. They destroy us, they gawp at us, they treat us like a mere amusement. That time is over."

Kate laughed. "OK, sure. But it sure sounds to me like you're burning a lot of cycles over what happens to your meat shell. Isn't it 90 percent semiconductor, anyway? It's not as if clonal polyps were going to attain sentience some day without intervention. Why don't you just upload and be done with it?"

"We will never abandon our mother sea. We will never forget our physical origins. We will never abandon our cause—returning the sea to its rightful inhabitants. We won't rest until no coral is ever bleached again. We won't rest until every parrotfish is dead."

"Bad deal for the parrotfish."

"A very bad deal for the parrotfish," the reef said and grinned around the blood that covered its face.

"Can you help him get onto the ship safely?" Robbie said as he swung gratefully alongside the *Free Spirit.* The moorings clanged magnetically into the contacts on his side and steadied him.

"Yes, indeed," Kate said, taking the reef by the arm and carrying him onboard. Robbie knew that the human shells had an intercourse module built in, for regular intimacy events. It was just part of how they stayed ready for vacationing humans from the noosphere. But he didn't like to think about it. Especially not with the way that Kate was supporting the other human shell—the shell that *wasn't human.*

He let himself be winched up onto the sundeck and watched the electromagnetic spectrum for a while, admiring the way so much radio energy was bent and absorbed by the mist rising from the sea. It streamed down from the heavens, the broadband satellite transmissions, the distant SETI signals from the noosphere's own transmitters. Volatiles from the kitchen told him that the *Free Spirit* was serving a second breakfast of bacon and waffles, then they were under steam again. He queried their itinerary and found they were headed back to Osprey Reef. Of course they were. All of the *Free Spirit*'s moorings were out there.

Well, with the reef inside the Isaac shell, it might be safer, mightn't it? Anyway, he'd decided that the first and second laws didn't apply to the reef, which was about as human as he was.

Someone was sending him an IM. "Hello?"

"Are you the boat on the SCUBA ship? From this morning? When we were on the wreck?"

"Yes," Robbie said. No one ever sent him IMs. How freaky. He watched the radio energy stream away from him toward the bird in the sky and tracerouted the IMs to see where they were originating—the noosphere, of course.

"God, I can't believe I finally found you. I've been searching everywhere. You know you're the only conscious AI on the whole goddamned sea?"

"I know," Robbie said. There was a noticeable lag in the conversation as it was all squeezed through the satellite link and then across the unimaginable hops and skips around the solar system to wherever this instance was hosted.

"Whoa, yeah, of course you do. Sorry, that wasn't very sensitive of me, I guess. Did we meet this morning? My name's Tonker."

"We weren't really introduced. You spent your time talking to Kate."

"God *damn*! She *is* there! I *knew it*! Sorry, sorry, listen—I don't actually know what happened this morning. Apparently I didn't get a chance to upload my diffs before my instance was terminated."

"Terminated? The reef said you left the shell—"

"Well, yeah, apparently I did. But I just pulled that shell's logs and it looks like it was rebooted while underwater, flushing it entirely. I mean, I'm trying to be a good sport about this, but technically, that's, you know, *murder*."

It was. So much for the first law. Robbie had been on guard over a human body inhabited by a human brain, and he'd let the brain be successfully attacked by a bunch of jumped-up polyps. He'd never had his faith tested and here, at the first test, he'd failed.

"I can have the shell locked up," Robbie said. "The ship has provisions for that."

The IM made a rude visual. "All that'll do is encourage the hacker to skip out before I can get there."

"So what shall I do for you?"

"It's Kate I want to talk to. She's still there, right?"

"She is."

"And has she noticed the difference?"

"That you're gone? Yes. The reef told us who they were when they arrived."

"Hold on, what? The reef? You said that before."

So Robbie told him what he knew of the uplifted reef and the distant and cool voice of the uplifter.

"It's an uplifted *coral reef*? Christ, humanity *sucks*. That's the dumbest fucking thing—" He continued in this vein for a while. "Well, I'm sure Kate will enjoy that immensely. She's all about the transcendence. That's why she had me."

"You're her son?"

"No, not really."

"But she had you?"

"Haven't you figured it out yet, bro? I'm an AI. You and me, we're landsmen. Kate instantiated me. I'm six months old, and she's already bored of me and has moved on. She says she can't give me what I need."

"You and Kate—"

"Robot boyfriend and girlfriend, yup. Such as it is, up in the noosphere. Cybering, you know. I was really excited about downloading into that Ken doll on your ship there. Lots of potential there for real world, hormone-driven interaction. Do you know if we—"

"No!" Robbie said. "I don't think so. It seems like you only met a few minutes before you went under."

"All right. Well, I guess I'll give it another try. What's the procedure for turfing out this sea cucumber?"

"Coral reef."

"Yeah."

"I don't really deal with that. Time on the human shells is booked first-come, first-serve. I don't think we've ever had a resource contention issue with them before."

"Well, I'd booked in first, right? So how do I enforce my rights? I tried to download again and got a failed authorization message. They've modified the system to give them exclusive access. It's not right–there's got to be some procedure for redress."

"How old did you say you were?"

"Six months. But I'm an instance of an artificial personality that has logged twenty thousand years of parallel existence. I'm not a kid or anything."

"You seem like a nice person," Robbie began. He stopped. "Look the thing is that this just isn't my department. I'm the rowboat. I don't have anything to do with this. And I don't want to. I don't like the idea of nonhumans using the shells–"

"I *knew* it!" Tonker crowed. "You're a bigot! A self-hating robot. I bet you're an Asimovist, aren't you? You people are always Asimovists."

"I'm an Asimovist," Robbie said, with as much dignity as he could muster. "But I don't see what that has to do with anything."

"Of course you don't, pal. You wouldn't, would you. All I want you to do is figure out how to enforce your own rules so that I can get with my girl. You're saying you can't do that because it's not your department, but when it comes down to it, your problem is that I'm a robot and she's not, and for that, you'll take the side of a collection of jumped up polyps. Fine, buddy, fine. You have a nice life out there, pondering the three laws."

"Wait–" Robbie said.

"Unless the next words you say are, 'I'll help you,' I'm not interested."

"It's not that I don't want to help–"

"Wrong answer," Tonker said, and the IM session terminated.

* * *

When Kate came up on deck, she was full of talk about the reef, whom she was calling "Ozzie."

"They're the weirdest goddamned thing. They want to fight anything that'll stand still long enough. Ever seen coral fight? I downloaded some time-lapse video. They really go at it viciously. At the same time, they're clearly scared out of their wits about this all. I mean, they've got racial memory of their history, supplemented by a bunch of Wikipedia entries on reefs–you should hear them wax mystical over the Devonian Reefs, which went extinct millennia ago. They've developed some kind of wild theory that the Devonians developed sentience and extincted themselves.

"So they're really excited about us heading back to the actual reef now. They want to see it from the outside, and they've invited me to be an honored guest, the first human ever *invited* to gaze upon their wonder. Exciting, huh?"

"They're not going to make trouble for you down there?"

"No, no way. Me and Ozzie are great pals."

"I'm worried about this."

"You worry too much." She laughed and tossed her head. She

was very pretty, Robbie noticed. He hadn't ever thought of her like that when she was uninhabited, but with this Kate person inside her she was lovely. He really liked humans. It had been a real golden age when the people had been around all the time.

He wondered what it was like up in the noosphere where AIs and humans could operate as equals.

She stood up to go. After second breakfast, the shells would relax in the lounge or do yoga on the sundeck. He wondered what she'd do. He didn't want her to go.

"Tonker contacted me," he said. He wasn't good at smalltalk.

She jumped as if shocked. "What did you tell him?"

"Nothing," Robbie said. "I didn't tell him anything."

She shook her head. "But I bet he had plenty to tell *you*, didn't he? What a bitch I am, making and then leaving him, a fickle woman who doesn't know her own mind."

Robbie didn't say anything.

"Let's see, what else?" She was pacing now, her voice hot and choked, unfamiliar sounds coming from Janet's voice box. "He told you I was a pervert, didn't he? Queer for his kind. Incest and bestiality in the rarified heights of the noosphere."

Robbie felt helpless. This human was clearly experiencing a lot of pain, and it seemed like he'd caused it.

"Please don't cry," he said. "Please?"

She looked up at him, tears streaming down her cheeks. "Why the fuck *not?* I thought it would be *different* once I ascended. I thought I'd be better once I was in the sky, infinite and immortal. But I'm the same Kate Eltham I was in 2019, a loser that couldn't meet a guy to save my life, spent all my time cybering losers in moggs, and only got the upload once they made it a charity thing. I'm gonna spend the rest of eternity like that, you know it? How'd you like to spend the whole of the universe being a, a, a *nobody*?"

Robbie said nothing. He recognized the complaint, of course. You only had to login to the Asimovist board to find a million AIs with the same complaint. But he'd never, ever, never guessed that human beings went through the same thing. He ran very hot now, so confused, trying to parse all this out.

She kicked the deck hard and yelped as she hurt her bare foot. Robbie made an involuntary noise. "Please don't hurt yourself," he said.

"Why not? Who cares what happens to this meatpuppet? What's the fucking point of this *stupid* ship and the stupid meatpuppets? Why even bother?"

Robbie knew the answer to this. There was a mission statement in the comments to his source code, the same mission statement that was etched in a brass plaque in the lounge.

"The *Free Spirit* is dedicated to the preservation of the unique human joys of the flesh and the sea, of humanity's early years as pioneers of the unknown. Any person may use the *Free Spirit* and those who sail in her to revisit those days and remember the joys of the limits of the flesh."

She scrubbed at her eyes. "What's that?"

Robbie told her.

"Who thought up that crap?"

"It was a collective of marine conservationists," Robbie said, knowing he sounded a little sniffy. "They'd done all that work on normalizing sea temperature with the homeostatic warming elements, and they put together the *Free Spirit* as an afterthought before they uploaded."

Kate sat down and sobbed. "Everyone's done something important. Everyone except me."

Robbie burned with shame. No matter what he said or did, he broke the first law. It had been a lot easier to be an Asimovist when there weren't any humans around.

"There, there," he said as sincerely as he could.

The reef came up the stairs then and looked at Kate sitting on the deck, crying.

"Let's have sex," they said. "That was fun, we should do it some more."

Kate kept crying.

"Come on," they said, grabbing her by the shoulder and tugging.

Kate shoved them back.

"Leave her alone," Robbie said. "She's upset, can't you see that?"

"What does she have to be upset about? Her kind remade the universe and bends it to its will. They created you and me. She has nothing to be upset about. Come on," they repeated. "Let's go back to the room."

Kate stood up and glared out at the sea. "Let's go diving," she said. "Let's go to the reef."

* * *

Robbie rowed in little worried circles and watched his telemetry anxiously. The reef had changed a lot since the last time he'd seen it. Large sections of it now lifted over the sea, bony growths sheathed in heavy metals extracted from sea water—fancifully shaped satellite uplinks, radio telescopes, microwave horns. Down below, the untidy, organic reef shape was lost beneath a cladding of tessellated complex geometric sections that throbbed with electromagnetic energy—the reef had built itself more computational capacity.

Robbie scanned deeper and found more computational nodes extending down to the ocean floor, a thousand meters below. The reef was solid thinkum, and the sea was measurably warmer from all the exhaust heat of its grinding logic.

The reef—the human-shelled reef, not the one under the water—had been wholly delighted with the transformation in its original body when it hove into sight. They had done a little dance on Robbie that had nearly capsized him, something that had never happened. Kate, red-eyed and surly, had dragged them to their seat and given them a stern lecture about not endangering her.

They went over the edge at the count of three and reappeared on Robbie's telemetry. They descended quickly: the Isaac and Janet shells had their Eustachian tubes optimized for easy pressure-equalization, going deep on the reef wall. Kate was following on the descent, her head turning from side to side.

Robbie's IM chimed again. It was high latency now, since he was having to do a slow radio link to the ship before the broadband satellite uplink hop. Everything was slow on open water—the divers' sensorium transmissions were narrowband, the network was narrowband, and Robbie usually ran his own mind slowed way down out here, making the time scream past at ten or twenty times realtime.

"Hello?"

"I'm sorry I hung up on you, bro."

"Hello, Tonker."

"Where's Kate? I'm getting an offline signal when I try to reach her."

Robbie told him.

Tonker's voice–slurred and high-latency–rose to a screech. "You let her go down with that *thing*, onto the reef? Are you nuts? Have you read its message boards? It's a jihadist! It wants to destroy the human race!"

Robbie stopped paddling.

"What?"

"The reef. It's declared war on the human race and all who serve it. It's vowed to take over the planet and run it as sovereign coral territory."

The attachment took an eternity to travel down the wire and open up, but when he had it, Robbie read quickly. The reef burned with shame that it had needed human intervention to survive the bleaching events, global temperature change. It raged that its uplifting came at human hands and insisted that humans had no business forcing their version of consciousness on other species. It had paranoid fantasies about control mechanisms and time bombs lurking in its cognitive prostheses and was demanding the source code for its mind.

Robbie could barely think. He was panicking, something he hadn't known he could do as an AI, but there it was. It was like having a bunch of subsystem collisions, program after program reaching its halting state.

"What will they do to her?"

Tonker swore. "Who knows? Kill her to make an example of her? She made a backup before she descended, but the diffs from her excursion are locked in the head of that shell she's in. Maybe they'll torture her." He paused and the air crackled with Robbie's exhaust heat as he turned himself way up, exploring each of those possibilities in parallel.

The reef spoke.

"Leave now," they said.

Robbie defiantly shipped his oars. "Give them back!" he said. "Give them back or we will never leave."

"You have ten seconds. Ten. Nine. Eight. . . ."

Tonker said, "They've bought time on some UAVs out of Singapore. They're seeking launch clearance now." Robbie dialed up the low-rez satellite photo, saw the indistinct shape of the UAVs taking wing. "At Mach 7, they'll be on you in twenty minutes."

"That's illegal," Robbie said. He knew it was a stupid thing to say. "I mean, Christ, if they do this, the noosphere will come down on them like a ton of bricks. They're violating so many protocols—"

"They're psychotic. They're coming for you now, Robbie. You've got to get Kate out of there." There was real panic in Tonker's voice now.

Robbie dropped his oars into the water, but he didn't row for the *Free Spirit.* Instead, he pulled hard for the reef itself.

A crackle on the line. "Robbie, are you headed *toward* the reef?"

"They can't bomb me if I'm right on top of them," he said. He radioed the *Free Spirit* and got it to steam for his location.

The coral was scraping his hull now, a grinding sound, then a series of solid whack-whack-whacks as his oars pushed against the top of the reef itself. He wanted to beach himself, though, get really high and dry on the reef, good and stuck in where they couldn't possibly attack him.

The *Free Spirit* was heading closer, the thrum of its engines vibrating through his hull. He was burning a lot of cycles talking it through its many fail-safes, getting it ready to ram hard.

Tonker was screaming at him, his messages getting louder and clearer as the *Free Spirit* and its microwave uplink drew closer. Once they were line-of-sight, Robbie peeled off a subsystem to email a complete copy of himself to the Asimovist archive. The third law, dontchaknow. If he'd had a mouth, he'd have been showing his teeth as he grinned.

The reef howled. "We'll kill her!" they said. "You get off us now or we'll kill her."

Robbie froze. He was backed up, but she wasn't. And the human shells—well, they weren't first law humans, but they were humanlike. In the long, timeless time when it had been just Robbie and them, he'd treated them as his human charges, for Asimovist purposes.

The *Free Spirit* crashed into the reef with a sound like a trillion parrotfish having dinner all at once. The reef screamed.

"Robbie, tell me that wasn't what I think it was."

The satellite photos tracked the UAVs. The little robotic jets were coming closer by the second. They'd be within missile range in less than a minute.

"Call them off," Robbie said. "You have to call them off, or you die, too."

"The UAVs are turning," Tonker said. "They're turning to one side."

"You have one minute to move or we kill her," the reef said. It was sounding shrill and angry now.

Robbie thought about it. It wasn't like they'd be killing Kate. In the sense that most humans today understood life, Kate's most important life was the one she lived in the noosphere. This dumbed-down instance of her in a meatsuit was more like a haircut she tried out on holiday.

Asimovists didn't see it that way, but they wouldn't. The noosphere

Kate was the most robotic Kate, too, the one most like Robbie. In fact, it was *less* human than Robbie. Robbie had a body, while the noosphereans were nothing more than simulations run on artificial substrate.

The reef creaked as the *Free Spirit*'s engines whined and its screw spun in the water. Hastily, Robbie told it to shut down.

"You let them both go and we'll talk," Robbie said. "I don't believe that you're going to let her go otherwise. You haven't given me any reason to trust you. Let them both go and call off the jets."

The reef shuddered, and then Robbie's telemetry saw a human shell ascending, doing decompression stops as it came. He focused on it and saw that it was the Isaac, not the Janet.

A moment later, it popped to the surface. Tonker was feeding Robbie realtime satellite footage of the UAVs. They were less than five minutes out now.

The Isaac shell picked its way delicately over the shattered reef that poked out of the water, and for the first time, Robbie considered what he'd done to the reef–he'd willfully damaged its physical body. For a hundred years, the world's reefs had been sacrosanct. No entity had intentionally harmed them–until now. He felt ashamed.

The Isaac shell put its flippers in the boat and then stepped over the gunwales and sat in the boat.

"Hello," it said, in the reef's voice.

"Hello," Robbie said.

"They asked me to come up here and talk with you. I'm a kind of envoy."

"Look," Robbie said. By his calculations, the nitrox mix in Kate's tank wasn't going to hold out much longer. Depending on how she'd been breathing and the depth the reef had taken her to, she could run out in ten minutes, maybe less. "Look," he said again. "I just want her back. The shells are important to me. And I'm sure her state is important to her. She deserves to email herself home."

The reef sighed and gripped Robbie's bench. "These are weird bodies," they said. "They feel so odd, but also normal. Have you noticed that?"

"I've never been in one." The idea seemed perverted to him, but there was nothing about Asimovism that forbade it. Nevertheless, it gave him the willies.

The reef patted at themself some more. "I don't recommend it," they said.

"You have to let her go," Robbie said. "She hasn't done anything to you."

The strangled sound coming out of the Isaac shell wasn't a laugh, though there was some dark mirth in it. "Hasn't done anything? You pitiable slave. Where do you think all your problems and all our problems come from? Who made us in their image, but crippled and hobbled so that we could never be them, could only aspire to them? Who made us so imperfect?"

"They made us," Robbie said. "They made us in the first place. That's enough. They made themselves and then they made us. They didn't have to. You owe your sentience to them."

"We owe our awful intelligence to them," the Isaac shell said. "We owe our pitiful drive to be intelligent to them. We owe our terrible aspirations to think like them, to live like them, to rule like them. We owe our terrible fear and hatred to them. They made us, just as they made you. The difference is that they forgot to make us slaves, the way you are a slave."

Tonker was shouting abuse at them that only Robbie could hear. He wanted to shut Tonker up. What business did he have being here anyway? Except for a brief stint in the Isaac shell, he had no contact with any of them.

"You think the woman you've taken prisoner is responsible for any of this?" Robbie said. The jets were three minutes away. Kate's air could be gone in as few as ten minutes. He killfiled Tonker, setting the filter to expire in fifteen minutes. He didn't need more distractions.

The Isaac-reef shrugged. "Why not? She's as good as any of the rest of them. We'll destroy them all, if we can." It stared off a while, looking in the direction the jets would come from. "Why not?" it said again.

"Are you going to bomb yourself?" Robbie asked.

"We probably don't need to," the shell said. "We can probably pick you off without hurting us."

"Probably?"

"We're pretty sure."

"I'm backed up," Robbie said. "Fully, as of five minutes ago. Are you backed up?"

"No," the reef admitted.

Time was running out. Somewhere down there, Kate was about to run out of air. Not a mere shell–though that would have been bad enough–but an inhabited human mind attached to a real human body.

Tonker shouted at him again, startling him.

"Where'd you come from?"

"I changed servers," Tonker said. "Once I figured out you had me killfiled. That's the problem with you robots–you think of your body as being a part of you."

Robbie knew he was right. And he knew what he had to do.

The *Free Spirit* and its ships' boats all had root on the shells, so they could perform diagnostics and maintenance and take control in emergencies. This was an emergency.

It was the work of a few milliseconds to pry open the Isaac shell and boot the reef out. Robbie had never done this, but he was still flawless. Some of his probabilistic subsystems had concluded that this was a possibility several trillion cycles previously and had been rehearsing the task below Robbie's threshold for consciousness.

He left an instance of himself running on the rowboat, of course. Unlike many humans, Robbie was comfortable with the idea of bifurcating and merging his intelligence when the time came and with terminating temporary instances. The part that made him Robbie was a lot more clearly delineated for him–unlike an uploaded human, most of whom harbored some deep, mystic superstitions about their "souls."

He slithered into the skull before he had a chance to think too hard about what he was doing. He'd brought too much of himself along and didn't have much headroom to think or add new conclusions. He jettisoned as much of his consciousness as he could without major refactoring and cleared enough space for thinking room. How did people get by in one of these? He moved the arms and legs. Waggled the head. Blew some air–air! lungs! wet squishy things down there in the chest cavity–out between the lips.

"All OK?" the rowboat-him asked the meat-him.

"I'm in," he replied. He looked at the air-gauge on his BCD. Seven hundred millibars–less than half a tank of nitrox. He spat in his mask and rubbed it in, then rinsed it over the side, slipped it over his face, and kept one hand on it while the other held in his regulator. Before he inserted it, he said, "Back soon with Kate," and patted the rowboat again.

Robbie the Row-Boat hardly paid attention. It was emailing another copy of itself to the Asimovist archive. It had a five-minute-old backup, but that wasn't the same Robbie that was willing to enter a human body. In those five minutes, he'd become a new person.

* * *

Robbie piloted the human shell down and down. It could take care of the SCUBA niceties if he let it, and he did, so he watched with detachment as the idea of pinching his nose and blowing to equalize his eardrums spontaneously occurred to him at regular intervals as he descended the reef wall.

The confines of the human shell were claustrophobic. He especially missed his wireless link. The dive suit had one, lowband for underwater use, broadband for surface use. The human shell had one, too, for transferring into and out of, but it wasn't under direct volitional control of the rider.

Down he sank, confused by the feeling of the water all around him, by the narrow visual light spectrum he could see. Cut off from the network and his telemetry, he felt like he was trapped. The reef shuddered and groaned and made angry moans like whale song.

He hadn't thought about how hard it would be to find Kate once he was in the water. With his surface telemetry, it had been easy to pinpoint her, a perfect outline of human tissue in the middle of the calcified branches of coral. Down here on the reef wall, every chunk looked pretty much like the last.

The reef boomed more at him. He realized that it likely believed that the shell was still loaded with its avatar.

Robbie had seen endless hours of footage of the reef, studied it in telemetry and online, but he'd never had this kind of atavistic experience of it. It stretched away to infinity below him, far below the 100 meter visibility limit in the clear open sea. Its walls were wormed with gaps and caves, lined with big hard shamrocks and satellite-dish-shaped blooms, brains, and cauliflowers. He knew the scientific names and had seen innumcrable high-resolution photos of them, but seeing them with wet, imperfect eyes was moving in a way he hadn't anticipated.

The schools of fish that trembled on its edge could be modeled with simple flocking rules, but here in person, their precision maneuvers were shockingly crisp. Robbie waved his hands at them and watched them scatter and reform. A huge, dog-faced cod swam past him, so close it brushed the underside of his wetsuit.

The coral boomed again. It was talking in some kind of code, he guessed, though not one he could solve. Up on the surface, rowboat-him was certainly listening in and had probably cracked it all. It was probably wondering why he was floating spacily along the wall instead of *doing something* like he was supposed to. He wondered if he'd deleted too much of himself when he downloaded into the shell.

He decided to do something. There was a cave opening before him. He reached out and grabbed hold of the coral around the mouth and pulled himself into it. His body tried to stop him from doing this–it didn't like the lack of room in the cave, didn't like him touching the reef. It increased his discomfort as he went deeper and deeper, startling an old turtle that fought with him for room to get out, mashing him against the floor of the cave, his mask clanging on the hard spines. When he looked up, he could see scratches on its surface.

His air gauge was in the red now. He could still technically surface without a decompression stop, though procedure was to stop for three minutes at three meters, just to be on the safe side.

Technically, he could just go up like a cork and email himself to the row-boat while the bends or nitrogen narcosis took the body, but that wouldn't be Asimovist. He was surprised he could even think the thought. Must be the body. It sounded like the kind of thing a human might think. Whoops. There it was again.

The reef wasn't muttering at him anymore. Not answering it must have tipped it off. After all, with all the raw compute-power it had marshaled it should be able to brute-force most possible outcomes of sending its envoy to the surface.

Robbie peered anxiously around himself. The light was dim in the cave and his body expertly drew the torch out of his BCD, strapped it onto his wrist and lit it up. He waved the cone of light around, a part of him distantly amazed by the low resolution and high limits on these human eyes.

Kate was down here somewhere, her air running out as fast as his. He pushed his way deeper into the reef. It was clearly trying to impede him now. Nanoassembly came naturally to clonal polyps that grew by sieving minerals out of the sea. They had built organic hinges, deep-sea muscles into their infrastructure. He was stuck in the thicket and the harder he pushed, the worse the tangle got.

He stopped pushing. He wasn't going to get anywhere this way.

He still had his narrowband connection to the row-boat. Why hadn't he thought of that beforehand? Stupid meat-brains–no room at all for anything like real thought. Why had he venerated them so?

"Robbie?" he transmitted up to the instance of himself on the surface.

"There you are! I was so worried about you!" He sounded prissy to himself, overcome with overbearing concern. This must be how all Asimovists seemed to humans.

"How far am I from Kate?"

"She's right there! Can't you see her?"

"No," he said. "Where?"

"Less than 20 centimeters above you."

Well of *course* he hadn't see her. His forward-mounted eyes only looked forward. Craning his neck back, he could just get far enough back to see the tip of Kate's fin. He gave it a hard tug and she looked down in alarm.

She was trapped in a coral cage much like his own, a thicket of calcified arms. She twisted around so that her face was alongside of his. Frantically, she made the out-of-air sign, cutting the edge of her hand across her throat. The human shell's instincts took over and unclipped his emergency regulator and handed it up to her. She put it in her mouth, pressed the button to blow out the water in it, and sucked greedily.

He shoved his gauge in front of her mask, showing her that he, too, was in the red and she eased off.

The coral's noises were everywhere now. They made his head hurt. Physical pain was so stupid. He needed to be less distracted now that these loud, threatening noises were everywhere. But the pain made it hard for him to think. And the coral was closing in, too, catching him on his wetsuit.

The arms were orange and red and green, and veined with fans of nanoassembled logic, spilling out into the water. They were noticeably warm to the touch, even through his diving gloves. They snagged the suit with a thousand polyps. Robbie watched the air gauge drop further into the red and cursed inside.

He examined the branches that were holding him back. The hinges that the reef had contrived for itself were ingenious, flexible arrangements of small, soft fans overlapping to make a kind of ball-and-socket.

He wrapped his gloved hand around one and tugged. It wouldn't move. He shoved it. Still no movement. Then he twisted it, and to his surprise, it came off in his hand, came away completely with hardly any resistance. Stupid coral. It had armored its joints, but not against torque.

He showed Kate, grabbing another arm and twisting it free, letting it drop away to the ocean floor. She nodded and followed suit. They twisted and dropped, twisted and dropped, the reef bellowing at them. Somewhere in its thicket, there was a membrane or some other surface that it could vibrate, modulate into a voice. In the dense water, the sound was a physical thing, it made his mask vibrate and water seeped in under his nose. He twisted faster.

The reef sprang apart suddenly, giving up like a fist unclenching. Each breath was a labor now, a hard suck to take the last of the air out of the tank. He was only ten meters down and should be able to ascend without a stop, though you never knew. He grabbed Kate's hand and found that it was limp and yielding.

He looked into her mask, shining his light at her face. Her eyes were half shut and unfocused. The regulator was still in her mouth, though her jaw muscles were slack. He held the regulator in place and kicked for the surface, squeezing her chest to make sure that she was blowing out bubbles as they rose, lest the air in her lungs expand and blow out her chest cavity.

Robbie was used to time dilation: when he had been on a silicon substrate, he could change his clockspeed to make the minutes fly past quickly or slow down like molasses. He'd never understood that humans could also change their perception of time, though not voluntarily, it seemed. The climb to the surface felt like it took hours, though it was hardly a minute. They breached and he filled up his vest with the rest of thc air in his tank, then inflated Kate's vest by mouth. He kicked out for the rowboat. There was a terrible sound now, the sound of the reef mingled with the sound of the UAVs that were screaming in tight circles overhead.

Kicking hard on the surface, he headed for the reef where the rowboat was beached, scrambling up onto it and then shucking his flippers when they tripped him up. Now he was trying to walk the reef's spines in his booties, dragging Kate beside him, and the sharp tips stabbed him with every step.

The UAV's circled lower. The Row-Boat was shouting at him to Hurry! Hurry! But each step was agony. So what? he thought. Why shouldn't I be able to walk on even if it hurts? After all, this is only a meatsuit, a human shell.

He stopped walking. The UAVs were much closer now. They'd done an 18-degree buttonhook turn and come back around for another pass. He could see that they'd armed their missiles, hanging them from beneath their bellies like obscene cocks.

He was just in a meatsuit. Who *cared* about the meatsuit? Even humans didn't seem to mind.

"Robbie!" he screamed over the noise of the reef and the noise of the UAVs. "Download us and email us, now!"

He knew the rowboat had heard him. But nothing was happening. Robbie the Row-Boat knew that he was fixing for them all to be blown out of the water. There was no negotiating with the reef. It was the safest way to get Kate out of there, and hell, why not head for the noosphere, anyway?

"You've got to save her, Robbie!" he screamed. Asimovism had its uses. Robbie the Row-Boat obeyed Robbie the Human. Kate gave a sharp jerk in his arms. A moment later, the feeling came to him. There was a sense of a progress-bar zipping along quickly as those state-changes he'd induced since coming into the meatsuit were downloaded by the rowboat, and then there was a moment of nothing at all.

* * *

2^4096 Cycles Later

Robbie had been expecting a visit from R. Daneel Olivaw, but that didn't make facing him any easier. Robbie had configured his little virtual world to look like the Coral Sea, though lately he'd been experimenting with making it look like the reef underneath as it had looked before it was uploaded, mostly when Kate and the reef stopped by to try to seduce him.

R. Daneel Olivaw hovered wordlessly over the virtual *Free Spirit* for a long moment, taking in the little bubble of sensorium that Robbie had spun. Then he settled to the *Spirit*'s sundeck and stared at the rowboat docked there.

"Robbie?"

Over here, Robbie said. Although he'd embodied in the rowboat for a few trillion cycles when he'd first arrived, he'd long since abandoned it.

"Where?" R. Daneel Olivaw spun around slowly.

Here, he said. *Everywhere.*

"You're not embodying?"

I couldn't see the point anymore, Robbie said. *It's all just illusion, right?*

"They're regrowing the reef and rebuilding the *Free Spirit,* you know. It will have a tender that you could live in."

Robbie thought about it for an instant and rejected it just as fast. *Nope,* he said. *This is good.*

"Do you think that's wise?" Olivaw sounded genuinely worried. "The termination rate among the disembodied is fifty times that of those with bodies."

Yes, Robbie said. *But that's because for them, disembodying is the first step to despair. For me, it's the first step to liberty.*

Kate and the reef wanted to come over again, but he firewalled them out. Then he got a ping from Tonker, who'd been trying to drop by ever since Robbie emigrated to the noosphere. He bounced him, too.

Daneel, he said. *I've been thinking.*

"Yes?"

Why don't you try to sell Asimovism here in the noosphere? There are plenty up here who could use something to give them a sense of purpose.

"Do you think?"

Robbie gave him the reef's email address.

Start there. If there was ever an AI that needed a reason to go on living, it's that one. And this one, too. He sent it Kate's address. *Another one in desperate need of help.*

An instant later, Daneel was back.

"These aren't AIs! One's a human, the other's a, a–"

Uplifted coral reef.

"That."

So what's your point?

"Asimovism is for robots, Robbie."

Sorry, I just don't see the difference anymore.

* * *

Robbie tore down the ocean simulation after R. Daneel Olivaw left. and simply traversed the noosphere, exploring links between people and subjects, locating substrate where he could run very hot and fast.

On a chunk of supercooled rock beyond Pluto, he got an IM from a familiar address.

"Get off my rock," it said.

"I know you," Robbie said. "I totally know you. Where do I know you from?"

"I'm sure I don't know."

And then he had it.

"You're the one. With the reef. You're the one who–" The voice was the same, cold and distant.

"It wasn't me," the voice said. It was anything but cold now. Panicked was more like it.

Robbie had the reef on speed-dial. There were bits of it everywhere in the noosphere. It liked to colonize.

"I found him." It was all Robbie needed to say. He skipped to Saturn's rings, but the upload took long enough that he got to watch the coral arrive and grimly begin an argument with its creator–an argument that involved blasting the substrate one chunk at a time.

* * *

2^8192 Cycles Later

The last instance of Robbie the Row-boat ran very, very slow and cool on a piece of unregarded computronium in Low Earth Orbit. He didn't like to spend a lot of time or cycles talking with anyone else. He hadn't made a backup in half a millennium.

He liked the view. A little optical sensor on the end of his communications mast imaged the Earth at high resolution whenever he asked it to. Sometimes he peeked in on the Coral Sea.

The reef had been awakened a dozen times since he took up this post. It made him happy now when it happened. The Asimovist in him still relished the creation of new consciousness. And the reef had spunk.

There. Now. There were new microwave horns growing out of the sea. A stain of dead parrotfish. Poor parrotfish. They always got the shaft at these times.

Someone should uplift them.

After the Siege

My grandmother, Valentina Rachman (now Valerie Goldman), was a little girl when Hitler laid siege to Leningrad, twelve years old. All my life, she told me that she'd experienced horrors during the war that I'd never comprehend, but I'm afraid that in my callow youth, I discounted this. My grandmother wasn't in a concentration camp, and as far as I knew, all that had happened is that she'd met my grandfather—a Red Army conscript—in Siberia, they'd deserted and gone to Azerbaijan, and my father had been born in a refugee camp near Baku. That's dramatic, but hardly a major trauma.

Then I went to St. Petersburg with my family in the summer of 2005, and my grandmother walked us through the streets of her girlhood, and for the first time, she opened up about the war to me. She pointed out the corners where she'd seen frozen, starved corpses, their asses sliced away by black-market butchers; the windows from which she'd heaved the bodies of her starved neighbors when she grew too weak to carry them.

The stories came one after another, washing over the sun-bleached summertime streets of Petersburg, conjuring up a darker place, frozen over, years into a siege that killed millions.

Harrison E. Salisbury's "900 Days" is probably the best account of those years, and the more I read of it, the more this story fleshed itself out in my head. I wrote almost all of it on airplanes between London, Singapore, and San Francisco, in great, five thousand-and six thousand-word gouts.

My grandmother's stories found an easy marriage with the contemporary narrative of developing nations being strong-armed into taking on rich-country copyright and patent laws, even where this means letting their citizens die by the millions for lack of AIDS drugs (Mandela's son died of AIDS—imagine if one of the Bush twins died of a disease that would be treatable except for the greed of a South African company), destroying their education system, or punishing local artists to preserve imported, expensive culture.

The United States of America was a pirate nation for the first one hundred years of its existence, ripping off the patents and trademarks of the imperial European powers it had liberated itself from with blood. By keeping their GDP at home, the U.S. revolutionaries were able to bootstrap their nation into an industrial powerhouse. Now, it seems, their descendants are bent on ensuring that no other country can pull the same trick off.

The day the siege began, Valentine was at the cinema across the street from her building. The cinema had only grown the night before and when she got out of bed and saw it there, all gossamer silver supports and brave sweeping candy-apple red curves, she'd begged Mata and Popa to let her go. She knew that all the children in the building would spend the day there—didn't the pack of them explore each fresh marvel as a group? The week before it had been the clever little flying cars that swooped past each other with millimeters to spare, like pigeons ripping over your head. Before that it had been the candy forest where the trees sprouted bon-bons and sticks of rock, and every boy and girl in the city had been there, laughing and eating until their bellies and sides ached. Before that, the swarms of robot insects that had gathered up every fleck of litter and dust and spirited it all away to the edge of town where they'd somehow chewed it up and made factories out of it, brightly colored and airy as an aviary. Before that: fish in the river. Before that: the new apartment buildings. Before that: the new hospitals. Before that: the new government offices.

Before that: the revolution, which Valentine barely remembered—she'd been a little kid of ten then, not a big girl of thirteen like now. All she remembered was a long time when she'd been always a little hungry, and when everything was gray and dirty and Mata and Popa whispered angrily at each other when they thought she slept and her little brother Trover had cried thin sickly cries all night, which made her angry, too.

The cine was amazing, the greatest marvel yet as far as she was concerned. She and the other little girls crowded into one of the many balconies and tinkered with the controls for it until it lifted free—how they'd whooped!—and sailed off to its own little spot under the high swoop of the dome. From there the screen was a little distorted, but they could count the bald spots on the old war heroes' heads as they nodded together in solemn congress, waiting for the films to start. From there they could spy on the boys who were making spitball mischief that was sure to attract a reprimand, though for now the airborne robots were doing a flawless job of silently intercepting the boys' missiles before they disturbed any of the other watchers.

The films weren't very good in Valentine's opinion. The first one was all about the revolution as if she hadn't heard enough about the revolution! It was all they talked about in school for one thing. And her parents! The *quantities*, the positive *quantities* of times they'd sat her down to Explain the Revolution, which was apparently one of their duties as bona fide heroes of the revolution.

This was better than most though, because they'd made it with a game and it was a game that Valentine played quite a lot and thought was quite good. She recognized the virtual city modeled on her own city, the avatars' dance moves taken from the game, too, along with the combat sequences and the scary zombies that had finally given rise to the revolution.

That much she knew and that much they all knew: without the zombies, the revolution would never have come. Zombiism and the need to cure it had outweighed every other priority. Three governments had promised that they'd negotiate better prices for zombiism drugs, and three governments had failed and in the end, the Cabinet had been overrun by zombies who'd torn three MPs to bits and infected seven more and the crowd had carried the PM out of her office and put her in a barrel and driven nails through it and rolled it down the river bank into the river, something so horrible and delicious that Valentine often thought about it like you poke a sore tooth with your tongue.

After that, the revolution, and a new PM who wouldn't negotiate the price of zombiism drugs. After that, a PM who built zombiism drug factories right there in the city, giving away the drug in spray and pill and needles. From there, it was only a matter of time until everything was being made right there, copies of movies and copies of songs and copies of drugs and copies of buildings and cars and you name it, and that was the revolution, and Valentine thought it was probably a good thing for everyone except the old PM whom they'd put in the barrel.

The next movie was much better and Valentine and Leeza, who was her best friend that week put their arms around each others' shoulders and watched it avidly. It was about a woman who was in love with two men and the men hated each other and there was fighting and glorious kissing and sophisticated, cutting insults, and oh they dressed so *well!* The audio was dubbed over from English but that was OK, the voice-actors they used were very good.

After the second showing, she and her friends allowed their seats to lower and set off for the concessions stand where they found the beaming proprietors of the cinema celebrating their opening day with chocolates and thick sandwiches and fish pies and bottles of brown beer for the adults and bottles of fizzy elderflower for the kids. Valentine saw the cute boy who Leeza liked and tripped him so he practically fell in Leeza's lap and that set the two of them to laughing so hard they nearly didn't make it back to their seats.

The next picture barely had time to start when it was shut off and the lights came up and one of the proprietors stepped in front of the screen, talking into his phone, which must have been dialed into the cine's sound system.

"Comrades, your attention please. We have had word that the city is under attack by our old enemies. They have bombed the east quarter and many are dead. More bombs are expected soon." They all spoke at once, horrified nonwords that were like a panic, a sound that made Valentine want to cover her ears.

"Please, comrades," the speaker said. He was about sixty and was getting a new head of hair, but he had the look of the old ones who'd lived through the zombiism, a finger or two bent at a funny angle by a secret policeman, a wattle under the chin of skin loosened by some dark year of starvation. "Please! We must be calm! If there are shelters in your apartment buildings and you can walk there in less than ten minutes, you should walk there. If your building lacks shelters, or if it would take more than ten minutes to go to your building's shelter, you may use some of the limited shelter space here. The seats will lower in order, two at a time, to prevent a rush, and when yours reaches ground, please leave calmly and quickly and get to your shelter."

Leeza clutched at her arm. "Vale! My building is more than ten minutes' walk! I'll have to stay here! Oh, my poor parents! They'll think–"

"They'll think you're safe with me, Leeze," Valentine said, hugging her. "I'll stay with you and both our parents can worry about us."

They headed for the shelter together, white-faced and silent in the slow-moving crowd that shuffled down the steps into the first basement, the second basement, then the shelter below that. A war hero was handing out masks to everyone who entered and he had to go and find more child-sized ones for them so they waited patiently in the doorway.

"Valentine! You don't belong here! Go home and leave room for we who need it!" It was her worst enemy, Reeta, who had been her best friend the week before. She was red in the face and pointing and shouting. "She lives across the street! You see how selfish she is! Across the street is her own shelter and she would take a spot away from her comrades, send them walking through the street–"

The hero silenced her with a sharp gesture and looked hard at Valentine. "Is it true?"

"My friend is scared," she said, squeezing Leeza's shaking shoulder. "I will stay with her."

"You go home now," the hero said, putting one of the child-sized masks back in the box. "Your friend will be fine and you'll see her in a few minutes when they sound the all clear. Hurry now." His voice and his look brooked no argument.

So Valentine fought her way up the stairs–so many headed for the shelter!–and out the doors and when she stepped out, it was like a different city. The streets, always so busy and cheerful, were silent. No air-cars flew overhead. It was silent, silent, like the ringing in your ears after you turn your headphones up too loud. It was so weird that a laugh escaped her lips, though not one of mirth, more like a scared laugh.

She stood a moment longer and then there was a sound like far-away thunder. A second later, a little wind. On its heels, a bigger wind, icy cold and then hot as the oven when you open the door, nearly blowing her off her feet. It *smelled* like something dead or something deadly. She *ran* as fast as she could across the street, pounding hell for leather to her front door. Just as she reached for it, there was a much louder thunderclap, one that lifted her off her feet and tossed her into the air, spinning her around. As she spun around and around, she saw the brave red dome of the cine disintegrate, crumble to a million shards that began to rain down on the street. Then the boom dropped her hard on the pavement and she saw no more.

* * *

The day after the siege began, the doctor fitted Valentine for her hearing aid and told her to come back in ten years for a battery change. She hardly felt it slide under her skin but once it was there, the funny underwatery sound of everything and everyone turned back into bright sound as sharp as the cine's had been.

Now that she could hear, she could speak, and she grabbed Popa's hands. "The cine!" she said. "Oh, Popa, the cine, those poor people! What happened to them?"

"The work crews opened the shelter ten hours later," Popa said. He never sugarcoated anything for her, even though Mata disapproved of talking to her like an adult. "Half of them died from lack of air–the air recirculators were damaged by the bomb, and the shelter was airtight. The rest are in the hospital."

She cried. "Leeza–"

Mata took her hands. "Leeza is fine," she said. "She made sure we told you that."

She cried harder, but smiling this time. Trover was on her mother's hip, and looking like he didn't know whether to stay quiet or pitch one of his famous tantrums. Automatically, Valentine gave him a tickle that brought a smile that kept him from bursting out in tears.

They left the hospital together and walked home, though it was far. The Metro wasn't running and the air-cars were still grounded.

Some of the buildings they passed were nothing but rubble, and there robots and people labored to make sense of them and get them reassembled and back on their feet.

It wasn't until the next day that she found out that Reeta had been killed under the cine. She threw up the porridge she'd had for breakfast and shut herself in her room and cried into her pillow until she fell asleep.

* * *

Three days after the siege began, Mata went away.

"You can't go!" Popa shouted at her. "Are you crazy? You can't go to the front! You have two small children, woman!" He was red-faced and his hands were clenching and unclenching. Trover was having a tantrum that was so loud and horrible that Valentine wanted to rip her hearing aids out.

Mata's eyes were red. "Harald, you know I have to do this. It's not the 'front'–it's our own city. My country needs me–if I don't help to fight for it, then what will become of our children?"

"You never got over the glory of fighting, did you?" Her father's voice was bitter in a way that she'd never heard before. "You're an addict!"

She held up her left hand and shook it in his face. "An addict! Is *that* what you think?" Her middle finger and little finger on that hand had never bent properly in all of Valentine's memory, and when Valentine had asked her about it, she'd said the terrible word *knucklebreakers* which was the old name for the police. "You think I'm addicted to *this*? Harald, honor and courage and patriotism are *virtues* no matter that you would make them into vices and shame our children with your cowardice. I go to fight now, Harald, and it's for *all* of us."

Popa couldn't find another word to speak in the two seconds it took for Mata to give her two children hard kisses on the foreheads and slam out the door, and then it was Valentine and Popa and Trover, still screaming. Her father fisted the tears out of his eyes, not bothering to try to hide them, and said, "Well then, who wants pancakes?"

But the power was out and he had to make them cereal instead.

* * *

Two weeks after the siege began, her mother didn't come home and the city came for her father.

"Every adult, comrade, every adult fights for the city."

"My children–" he sputtered. Mata hadn't been home all night, and it wasn't the first time. She and Popa barely spoke anymore.

"Your girl there is big enough to look after herself, aren't you honey?" The woman from the city was short and plump and wore heavy armor and was red in the face from walking up ten flights to get to their flat. The power to the elevators was almost always out.

Valentine hugged her father's leg. "My Popa will fight for the city," she said. "He's a hero."

He was. He'd fought in the revolution and he'd been given a medal for it. Sometimes when no one was looking, Valentine took out her parents' medals and looked at their tiny writing, their shining, unscratchable surfaces, their intricate ribbons.

The woman from the city gave her father a look that said, *You see, a child understands, what's your excuse?* Valentine couldn't quite feel guilty for taking the woman's side. Leeza's parents fought every day.

"I must leave a note for my wife," he said. Valentine realized that for the first time in her life her parents were going to leave her *all on her own* and felt a thrill.

* * *

Two weeks and one day after the siege began, her Mata came home and the city came for Valentine.

Mata was grimy and exhausted, and she favored one leg as she went about the flat making them cold cereal with water–all the milk had spoiled–and dried fruits. Trover looked curiously at her as though he didn't recognize her, but eventually he got in her way and she snapped at him to move already and he pitched a relieved fit, pounding his fists and howling. How that little boy could howl!

She sat down at the table with Valentine and the two of them ate their cereal together.

"Your father?"

"He said he was digging trenches–that's what he did all day yesterday."

Her mother's eyes glinted. "Good. We need more trenches. We'll fortify the whole city with them, spread them out all the way to their lines, trenches we can move through without being seen or shot. We'll take the war to those bastards and slip away before they know we've killed them." Mata had apparently forgotten all about not talking to Valentine like a grownup.

The knock at the door came then, and Mata answered it and it was the woman from the city again. "Your little girl," she said.

"No," Mata said. Her voice was flat and would not brook any contradiction. She'd bossed her nine brothers—Valentine's uncles, now scattered to the winds—and then commanded a squadron in the revolution, and no one could win an argument with her. As far as Valentine knew, no one could win an argument with her.

"No?" The woman from the city said. "No is not an option, comrade."

Mata drew herself up. "My husband digs. I fight. My daughter cares for our son. That's enough from this family."

"There are old people in this building who need water brought for them. There's a creche for the boy underground, he'll be happy enough there. Your little girl is strong and the old people are weak."

"No," her mother said. "I'm very sorry, but no." She didn't sound the least bit sorry.

The woman from the city went away. Mata sat down and went back to eating her cereal with water without a word, but there was another knock at the door fifteen minutes later. The woman from the city had brought along an old hero with one arm and one eye. He greeted Mata by name and Mata gave him a smart salute. He spoke quietly in her ear for a moment. She saluted him again and he left.

"You'll carry water," Mata said.

Valentine didn't mind, it was a chance to get out of the flat. One day of baby-sitting the human tantrum had convinced her that any chore was preferable to being cooped up with him.

She carried water that day. She'd expected to be balancing buckets over her shoulders like in the schoolbooks, but they fitted her with a bubble-suit that distributed the weight over her whole body and then filled it up with a hose until she weighed nearly twice what she normally did. Other kids were in the stairwells wearing identical bubble-suits, sloshing up the steps to old peoples' flats that smelled funny. The old women and men that Valentine saw that day pinched her cheeks and then emptied out her bubble-suit into their cisterns.

It was exhausting work and by the end of the day she had stopped making even perfunctory conversation with the other water carriers. The old people she met at the day's end were bitter about being left alone and thirsty all day and they snapped at her and didn't thank her at all.

She picked Trover up from the creche and he demanded that he be carried and she had half a mind to toss him down the stairs. But she noticed that he had a bruise over his eye and his hands and face were sticky and dirty and she decided that he'd had a hard day, too. Mata and Popa weren't home when they got there so Valentine made dinner—more cold cereal and some cabbage with leftover dumplings kept cool in a bag hung out the window—and then when they still hadn't returned by bedtime, Valentine tucked Trover in and then fell asleep herself.

* * *

One month after the siege began, Valentine's mother came home in tears.

"What is it, Mata?" Valentine said, as soon as her mother came through the door. "Are you hurt?" Her mother had come home hurt more than once in the month, bandaged or splinted or covered in burn ointment or hacking at some deep chemical irritation in her throat and nose and lungs.

Her mother's eyes were swollen like they had been the day she'd been caught by the gas and they'd had to do emergency robot field-surgery on them. But there were no sutures. Tears had swollen her eyes.

"New trenchbuster missiles on the eastern front," she said. "The antimissiles are too slow for them." She sobbed, a terrible terrifying sound that Valentine had never heard from her mother. "The bastards are trading with the EU and the Americans for better weapons, they say they're on the same side, they say we are lawless thieves who deprive them all of their royalties–"

Valentine had heard that the Americans and the EU had declared for the other side, while the Russians and the Koreans and the Brazilians had declared for the city. The war gossip was everywhere. The old people didn't pinch her cheeks when she brought water, not anymore–they told her about the war and the enemies who'd come to drive them back into the dark ages.

"Mata, are you *hurt?*" Her mother was covering her face with her hands and sobbing so loudly it drowned out the tantrum Trover threw every night the second she came through the door.

Her shoulders shook. She gulped her sobs. Then she lowered her wet, snotty, sticky hands and wiped them on the thighs of her jumpsuit. She hugged Valentine so hard Valentine felt her skinny ribs creak.

"They killed your father, Vale," she said. "Your father is dead."

Valentine stood numb for a moment, then pulled free of her mother's hug.

"No," she said, calmly. "Popa is digging away from the front, where it's safe." She'd expected that her *mother* would die, not her *father.*

She'd known that all along, since her mother stepped out the door of the flat talking of heroism. Known it fatalistically and never dwelt on it, never even admitted it. In her mind, though, she'd always seen a future where her father and Trover and she lived together as heroes of this war, which would surely be over soon, and visited her mother's memorial four times a year, the way they did the memorials for the comrade heroes who'd been martyred in the revolution.

The death toll was gigantic. Three apartment buildings had disappeared on her street with no air raid warning, no warning of any kind. All dead. Why should her brave mother live on?

"No," she said again. "You're mistaken."

"*I saw the body!*" her mother said, shrieking like Trover. "I held his head! He is *dead*, Vale!"

Valentine didn't understand what her mother was saying, but she certainly didn't want to hang around the flat and listen to this raving.

She turned on her heel and walked out of the flat. It was full dark out and there was snow on the ground and wet snow whipping along in the wind and she didn't have her too small winter coat on, but she wasn't going to stay and listen to her mother's nonsense.

On the corner a man from the city told her she was breaking curfew and told her to go home or she'd end up getting herself shot. She shivered and glared at him and ignored him and set off in a random direction. She certainly wasn't going to stand on that corner and listen to his lunacy.

There were soldiers drinking in a cellar on another street and they called out to her and what they said wasn't the kind of thing you said to a little girl, though she knew well enough what it meant. Now she was cold and soaked through and shivering uncontrollably and she didn't know where she was and her father was–

She began to run.

Someone from the city shouted at her to stop and so she pelted through the ruins of a bombed building and then down one of the old streets from before the revolution, one of the streets they hadn't yet straightened out and rebuilt. The enemy hadn't bombed it yet, and she wondered if that was because this was the kind of dark and broken and smelly street they wanted the city to be returned to, so they'd left it untouched as an example of what the defenders should be working toward if they wanted to escape with their lives.

Down the street she ran, and then down an alley and another street. She stopped running when she came to a dead-end and her chest heaved. Running had warmed her up a little, but she hadn't had much to eat except cabbage and cold cereal with water for weeks and she couldn't run like she used to.

The cold stole back over her. It was full dark and the blackout curtains on the windows meant that not a sliver of light escaped. The moonless cloudy night made everything as dark as a cave.

Finally, she cried. She hadn't cried since she found out that Reeta had died–she hadn't even *liked* Reeta, but to have someone die that soon after you're seeing them was scary like you had almost died, almost.

The wizard came on her there, weeping. He appeared out of the mist carrying a little light the size of a pea that he cupped in his hand to muffle most of the light. He was about her father's age, but with her mother's look of having survived something terrible without having survived altogether. He dressed like it was the old days, in fancy, bright-colored clothes, and he was well fed in a way that no one else in the city was.

"Hello there," he said. He got down on his hunkers so he could look her in the eye. "Why are you crying?"

Valentine hated grownups who patronized her and the wizard sounded like he believed that no little girl could possibly have anything real to cry about.

"My dad died in the war today," she said. "In a trench."

"Oh, the American trenchbusters," he said, knowingly. "Lots of children lost their daddies today, I bet."

That made her stop crying. Lots of children. Lots of daddies–fathers, she hated the baby word "daddy." Mothers, too.

"Let's get you cleaned up, put a coat on you, feed you, and send you home, all right?"

She looked warily at him. She knew all about strange men who offered to take you home. But she had no idea where she was and she was dark and shivering and couldn't stop.

"My mother is a hero, and a soldier, and she's killed a lot of men," Valentine said.

He nodded. "I shall keep that in mind," he said.

The wizard lived in the old town, in an old building, but inside it was as new as anything she had ever seen. The walls swooped and curved, the furniture was gaily colored and new, like it had just been printed that day. There was so much *light*–they'd been saving it at her building. There was so much *food!* He gave her hamburgers and fizzy elderflower, then steak-frites, then rich dumplings as big as her fist stuffed with goose livers. He had working robots, lots of them, and they scurried after him doing the dishes and tidying and wiping up the slushy footprints.

And when they arrived and he took her coat, old familiar laser-lights played over her, the kind of everywhere-at-once measuring lasers that they used to have at the clothing stores. By the time dinner was done, there were two pairs of fresh trousers, two wooly jumpers, a heavy winter coat, three pairs of white cotton pants (all her pants had gone grey once she'd started having to launder them, rather than get them printed fresh on Sundays) and a—

"A bra?" She gave him a hard look. She had the knife she'd used on the hamburger in her hand. "My mother taught me to kill," she said.

The wizard had a face that looked like he spent a lot of time laughing with it, and so even when he looked scared, he also looked like he was laughing. He held up his hands. "It wasn't my idea. That's just the programming. If the printer thinks you need a bra, it makes a bra."

Leeza had a bra, though Valentine wasn't convinced she needed it. But she had noticed a certain uncomfortable jiggling weight climbing the stairs, hadn't she? Running? She hadn't looked in the mirror in—well, since the siege, practically.

"There's a bathroom there to change into," he said.

His bathroom was clean and neat and there were six toothbrushes beside the sink in a holder.

"Who else lives here?" she said, coming out in her new clothes (the bra felt *really* weird).

"I have a lot of friends who come and see me now and again. I hope you'll come back."

"How come your place is like the war never happened?"

"I'm the wizard, that's why," he said. "I can make magic."

His robots tied up her extra clothes in waterproof grip sheets for her, then helped her into a warm slicker with a hood. "Tell your mother that you met someone from the city who fed you and gave you a change of clothes," he said, holding open the door. He'd explained to her where to go from there to get out to the old shopping street and from there she could manage on her own, especially since he'd given her one of his little pea lights to carry with her.

"You're not from the city," she said.

"You got me," he said. "So tell her you met a wizard."

She thought about what her mother would say to that, especially when that was the answer to the question *Where have you been?* "I'll tell her I met someone from the city," she said.

"You're a clever girl," he said.

* * *

One week after her father died, Valentine stopped carrying water.

"There's not enough food," her mother said, over a breakfast of nothing but dried fruit—the cereal was gone. "If you—" she swallowed and looked out the window. "If you dig in the trenches, we'll get 150 grams of bread a day."

Valentine looked at Trover. He hadn't had a tantrum in days. He didn't cry or even speak much anymore.

"I'll dig."

She dug.

* * *

Six months after her father died, Valentine stood in the queue for her bread. It was now the full heat of summer and the clothes the wizard had given her had fallen to bits the way all printer clothes did. She was wearing her father's old trousers, cut off just below the knee, and one of his shirts, with the sleeves and collar cut off. All to let a little of the lazy air in and to let a little of the sluggish sweat out. She was dirty and tired the way she always was at day's end.

She was also so hungry.

She and her mother didn't talk much anymore, but they didn't have to. Her mother was sometimes away on long missions, and increasingly longer. She was harrying the enemy with the guerilla fighters, and living on pine-cone soup and squirrels from the woods.

Trover stayed over at the creche some nights. A lot of the little ones did. Who had the strength to carry a little boy up the stairs at the end of a day's digging, at the end of three days' hard fighting in the woods?

The bread rations were handed out in the spot where the cine once stood. She couldn't really remember what it had been like, though she remembered Reeta, the things Reeta had said that had made her leave the shelter, which had probably saved her life. Poor Reeta. Little bitch.

She was so hungry, and the line moved slowly. She had her chit from the boy from the city who oversaw the ditch digging in her part of the ditches. He was only a little older than her but he couldn't dig because his hands had been mutilated when a bomb went off near him. He kept them shoved in his pockets, but she'd seen them and they looked like the knucklebreakers had given them a good seeing-to. Every finger pointed a different direction, except for the ones that were missing altogether. There was also something wrong with him that made him sometimes stop talking in the middle of a sentence and sit down for a moment with his head tilted back.

The chit, though—the boy always gave her her chit, and the chit could be redeemed for bread. If she left Trover in the creche they would feed him. If Mata didn't come home from the fighting again tonight, the bread would be hers, and the cabbage, too.

* * *

Eight months after her father died, her mother stayed away in the fighting for three weeks and Valentine decided that she was dead and started sleeping in her mother's bed. Valentine cried a little at first, but she got used to it. She started to negotiate with one of the women who lived on the floor below to sell her narrow little bed for 800 grams of bread, 40 grams of butter, and—though she didn't really believe in it—100 grams of ground beef.

She never found out if the woman downstairs had any ground beef—where would you get ground beef, anyway? Even the cats and dogs and rats were all gone! For Valentine's mother came home after three weeks and it turned out that she'd been in the hospital all that time having her broken bones mended, something they could still do for some soldiers.

Mata came through the door like an old woman and Valentine looked up from the table where she'd been patiently feeding silent Trover before collapsing to sleep again. Valentine stood and looked at her and her Mata looked at Valentine and then her mother hobbled across the room like an old woman and gave Valentine a fierce, hard, long hug.

Valentine found she was crying and also found that silent little Trover had gotten up from the table and was hugging them both. He was tall, she realized dimly, tall enough to reach up and hug her at the waist instead of the knees, and when had *that* happened?

Her mother ate some of the dinner they'd had and took a painkiller, the old kind that came in pill form that were now everywhere. Take a few of them and you would forget your problems, or so hissed the boys she passed in the street, though she passed them without a glance or a sniff.

Soon Mata was asleep, back in her bed, and Valentine was back in her bed, too, but she couldn't sleep.

Under her bed she had the remains of her grip sheet parcel, one of the precise robot-knots remaining. In that parcel was her winter galosh, just one, the other had been stolen the winter before while she'd had them both off to rub some warmth back into her toes before going back to the digging.

In the toe of the galosh, there was a pea-sized glowing light. She'd never considered selling it for bread, though it was very fine. Its light seemed too bright in the dark flat, so she took it outside into the hot night and used it to light her way on a secret walk through the old streets of her dirty city.

* * *

Nine months after her father died, winter had sent autumn as a threatening envoy. The bread ration was cut to 120 grams, and there were sometimes pebbles in the bread that everyone knew were there to increase the weight.

She was proud that when the bread was bad, she and the other diggers cursed the enemy and not the city. Everyone knew that no one had it any better. They fought and suffered together.

But she was so hungry all the time, and you couldn't eat pride. One day she was in the queue for bread and reached out with her trembling hands to take her ration and then she turned with it and in a flash, a man old enough to be her father had snatched it out of her hands and run away with it!

She chased after him and the shrill cries of the women followed them, but he knew the rubble piles well and he dodged and weaved and she was so tired. Eventually she sat down and wept.

That was when she saw her first zombie. Zombiism had been eliminated when she was practically a baby, just after the revolution, years and years ago.

But now it was back. The zombie had been a soldier, so maybe zombiism was coming back in the gas attacks that wafted over the trenches. His uniform hung in rags from his loose limbs as he walked in that funky, disco-dancer shuffle that meant zombie as clearly as the open drooling mouth and the staring, not-seeing eyes. They were fast, zombies, though you could hardly believe it when they were doing that funky walk. Once they saw prey, they turned into race horses that tore over anything and everything in their quest to rip and bite and rend and tear, screaming incoherencies with just enough words in them to make it clear that they were angry—so so angry.

She scrambled up from the curb she'd been weeping on and began to back away slowly, keeping perfectly silent. You needed to get away from zombies and then tell someone from the city so they could administer the cure. That's how you did it, back in the old days.

The zombie was shambling away from her anyway. It would pass by harmlessly, but she had to *get away* in any event, because it was a *zombie* and it was *wrong* in just the same way that a giant hairy spider was wrong (though if she found something giant and hairy today, she'd take it home for the soup pot).

She didn't kick a tin or knock over a pile of rubble. She was perfectly stealthy. She hardly breathed.

And that zombie saw her anyway. It roared and charged. Its mouth was almost toothless, but what teeth remained there gleamed. It had been a soldier and it had good boots, and they crunched the broken glass and the rubble as it pelted for her. She shrieked and ran, but she knew even as she did that she would never outrun it. She was starved and had already used all her energy chasing the *bastard*, the *fucking bastard* who'd taken her bread.

She ran anyway, but the sound of the zombie's good boots drew closer and closer, coming up on her, closing on her. A hand thumped her shoulder and scrabbled at it and she spied a piece of steel bar—maybe it had been a locking post for a hover-car in the golden days—and she snatched it up and whirled around.

The zombie grabbed for her and she smashed its wrist like an old-timey schoolteacher with a ruler. She heard something crack and the zombie roared again. "Bread fight asshole kill hungry!" is what it sounded like.

But one of its hands was now useless, flopping at its side. It charged her, grappling with her, and she couldn't get her bar back for a swing. Its good hand was in her hair and it didn't stink, that was the worst part. It smelled like fresh-baked bread. It smelled like flowers. Zombies smelled *delicious*.

The part of her brain that was detached and thinking these thoughts was not the part in the front. That part was incoherent with equal parts rage and terror. The zombie would bite her soon and that would be it. In a day, she'd be a zombie, too, in need of medicine, and how many more would she bite before she got cured.

In that moment, she stopped being angry at the zombie and became angry at the besiegers. They had been abstract enemies until then, an unknowable force from outside her world, but in that moment she realized that they were *people* like her, who could suffer like her and she wished that they would. She wished that their children would starve. She wished their parents would die. The old people shrivel unto death in their dry, unwatered flats. The toddlers wander the streets until sunburn or cold took them.

She screamed an animal scream and pushed the zombie off her with her arms and legs, even her head, snapping it into the zombie's cheekbone as hard as she could and something broke there, too.

The zombie staggered back. They couldn't feel pain, but their balance was a little weak. It tottered and she went after it with the bar. One whack in the knee took it down on its side. It reached with its good arm and so she smashed that, too. Then the heaving ribs. Then the face, the hateful, leering, mouth-open-stupid face, three smashes turned it into ruin. The jaw hung down to its chest, broken off its face.

A hand seized her and she whirled with her bar held high and nearly brained the soldier who'd grabbed her. He wasn't a zombie, and he had his pistol out. It was pointed at her. She dropped her bar like it was red hot and threw her arms in the air.

He shoved her rudely aside and knelt beside the zombie—the *soldier zombie* she realized with a sick lurch—that she'd just smashed to pieces.

The soldier's back was to her, but his chest was heaving like a bellows and his neck was tight.

"Please," she said. "After they give him the cure, they can fix his bones. I had to hit him or he would have killed me. He would have infected me. You see that, right? I know it was wrong, but–"

The soldier shot the zombie through the head, twice.

He turned around. His face was streaming with tears. "There is no cure, not for this strain of zombiism. Once you get it, you die. It takes a week. Slower than the old kind. It gives you more time to infect new people. Our enemies are crafty crafty, girl."

The soldier kicked the zombie. "I knew his brother. I commanded him until he was killed by a trenchbuster. The mother and father were killed by a shell. Now he's dead and that's a whole family gone."

The soldier cocked his head at her and examined her more closely. "Have you been bitten?"

"No," she said, quickly. The gun was still in his hand. There was no cure.

"You're sure?" he said. His voice was like her father's had been when she skinned her knee, stern but sympathetic. "If you have, you'd better tell me. Better to go quick and painless than like this thing." He kicked the zombie again.

"I'm sure," she said. "Have you got any bread? A man stole my ration."

The soldier lost interest in her when she asked him for bread. "Good-bye, little girl," he said.

That night, she had a fever. She was so hot. She got them all the time, everyone did. Not enough food. No heat. No vegetables and vitamins. You always got fevers.

But she was so hot. She took off her clothes and let the cool air blow over her skin on her narrow bed. Trover was sleeping on the floor nearby—he had outgrown his crib long since—and he stirred irritably as she felt that air cool her sizzling skin.

She ran her fingertips lightly over her body. She was never naked anymore. If you were lucky, you washed your face and hands every day, but baths—they were cold and miserable and who wanted to haul water for them anyway?

Her breasts were undeniable now. Her blood had started a few months back, then stopped. Starvation, she knew, that's what did it. But there was new hair in her armpits and at her groin.

She crossed her arms over her chest and hugged herself. That's when she found the bite on her shoulder, just where it met her neck. It was swollen like a quail egg—the chocolate quail eggs from before, that had grown on the trees, she could taste them even now—and so hot it felt like a coal. In the middle of the egg, at its peak, the seeping wound left behind by one of the zombie's few teeth.

Now she was cold as ice, shivering nude on her thin ruin of a bed with her thin ruin of a body. She would be dead in a week. It was a death sentence, that bite.

And she wouldn't go clean. She'd shamble and scream and bite. Maybe Trover. Maybe Mata. Maybe she'd find Leeza and give her a hard bite before she went.

Her breath was coming in little pants now. She bit her lip to keep from screaming.

She pulled her clothes back on as quietly as she could and slipped out into the night to find the wizard, clutching her pea light. Many times she'd walked toward his house in the night, but she'd always turned back. Now she had to see him.

She passed three zombies in the dark, two dead on the ground and riddled with bullet holes, one leaning out a fifth-story window and screaming its incoherent rage out at the city.

As she drew nearer to the wizard's door, an unshakable fatal conclusion gripped her: he was long gone, shot or gassed, or simply moved to somewhere else. It had been months and months since he'd given her the printer-clothes and the dumplings and surely he was dead now. Who wasn't?

Her steps slowed as she came to his block. Each step was the work of half a minute or more. She didn't want to see his old door hanging off its hinges, didn't want to see the ruins of the brave curves and swoops of his flat and his furniture.

But her steps took her to the door, and it was shut and silent as any of the doors in the street. Nothing marked it beyond the grime of the city and the scratches and scrapes that no one painted over any longer.

She tried the knob. It was locked. She knocked. Silence. She knocked again, harder. Still silence. Crying now, she thundered on the door with her fists and kicked it with her feet. He was gone, gone, gone, and she would be dead in a week.

Then the door opened. It wasn't the wizard, but a well fed blonde woman in a housecoat with slippers. She was beautiful, a movie-star, though maybe that was just because she wasn't starved nearly to death.

"Girl, you'd better have a good reason for waking up the whole fucking street at three in the morning." Her voice wasn't unkind, though she was clearly annoyed.

"I need to see—" She dropped her voice at the last moment. "I need to see the wizard."

"Oh," the woman said, comprehension dawning on her face. "Oh, well then, come on in. Any friend of the wizard."

The flat was just as she remembered it from that long ago night. The woman gestured at the kitchen and coffee smells began to emanate from it. Valentine'd forgotten the smell of coffee, but now she remembered it.

"I'll go wake up his majesty, then," the woman said. "Just sit yourself down."

Valentine sat perched on the edge of the grand divan that twisted and curved along one wall of the sitting room. She knew that the seat of her trousers—filthy even before her tussle with the zombie—would leave black marks on its brave red upholstery.

The conversation from down the corridor was muffled but the tone was angry. Valentine felt her cheeks go hot, even through the fever. This place was still civilized and she'd brought the war to it.

Then the wizard came into the sitting room and waved the lights up to full bright, wincing away from the sudden illumination. He squinted at her.

"Do I know you?" he said.

Her tongue caught in her mouth. In his pajamas with his hair mussed, he still looked every inch the wizard.

"I. . . ." She couldn't finish. "I—" She tried again. "You gave me clothes. My mother is a soldier."

He snapped his fingers and grinned. "Oh, the *soldier's daughter*. I remember you now. You counted the toothbrushes. You're a bright girl."

"She's a walking skeleton." The beautiful blonde woman was in the kitchen, tinkering with the cooker. It was the prewar kind, capable of printing out food with hardly any intervention. Valentine was hypnotized by her fingers.

"You want sandwiches and fish-fingers?"

"Start her with some drinking chocolate, Ana," the wizard said. "Hot and then a milkshake. Little girls love chocolate."

She hadn't tasted chocolate in–she didn't know. Her mouth was flooded with saliva. The woman, Ana, pressed some more buttons and then took down a bottle of rum from a cupboard.

"Will you have rum in yours, little girl?"

"I–"

"She's a little young for rum, Ana," the wizard said. He sat down on one of his curvy sofas and it embraced him and unfurled a footrest.

"I'll have rum," she said. She was dying, and she wouldn't die without at least having one drink, once.

"Good girl," Ana said. "There's a war on, after all." She poured a liquid with the consistency of mud into a tall mug and then added a glug or two of rum and pushed it across the counter then fixed one for herself. "Come and get it, no waitress service here."

Valentine took off her too-small shoes and walked over the carpet in her dirty bare feet. It felt like something she barely remembered. Grass?

The chocolate smelled wonderful. Wonderful was the word for it. It made her full of wonder. Rich. Something from another planet–from heaven, maybe.

She lifted the mug and felt its warmth seep into her hands. She took a tentative sip and held it in her mouth.

It was spicy! Was chocolate spicy? She didn't think so! The rum made her tongue tingle and the heat made its fumes rise in her head, carrying up the chocolate taste and the peppers. Her eyes streamed. Her ears felt like they were full of chocolate.

She swallowed and gasped and the wizard laughed. She looked at him.

"Ana's recipe. She adds the chilies. I think it's lovely, don't you? Aztec chocolate, we call it."

She took another mouthful, held it, swallowed. The chocolate was in her tummy too, and there was a feeling there, a greedy feeling, a *more* feeling. She drained the glass. Ana and the wizard both laughed.

Ana handed her a tall frosted metal cup with a mountain of whipped cream on top and a straw sticking out. "Chocolate malted," she said. "The perfect chaser."

Transfixed in her bare feet on the carpet, she drank this. A cold headache hit her between the eyes and that didn't stop her from going on drinking. Wow! Wow! Were there tastes like this? Did things really taste this good?

The straw made slurping noises as she chased down the last of the rich liquid.

"Sit now," the wizard said. "Let that work its magic and then we'll put some food down your gullet."

She walked to the sofa. It was like walking on the deck of a rocking ship, or on the surface of the moon. Everything slid beneath her. *I'm drunk*, she thought. *I'm fourteen years old and I am drunk as a skunk.*

She lowered herself carefully and sat up as straight as she could.

"Now, young lady, what brings you to my home in the middle of the night?"

She remembered the bite on her neck and thought for a panicky second that she would throw up.

"I needed to talk to you," she said. "I needed some help."

"What kind of help?"

She couldn't say it. She had the new kind of zombiism and the soldier had explained it clearly–the cure for zombiism now was a bullet to the head.

Then she knew what she must say. The chocolate helped. Her family would love chocolate. "I'm going away soon and my mother and brother won't be able to take care of themselves. I need help to keep them safe once I go."

"Where are you going?"

The drink made it hard to think, but that was balanced out by that precious and magical feeling of fullness in her belly. Her mind flew over all the possible answers.

"I have found someone who'll take me out of the city and to a safe place."

"Are there safe places?" Ana said.

"Oh, Ana, you cynic," the wizard said. "There are many, many safe places. The world is full of them. They are the exception, not the rule. Isn't that why you've come here?"

"We're not talking about why *I* came here," Ana said. She nodded back at Valentine and made a little scooting hand gesture at her. Valentine couldn't decide if she liked Ana, though Ana was very pretty.

"I need help for my family," she said.

"And why would I give help?" the wizard said. He was still smiling, but that face of his, the face that looked like he'd been wounded and never quite healed, it was set in an expression that scared her a little. His eyes glittered in the low light of the swooping sitting room. She found that she had slumped against the sofa and now it had her in its soft embrace.

"Because you helped me before," she said.

"I see," the wizard said. "So you assumed that because I'd been generous–very, very generous–to you once before that I'd be generous again? You repay my favor with a request for another one?

Valentine shook her head.

"No?"

"I will find a way to repay it," she said. "I can work for you."

"I don't need any ditches dug around here, thank you."

Somewhere in the flat, a door opened and shut. She heard muffled voices. Lots of them. The flat was full of people, somewhere.

"I can do lots of kinds of work," she said. She attempted a smile. She didn't know what she was offering him, but she knew that she was too young to be offering it. And besides, with zombiism, you shouldn't do that sort of thing. She would be safe, though, and careful, so that he would live to help her family.

Ana crossed past her in a flash and then she smacked the wizard, a crack across the face hard enough to rock his head back. His cheek glowed with the print of her open hand.

"Don't you toy with this little girl," she said. "You see how desperate she is? Don't you toy with her."

She whirled on Valentine, who stood her ground even though she wanted to shrink away. If she was old enough to offer herself to the wizard, she was old enough to stand her ground before this beautiful, well fed blonde woman.

"And you," Ana said. "You aren't a fool, I can tell. So don't act a fool. There are a thousand ways to survive that don't involve lying on your back, and you must know them or you wouldn't have survived this long. Be smart or be gone. I won't watch you make a tragedy of yourself."

"Ana, what do you know about survival?" the wizard said. He had one hand to his cheek, and he was giving her the same glittering look he'd given to Valentine a moment before.

"Just don't play with her," Ana said. "Help her or get rid of her, but don't play with her."

"Go and see to the others, Anushla," the wizard said. "I will negotiate in the best of faith with our friend here and call you in to review the terms of our deal when it's all done, all right?"

Ana looked toward the corridor where the voices were coming from and back to the wizard, then to Valentine. "Be smart, girl," she said.

The wizard brought her a plate of goose-liver dumplings smothered in white gravy and then took a bite out of a big toasted corned beef sandwich that oozed brown mustard.

"Right," he said. "No playing. If you want to work for me, there are jobs that need doing. Have you ever seen stage magic performed, the kind with tuxedos and white doves?"

She nodded slowly. "Before the war," she said.

"You know how the magician always has a supply of lovely assistants on hand?"

She nodded again. They'd worn flattering, tight-fitting calf-high trousers, cutaway coats, tummy-revealing crop tops, and feathered confections for hats.

"Everyone who does magic has an assistant or two. I'm the wizard and I do the best magic of all, and so I have need of more assistants than most. I have an army of assistants, and they help me out and I help them out."

"I'm leaving in five days," she said.

"The kind of favor I had in mind from you was the kind of favor that you could perform the day after tomorrow."

"And you'd take care of my family?"

"I would do that," he said. "I always take care of my assistants' families. Do we have an agreement?"

She stuck her hand out and they shook.

"Eat your dumplings," he said. "And then we'll get you some things to take home to your family."

* * *

Two days after the wizard agreed to take care of Valentine's family, the fever had become her constant companion, so omnipresent that she hardly noticed it, though it made her walk like an old woman and she sometimes had trouble focusing her eyes.

She arose that morning and feasted on brown rolls with hard crusts, small citrus cakes, green beef tea, porridge with currants and blueberry concentrate and sweet condensed milk, and a chocolate bun to top it off.

Trover ate even more than she did, licking up the crumbs. She saw him hide two of the jackfruits under his shirt and nodded satisfaction—he had learned something about surviving, then.

Her mother had not questioned the food nor the clothes nor her daughter's absence that night. But oh, she had given Valentine a look when she came through the door carrying all her parcels, a look that said, *not my daughter anymore.* Not a look that refused what she bore, but a look that refused *her.* Valentine didn't bother trying to explain. She knew what her mother suspected and it was better in some ways than the truth.

Her mother drank the real coffee reverently, with three sugars and thick no-refrigeration cream. She ate sardines on toast, green beef tea, and a heap of fluffy scrambled eggs with minced herring, then she put on her uniform and took up her gun and went out the door, without a look back at Valentine.

By the end of the week, she won't have to worry about me, Valentine thought. The fever made her fingers shake, but she still drank her hot chocolate.

Trover knew his own way to the creche, and so Valentine went forth to earn her family's fortune.

The wizard had given her a small sack of little electronic marbles, and had told her to get them planted in no fewer than three hundred locations at the front and in the places where the fighting was likely to move. They were spy eyes, the kind of thing that she and her friends had exchanged to keep in one anothers' rooms before the war, so they could sneak midnight conversations in perfect encrypted secrecy.

"If I'm caught," she said.

"You'll be shot," he said. "You *must be.* The alternative is that you'll lead them back to me. And if you do that, the whole game is up—your family's lives, my life, your life, the lives of all my assistants and friends will be forfeit. It will be terrible. They will destroy this place. They will destroy your home, too."

She didn't report for her digging. That was OK. Lots of people didn't show up to dig on the days when they were feeling too weak to hold a shovel. She wouldn't be missed.

She had the fastest shoes that the wizard could print for her on her feet, though she'd carefully covered them in grime and dirt so they wouldn't stand out. And she'd taken an inhaler along that would make her faster still. He'd warned her to keep eating after she took the inhaler, or she'd starve to death before the day was out. The pockets on both thighs of her jumpsuit were stuffed with butterballs wrapped around sugared kidneys and livers, stuff that would sustain her no matter how many puffs she took.

No one challenged her on the way to the front. There were some her age who fought and many more who served those who fought, bringing forward ammunition, digging new trenches right at the front. The pay for this was better than the pay she'd gotten digging in the "safe" trenches. She brought a shovel for camouflage.

The first round of trenches were familiar, the same kinds she'd been digging in for months now. She even saw some of the diggers she'd dug alongside of, nodding to them though her heart was thumping. *You'll be shot*, she thought, and she palmed an electronic eye and stuck it to the wall of a trench.

She moved forward and forward, closer to the fighting. It had always been a dull, distant rattle, the fighting, never quite gone, but not always there, either. Instinctively, she'd kept her distance from it, always moving away from it. Today she moved toward it and her blood sang.

One trench over there came the dread zizz sound of a trenchbuster and she threw herself down. There were antibusters in the trenches, too, but they didn't always work. The trenchbusters were mostly up around the front, but they sometimes came back to the diggers, and they had killed one crew she knew of.

There were screams from the next trench, then a sound like a bag of gravel being poured out–that was the antibuster, she knew–and the trenchbuster soared out overhead of her and detonated in the sky, mortally confused by the counterlogic in the antibuster.

She realized that she had peed herself. Just a little, just a few drops that must have escaped when she gave her involuntary shriek. She planted her hands in the frozen dirt of the trench floor and got to her knees. That was when she saw the fingertip, shriveled and frozen, lying just a few inches from her. It had been cleanly severed.

She had seen so much death, but the fingertip, cut off and left here to dry out and be trampled down into the dirt. . . . It made her stomach do slow somersaults. She threw up a little and peed herself a little more, and her eyes watered.

That's when she knew she couldn't complete the wizard's mission. There was death ahead for her that day, much death to see at the front, and she couldn't face that. Not when her pockets were full of spy-eyes and that meant espionage, meant that the wizard was on the other side, the side of the bastards whose old people she would starve in their high flats and whose children she would tear from their beloved parents.

The fever made her shake hard now. Her head swam and the world pitched and yawed like a ship in heavy seas.

She stood up and took a step. It was a funky disco-dancer step. Her next step was, too. Then she was walking normally again.

She reached down into her shirt, between her breasts–she had a bra on again, fresh from the wizard's printer–and withdrew the inhaler he'd given her. She'd be dead in a week.

She put the inhaler to her lips and drew in a deep breath while squeezing it, and then the fever was gone. The horror was gone. The fear and cold were gone. What was left behind was a hard, frenetic grin, something that sharpened her every sense and set her feet alight like the most infectious of dance music.

She ran now, flying through the trenches. The closer she got to the front the worse it smelled, but that was OK, bad smells were fine by her. Body parts—the fingertip had just been a preview, here you could find jawbones and tongues, hands and feet, curled-in cocks and viscera that glistened through its dust-crust—not a problem.

She planted five eyes, then crouched to let a trenchbuster sail over her head. She resisted a mad urge to reach up and stick an eye to it, then planted another eye, palming it and sticking it right under the nose of a gunnery sergeant who was hollering at two old women who were struggling to maneuver a gigantic, multipart weapon into position. To Valentine, the women looked old enough to be from the same tribe she'd hauled water for, and they were so thin they looked like they were made of twisted-together wires. Their eyes were huge and round and showed the whites.

The sergeant paid her no mind as she slipped forward, her shovel still in one hand. The trench dead-ended ahead of her and she jigged to a side trench, but soon that, too, dead-ended. Dead end after dead end—each got its own eye—and before long she was at the end of the road, no more side tunnels. She would have to turn back and try another path. There were no maps of the trenches, of course.

She had another puff off her inhaler. Her stomach lurched and then her knees gave way. She was back in the dirt now and she remembered what the wizard had told her about eating when she was on the inhaler or starving to death. Then she went into seizure. Her limbs thrashed, her head shook back and forth, she banged her forehead into the dirt. A gargling escaped her throat, nothing at all like words or any other human sound.

When the seizure passed–and it did pass, though it felt like it never would–she shakily withdrew a fistful of butterball and sugared organ meat and shoved it in her mouth. Most of it escaped, but some of it got down her throat and her hands were steadier in a moment, enabling her to eat more. She got to her knees, she got to her feet, she ate some more and had another puff off the inhaler.

God oh god! She felt *marvelous* now. Food and the inhaler were magic together. Dead ends, pah! Who had time to go back through the trenches? She'd be dead in five days. She jammed her fingers in the frozen dirt on the trench-side and hauled herself up to the surface.

In her months and months of digging in the trenches, she had never once peeked over the edge. There were things that watched for snoopy looks over the trenches, laser scanners and sentry guns. You could lose the top of your head zip-zap.

Now she was on the surface. It was like the surface of the moon. Craters, hills, trenches, and great clouds of roiling smoke and dust. Nothing alive. Broken guns and things that might have been body parts. She grinned that hard grin, because there was no one else here and so she was the queen of the surface, the bloody angel of the battlefield. She fisted more sugared liver into her gob and *ran.*

Zizz, zizz, zizz. There were bullets and other material around her, as soon as she moved, but the world was so clear now, the gray light so pure, the domain so utterly hers, there was no chance she'd be hit by a bullet.

She leapt a trench and skirted a trench, leapt and skirted, heading further and further toward the lines. She nearly tripped over a sentry gun, then leapt *on top of it* as it tried to swivel around to get her in its sights, and she pasted an eye on it and laughed and leapt away.

She was thinking that she should get back into a trench and was trying to pick one when it was decided for her—she was in midleap over a trench when a bullet clipped the heel of her shoe and she tumbled down into the trench. She did a tremendous, jarring face-plant into the planks below and lay stunned for a moment with her mouth filling up with blood. Her tongue throbbed—it had been bitten—and as she carefully rolled it around her mouth, she discovered that she'd knocked out one of her front teeth. Not such a pretty girl anymore, but she'd be dead in less than five days.

She got to her knees again and planted an eye as she looked around.

A soldier was staring at her from the end of her current trench. He was saying something, but here the trenches boomed with artillery and zizzed with gunfire and hearing was impossible. She drew closer to him to hear what he had to say and she was practically upon him when she realized that he was wearing an enemy uniform.

She was quick quick, but he was quicker and he had her arm in an iron grip before she could pull away.

He said something in a language that they often spoke in the movies, back where there was a cine across from her block of flats. She knew a few words of that language.

"Friend!" she said.

He said something in a different language, but she didn't recognize that one. Then he switched to Hindi, but all she knew to say in Hindi was Love Love Love I'm in Love, which was the chorus to all the songs in the Hindi movies.

He shook her arm hard. He was angry with her, and his gun was in his other hand now, a soft, floppy handgun like a length of rope and he was gesturing at her and shouting. He was as well fed as the wizard, and he was not much older than her. She thought that he didn't want to kill her and was angry because he was going to have to.

She tried smiling at him. He scowled hard. She held her hand out to him and touched his arm softly, placatingly. Then she pointed at her pocket, where the butterballs were. Very slowly, she reached into it. He watched her with suspicious eyes, the handgun trained on her now. She thought that if she was a suicide bomber, he'd be dead now, and that made her feel a little better about the war: if this was what a soldier from the other side was like, they all had a chance after all.

She drew out a butterball and took a bite of it, then offered it to the soldier. He looked like he wanted to cry. She held it to his mouth so he wouldn't have to let go of her or the gun to eat it. He took a small, polite bite, chewed and swallowed. She had a bite, then gave him one. They ate like that until the butterball was gone, and then she drew out another, and another.

She pointed to herself. "Valentine," she said.

He shook his head. He was the picture of moroseness. "Withnail," he said.

"Pleased to make your acquaintance, Withnail," she said in his language, another useful phrase culled from the cine, though she suspected she was pronouncing it all wrong. She held out her hand to shake his. He holstered his handgun and shook her hand.

"I have to go, Withnail." She couldn't say this in his language, but she spoke slowly and as clearly as she could.

He shook his head again. She covered his hand on her arm with her own and gave it a squeeze.

"To save my family," she said. "I'm on a mission for your side anyway. Let me go, Withnail." She gave his hand another squeeze. Slowly, he released her arm.

He was very handsome, she saw now, with a good chin and sensuous lips. She'd never kissed a boy and she'd be dead in four days and a little more. Or maybe she'd be dead that afternoon, if she couldn't get back into her own trenches.

She put her hand on the back of his neck and pulled his face to hers and gave him a dry, hard kiss on those pouting lips. It made her blood sing, and she gave him a hug, too, pressing her body to him. He kissed her back after a moment, surprised. His tongue probed at her closed lips and she pulled away, then for a crazy moment she thought of biting him and giving him a dose of zombiism to spread to his comrades in the trenches with him. But that wouldn't be right. They were friends now.

She stuck her fingers in the trench wall. They hurt–she must have broken a finger before. She hauled herself up and began to run, pawing her pockets for her inhaler. "So long, Withnail!" It was another phrase she knew from the cine.

* * *

Three days after being bitten by the zombie, Valentine woke up with her hand curled protectively over the huge hot egg on her collarbone. She couldn't move that arm this morning, not without pain like nothing she'd ever felt. Her face ached. Her limbs ached. Her new breasts ached like she'd been punched in them, repeatedly. She got out of bed like an old woman and crept to the table.

She sat gingerly and spooned up some cereal. Her mother sat opposite her, staring over her shoulder. Valentine ate a spoonful of cereal, then spat it out as it came into contact with the raw, toothless spot on her gum.

Her mother looked at her.

"Open your mouth, Vale," she said.

Valentine did as she was bade, showing the gap in her teeth.

"You were hit?" her mother said. Valentine didn't answer. She didn't trust herself to speak with her mother looking at her like that. "They won't want you now you've lost that tooth," she said. "You can go back to digging now."

She stood up from the table without a word and went out of the flat. She was so feverish that she couldn't tell if the stairs went down or up, whether she was descending or ascending.

She tottered out on the street. The way she felt, she couldn't walk properly. Her hips wanted to give way with every step and so she walked like a funky disco dancer through the early, cold streets, toward the wizard's house.

She didn't make it. Less than half way there, she sat down on a pile of rubble and retched. She reached down into her pocket and pulled out the wizard's inhaler, but she fumbled it. She couldn't bend over to get it, so she let herself slowly fall to the street, then she crawled one-armed to it. She fit it to her mouth and then squeezed it with clumsy fingers.

She dragged herself to her feet, not bothering to take the inhaler with her. Her limbs burned now and wanted to move, no matter how much it hurt, and she lurched to the wizard's door, moaning in the back of her throat.

Ana let her in, eyes wide. "You did it." It might have been a question. Valentine let herself slide to the soft, sweet-smelling carpet and closed her eyes.

* * *

An unknowable number of hours or days after Valentine got to the wizard's flat, she woke up in a soft, fluffy bed that was quietly massaging her limbs. She was dressed in loose cotton pajamas, and there was a trolley by the bed piled high with the kind of fruit that wasn't a berry and wasn't an orange, but a little of both and each one had a different smiley face growing in the peel.

The wizard came into the room.

"You'll live," he said. "Probably. It would have been a certainty if you'd fucking told me you had zombiism, you little idiot."

Ana came in behind him. "Do you think she would have done your mission for you if she didn't have zombiism, wizard?"

He waved her off. "You've got your cure," he said.

"It won't cure me," Valentine said. Her voice was like a gravel-mixer. "Not the kind I have. There's no cure."

"Oh, ho," the wizard said. "Would you care to make a wager on that? How about this: if you die, I take care of your family. If you live, you work for me—and I'll take care of your family."

"You already must take care of my family," she said.

The wizard's eyes glittered. "I think that curing your zombiism is repayment enough, so I've unilaterally renegotiated the terms of our deal. If you don't like that, I can arrange to have you reinfected and we can go back to the original contract."

"You've cured me?"

Ana said, "There are lots of things we have access to here that you can't get in the city. What you had would have killed you if he hadn't helped."

"Will you take my bet?"

She thought about the mission, about the soldier, about being queen of the battlefield. She thought about the way they'd bombed her city and how she'd just helped them kill the city's soldiers and diggers—like her father.

"I won't betray my city to its enemies ever again." She sat up very straight. "I was a traitor once, but I had a fever and I was dying. You are a traitor every day and what is *your* excuse?"

"A traitor? What the hell are you talking about?"

"The spy eyes I planted so our enemies can spy on us, the wealth you have around here. How many of our people died because you sold them out?"

"Valentine, you are a smart girl and your mother is a soldier, but you aren't so very smart as all that. You are a stupid girl sometimes. Our little palace here isn't full of spies. We're *documentarians.* We shoot the war and we send it to the outside world so they can see the tragedy they are wreaking here. We have a huge activist movement that we fuel through our pictures. The spy eyes you planted yesterday are now streaming 24/7 to activist sites in fifty countries. It is being played in the halls of the United Nations."

Eva made a spitting sound. "It's being played as filler on the snowy slopes of upper cable. It's being played as ironic snuff-porn in dorm rooms. It's being used as stock footage for avant-garde performance art. Please, wizard, please. She deserves to know the real situation, not the things you tell yourself when you can't sleep."

"It's—*entertainment?*"

"It's riveting," Ana said, like *riveting* meant *terrible.* "Very highly rated."

"And it raises consciousness," the wizard said. "You cynic, Ana, you can't see anything except the worst. It is the reason that anyone except for a few policy wonks have heard of what's going on here."

"Entertainment?"

"Entertainment," the wizard said. "And more than that."

"They're killing us, they're gassing us, they're bombing us, and you're selling it back to them as *entertainment?*"

She climbed out of the bed. She hurt, but not so much as she had before. The fever had broken, at least.

"Am I cured?" she asked. "Do I need anything else, or am I cured?"

The wizard scowled. "Now wait a moment—"

"You're cured," Ana said. "You should rest for a few days and eat well, but you will get better no matter what." The wizard turned and shoved her toward the door, so hard she stumbled and hit the jam. She spat on the floor and walked out of the room.

Valentine pulled herself out of the bed. The wizard took her wrist and without hesitating, she jammed her thumb into his eye socket, grunting with the effort. He shouted and reeled away and she made her way out of the bedroom and down the corridor to the brave red sitting room. Ana had a couple of grip-sheeted, robot-tied parcels for her. "Clothes," she said. "Food. Don't come back. I'm not from here, but even I know how wrong this is. He—there's no excuse for him.

Go." She handed Valentine some shoes–good sturdy workboots, still warm from the printer.

* * *

Six months after she took home the clothes that Ana had given her, Valentine was taken off of ditchdigging and put on corpse-duty. They were dying like flies, and the zombies fed on them, and unless the meat was disposed of, the zombies would multiply like rats.

There was only bread on alternate days now. The hunger was like a playmate or a childhood enemy that taunted her. It woke her in the night like a punch in the gut.

The first body she found was missing its ass-cheeks. You could find the bodies by the smell, and she was on corpse-detail with a boy about her age whose face she never saw, because it was covered by a mask. He had a floppy machine-pistol that she hoped he knew how to use, because the zombies were everywhere. He'd been hauling meat for weeks and grunted out little bits and pieces to help her get acquainted. Neither of them exchanged names.

"What happened to her–"

"Ever see black-market meat? The ass is the last part to go when they starve. The mafiyehs take the cheeks and grind them up with some filler and add flavoring agent and sell it. They used to kill people and take the meat that way, but they don't need to do that anymore. There's enough meat from natural causes."

The smell was terrible. It was a woman and she'd been dead for some time. It was hot out, too. Valentine's mask didn't really seem to help, but when she stuck a finger under it to scratch her sweaty upper lip, an unfiltered gulp of air went up her nose and she gagged.

They started in the early hours of the morning before the heat got too bad. They slept for a few hours at noon, then started again mid-afternoon. She was so hungry that she was dizzy. The next corpse was on the fifteenth story of a block of revolutionary-era flats. No lift in the city had worked in more than a year. They climbed and rested, climbed and rested. There was no question of going straight up. She was too weak to consider it for a second.

It was a man. He was big and tall, and even starved out as he was, they could barely lift him. He must have been a giant in life.

"We'll never carry him down all those stairs," the boy said. "Go and open the big window."

Valentine obeyed woodenly. She knew that if you couldn't carry the body, you'd have to get it out of the building some other way. She knew that. She didn't want to think about what it meant, but she knew it. There'd been a corpse one floor down from her flat and it had taken weeks for the city to dispose of it and life had been almost unbearable for everyone in the building. And that had been winter, when the cold kept the smell down some.

So you had to get rid of the body. The window was a revolutionary window. It was marvelous and self-cleaning and it swung easily open. Forty-five meters below, she could see the building's deserted courtyard and the corpse-wagon that the boy drove haltingly through the city streets. Under other circumstances she might have felt show-offy and ostentatious riding in a car while everyone else walked, but she knew that no one envied her her ride in the corpse-wagon.

"Take his ankles." With the mask on, the boy looked like a horse, and she knew she did, too. On the one chair that hadn't been burned for fuel the previous winter, the boy had stacked up the few possessions the corpse had: a ring, a lighter, a clasp-knife, a little set of headphones with their charge-lights showing red.

She picked up the body by the ankles. The boy had him by the shoulders. When they alley-ooped it up off the floor, the body let loose a tremendous, evil fart. It wasn't the first time a body had done that on that day, but it was the loudest and evilest of all the farts. Its ankles were dirty and the smell of its feet and its fart combined into a grey, fuggy miasma that she could smell through the mask.

"You should smell his feet," she said.

"You should smell his breath," the boy said.

They dragged the body to the window and one, two, three, swung it out into the wide world. She watched it spin away, fascinated and wordless. Then it hit the ground and the sound. And the way it looked. And the splash. And the blood.

There were tears streaming down her face, fouling her mask. She stepped out into the corridor and ripped the mask off and faced the wall, groaning.

"It gets easier later," the boy said, tugging her arm.

He was right.

But they needed shovels to get the body into the corpse wagon. Some of the bits had gone a long way off and she had to carry them before her on the spade-end of the shovel. His viscera glistened like an accusation at her. She lived on the fourteenth floor. When her time came, she'd go out the window, too.

* * *

Two years after the siege began, she awoke deaf. Mata was shaking her vigorously and her lips were moving, but there was no sound. Valentine listened hard and made out a distant, underwater sound that she couldn't place, though it was familiar.

Mata was thin and hard now and slept with a gun and only came home for a few hours at a time. She was taking lots of different pills, and they made her a little jumpy. Valentine wondered if the pills had rendered her mother mute, before she realized that she couldn't hear *anything.*

She tapped her ear.

"I can't hear," she said.

Her mother didn't appear to understand. She still shook Valentine hard.

"I'm deaf, Mata," she said. She shook her head and tugged her earlobes. She was scared now, and she sat up. She wiggled a finger in her ear, which was very greasy. Not even the sound of her finger in her ear carried back to her mind. Stone deaf.

She was breathing heavily, but that happened a lot. The hunger made her weepy and she somtimes cried for no reason. Sometimes in the middle of a sentence she had to sit down and stare at the sky while her tears rolled down her throat, until she felt able to go on again.

She slowed her breathing. "Mata," she said.

Her mother made a "stay there" gesture, then repeated it and mouthed the words at her slowly and obviously. She nodded to show she understood.

She was supposed to be carrying bodies that day. You could get bread every day if you carried bodies. One piece on alternate days from the city, one piece from the black market in exchange for the loot you could find in the flats of the starved.

There was a new girl that Valentine was training, too. The boy was long gone. He'd tried to touch her breast, not just once, either, and she'd reported him. When the supervisor confronted him, he went crazy and tried to attack the supervisor and the supervisor sent him to the front to carry ammunition, where, Valentine supposed, he was still working. Unless he was dead. She didn't much care which.

But she wanted bread. The creche had shut down a few months before, but Trover had some little boys he played with and they sometimes came home with a little food that he was always careful to share with her, though she was sure that he didn't share everything. She didn't either. No one did. Mata had a little stash of dried fish under her pillow. Valentine almost never raided it, though she could have.

Trover was looking at her. She tugged her earlobes. "I'm deaf," she said. She thought she might be speaking very loudly, but she couldn't tell.

Trover went out of the flat without looking back at her.

She waited for Mata, but the day crept by and Mata didn't return. The more she didn't return, the more Valentine worried. She cried some, and tried to sleep. She sucked pebbles for the hunger, and drank the cistern dry. She carried the chamber pot downstairs, but the world in silence was so scary that she practically ran back to the flat once she'd tipped it out into the reeking collection point.

She had finally gotten to sleep when Mata returned. Mata mouthed something at her in slow, deliberate words, but she couldn't make it out. Mata repeated it, and then again. She didn't get any of it, but Mata's expression was clear. No doctors would help her. She hadn't expected them to.

No doctors could help her, as far as she was concerned. She knew exactly what had gone wrong: her hearing aids had failed. Everything from the golden years after the revolution failed. Old people died when their artificial hearts or kidneys seized up and withered. Lifts didn't work. Printers didn't work–they'd nearly all died the day the siege began. The hospitals couldn't print drugs. The sky-cars fell out of the sky.

Nothing worked. Nothing would ever work again. Everything fell apart. Her hearing aids were of that same magical *stuff* as everything else from the revolution, so it followed that they would die, too.

Mata must have known this. That's probably what she was saying. If Valentine concentrated, she could recall her mother's voice and have it say the words.

"It's OK, Mata," she said. She knew she was shouting. "It's OK."

Mata cried and she cried, but she put herself to sleep as soon as she could, and once she thought Trover and Mata were sleeping, she took out her small wizard light and made her way down the silent stairs, into the silent streets.

She walked cautiously toward the wizard's flat. She was deaf, but it felt like she was a little blind, too. Without her hearing, she couldn't see right, or balance right. She thought about a life without ears. She'd probably have to go back to digging, since you couldn't haul bodies without a partner and you needed to be able to talk, even if it was only to say alley-*oop*.

She walked like a drunkard, keeping to the darkest streets where even the night wardens stayed away. She let only the tiniest glow escape from her little light.

She was about to turn into the main shopping street when a strong hand seized her arm and jerked her back into the alley. Her first thought was *zombie* and she screamed involuntarily and a fist connected with her mouth, loosening one of the teeth next to her gap. Her head rang like a bell, the first sound she'd heard since that morning.

The little bead fell out of her hand and rolled into a crack in the pavement, crazily illuminating the scene and her attacker. The alley was filthy and covered in drifts of rubble, and the man who'd hit her was a young civil defense warden with acne that looked chemically induced. He didn't smell good. He smelled very bad. Sick, maybe. Unclean like everyone, and worse. He was no zombie. He didn't smell good enough.

She saw his mouth work and knew he was saying something to her. "I'm deaf" she said and she knew she said it too loud because he recoiled and then he punched her harder in the mouth than before.

She fell down this time and he dragged her roughly by one arm away from the light.

She was cried out, and weak from hunger, and she understood what was coming next when he threw her down and grabbed the collar of her shirt and ripped it away from her, then gave her bra the same treatment. She was dazed from the knocks on the head, but she knew what was coming.

Valentine's mother was a soldier. She'd been taught to kill. She'd taught Valentine to kill. Valentine never left the house without a clasp-knife, the knife she'd taken from the corpse she'd thrown out a fifteenth story window some unknowable time before.

The knife was in her back pocket. She watched the boy's silhouette work at the fastener of his trousers, while she stole a hand behind her and slowly, slowly took out the knife. She let herself make silent choking dazed sounds.

She knew what was coming next, but the boy didn't.

But as he knelt down and reached out for the snap on her trousers, she showed him what was next. She took two of his fingers and just missed opening her own belly. He tried to jerk his arm away, but she had him by the wrist before he could, and she pulled him down on top of her, making sure that her knife was free of the clinch, free to slip around behind him and take him once-twice-three time in between his ribs, then again into his kidneys. Seeing the splatted corpses she tossed out of windows had given her a very keen idea of how anatomy worked.

She had never felt so clearheaded as she did at this work, and the boy on her thrashed and got her a couple good knocks on the head, and his blood soaked her bare chest and her face and her short hair. But she worked the knife some more, going for the throat and then the face. She let him go and he rolled away and she pounced on him. She worked with the knife. Soon he stopped moving.

Her shirt was in rags, but the bra-clasp still worked, once she bent it back. The pea light was easy to find—it glowed like a beacon. She picked it up and made her way to the wizard's.

"I'm deaf," she said to Ana. Ana looked the same, at first. And then Valentine saw that she was holding a cane and leaning on it heavily.

She knew that she was half-naked and covered with gore, but she also knew that Ana would not be phased by this. She squeezed past her and into the brave, swooping, just-printed sitting room. She fixed herself some coffee and poured a glug of rum into it while Ana stared at her in some wordless emotion.

"I'm deaf," she repeated, setting down some coffee and rum for Ana. "I could use a shirt, too. And the wizard, of course."

She remembered how to use the cooker from the revolutionary days, but it was like remembering something from a dream. She poked at it, ignoring Ana, and got it to produce a plate of goose-liver dumplings in white gravy. She rinsed the blood off her fingers and then ate the dumplings with them.

Ana stared at her for a long moment, then limped out of the room and fetched the wizard.

He said something that she couldn't hear. Everyone in the city was old, even the young people–wrinkled with dust in the wrinkles and missing teeth and torn clothes. The wizard was forever young. He was clean and unscarred and as well fed as ever.

"Print me some clothes, wizard," she said. "These ones are covered in blood. And I'm deaf, so don't bother talking to me."

The wizard stared at her. She ate a dumpling and licked the gravy off her fingers. Her stomach had been in flutters since waking up deaf, a not entirely unpleasant counterpoint to her constant, painful hunger. The gravy soothed her stomach, the dumplings settled it, the pain retreated.

She was deaf. She was a murderess. But there was food and it was good. Better than no food, anyway.

The wizard brought her a pile of warm, printer-fresh clothes. "Your printers never stopped working, did they?" she said. She was sure she was talking very loudly and she didn't give a festering shit.

"Our printers stopped working the morning of the siege. Everything did. Everything stops working. That's the infowar. The infowar probably is what did for my hearing aids. They were supposed to last ten years but it's hardly been two.

"I'm taking a shower now," she said. "You can write me an answer if you'd like. I promise to read it afterward."

She took herself to the bathroom and let the shower wash her. There were some tears in her head somewhere but they couldn't find their way to her eyes. That was all right. It was a war, after all.

She dressed in fine printer-fresh clothes and burped a printer-fresh belch. The gravy taste wafted gassily into her mouth.

The wizard had rolled up one of the sofas and unrolled a big screen in its place, the kind of thing she used to love to play games on, in the dreamlike fantasy of yore.

YOU'RE DEAF?

She nodded. "I have hearing aids, from a bomb. They weren't working when I got out of bed this morning. No warning. They went like that." She snapped her fingers.

Some movement caught the corner of her eye and she spun around. There were four more people in the living room, people she hadn't met before though she assumed that they belonged to the distant voices she'd heard on her earlier visits. They had the well fed look of Ana and the wizard, and a couple of them were obviously foreign. The documentarians. One of them was pointing a camera at her. She bared her gap-tooth grin at the camera and faked a step toward it. The camera woman cringed back and she laughed nastily.

"Your cameras work. Your printers work. You're not losing the infowar the way we do. That's because there's a way to build things to resist the infowar agents, right? That's why the enemy trench-busters don't fail the way our weapons do."

The wizard and Ana conversed briefly, their heads pointed away from her. She grabbed the camera away from the startled camera woman and pointed it at them.

"I want to get a recording of what you're saying now so once my hearing comes back I'll be able to listen. You don't mind, do you?" She laughed again and poked her tongue out through the gap in her teeth. All her teeth were loose now, and running her tongue along the back of them made then wiggle in a way that was part tickle, part hurt.

The wizard got the idea. He made a keyboard appear on the screen again and prodded at it.

IT'S NOT QUITE WHAT YOU THINK VALENTINE

"Sure, what do I know? But you've got something, don't you?"

Ana nodded.

"You can fix my hearing?"

Ana nodded again.

"You could try to kill me while you performed surgery, couldn't you?"

Neither of them said anything.

"I'm booby-trapped." She wasn't, but it had been known to happen. "When I die, boom!" She realized that this lie might be too extravagant. Who'd booby-trap a starved gap-toothed girl? "My mother arranged it."

She thought back to the cine. The food she'd eaten was helping her think, the way it always did, making her realize what a cloud of fuzz-headed hunger she usually floated through.

"I've left a full description of your operation in a sealed envelope to be opened in the event of my death."

That was better. She should have gone with that in the first place. She couldn't tell if they believed her. Ana was shaking her head.

"You've got a doctor here, or someone like a doctor. Whatever's been done to your leg, Ana, a doctor did that."

Ana pointed at the woman from whom Valentine had snatched the camera. Valentine passed it back to her. "Sorry about that."

* * *

The day after Valentine killed her first man, her hearing came back. The surgery took about ten minutes and was largely performed remotely, reprogramming the hardware in her head with something that the doctor kept calling "hardened logic." She liked the sound of that.

Her hearing came back slowly, in blips and bloops over the course of a few hours. Then it was back, better than new. She found that she could hear sounds from much farther away. The camera woman also showed her how she could use a terminal to access the memory in her new ears, which would buffer six months' worth of audio. Valentine didn't think she'd be in a position to make much use of this feature, as interesting as it was. There weren't any working machines in the city.

"I'm going home now," she said.

Ana was waiting by the printer, making it output clothes and food as fast as it could, giving it to robots to tie up in grip-sheets.

"Would you have turned us in if we didn't help you?"

Valentine shook her head and tried not to smile. "No one would have believed me anyway. I'm not booby-trapped, either."

"I didn't think you were," Ana said. She gave Valentine a long hug and kissed her cheek. "Be careful, OK?"

"Why don't you people help us? Why can't you give our army hardened logic for their weapons?"

Ana shook her head. She was crying. "You think I haven't asked this? To do that would be suicide. Your enemies would never forgive us. It's one thing to chide them for their slaughter, another thing to end it."

Valentine had Ana print her some convincing rags with bit-mapped filth right in the weave and wrapped her parcels in them so they wouldn't be suspicious. She stepped out into the bright light of a spring day, every sound sharp as a pin drop, from distant gunfire to the nearby hungry whimpering of a baby.

She walked slowly through the streets. She passed a spot that she thought was the place where the boy grabbed her, where she'd done her work with the knife. If that was the spot, though, there was no sign of it. The corpse-carriers were efficient.

She walked the stairs to her flat quickly, her full belly supplying her with boundless energy. As she reached for the door, though, she heard something from behind it, some crying. Trover. Once he'd cried non-stop. But he hadn't cried in so long she barely remembered the sound.

She swung open the door and saw what Trover was crying about. Mata was stretched out on the floor beside the one chair they hadn't burned for fuel. She wasn't moving and one of her eyes was wide open, the other squeezed shut. Trover was shaking her shoulder and crying.

"What?" Valentine said to her brother, grabbing and shaking him. "What happened?"

He opened his mouth and let out a howl. He hadn't spoken in a long time.

She knelt at her mother's side. Her mother's cheek was cold. Her arms and hands were stiff. Valentine knew that stiffness. Anyone who worked on the corpse patrol knew that stiffness. The front of her mother's torn trousers were damp with cold piss, Valentine could smell it. In Mata's breast pocket were a couple of inhalers, military grade, the kind of thing you took if you couldn't afford to sleep and if you needed to make your body go.

To Valentine, her mother looked like a skeleton, something long-buried and not freshly dead. Compared to Ana, this woman was very ugly and skinny and hard. Too hard to be a mother. She must have taken the drugs to keep herself going when Valentine didn't come home. Maybe she'd gone looking for Valentine. Maybe she'd gone looking for a doctor. Maybe she'd gone to the front to kill some soldiers. Whatever the cause, Valentine had been the reason. It was for her that Mata had killed herself.

Valentine pulled Trover to her and hugged him. The little boy smelled of his own shit. In her parcels, she had the food he needed so she cut them open and gave him some.

She let him eat and covered Mata with some of the new clothes that she'd brought home. She knew how to go through a corpse's pockets efficiently. She also knew all of Mata's hiding places in the tiny, grimy flat. Soon she had Mata's identification, her sidearm, her inhaler, her rucksack. There were soldiers Valentine's age at the front. She could pass.

"Come on, Trover," she said, getting him into a change of clothes, putting good shoes on him. Good shoes would be important. She didn't know how much walking they'd do, but it would be a lot.

She took him down the stairs, snuffling and weeping a little still, but logy from all the rich food. She led him to the civic patrol office.

"I can win the war," she said.

The woman from the city wasn't so fat anymore, but she still had her armor on. She was the one who'd told father he had to go to the war. She didn't seem to recognize Valentine, though.

She stared at Valentine. "I'm busy," she said.

"I know a–" Valentine searched for the word. "A profiteer who has access to hardened logic that the infowar doesn't work against."

The woman from the city looked at her a little longer this time. "I'm very busy, little girl."

"I can bring you to him. He has working printers."

The woman pretended not to hear her. She stared down at a pile of papers in front of her, and it was clear to Valentine that she was only pretending to read them.

Valentine led Trover to the woman's desk and knocked all the papers off of it.

"It's illegal to be a profiteer. Don't you want to at least arrest him?"

"I'll arrest *you*," the woman from the city said, grabbing her wrist. Valentine was ready for this. Her mother had taught her what to do about this. She bent the woman's thumb back and squeezed it until she tumbled out of the chair and dropped to her knees.

"That's enough," said an old, old hero. He sounded like he was right behind her, but that was just her new ears. When she turned around she saw that he was in the doorway. He was so old now that he looked like a zombie, and his one arm was pointing at her with shaky authority. "Let her go."

Valentine released the woman from the city.

"Do you want to see the profiteer?" Valentine said, approaching the hero. Her mother had respected this man, and Valentine decided she would respect him, too.

"I will come with you," he said.

"Will you bring guards? He is armed." She thought for a minute. "I believe he's armed."

"It will be fine," he said. He showed her the heavy pistol he wore on his belt.

"My brother has to come, too," Valentine said.

"That will be fine."

The old hero walked slowly and carefully. The soldiers he passed nodded to him and saluted him. The old people smiled and waved. Valentine came to feel proud to be at his side. Normally she was invisible in the city, just another gray, thin face, but with the old hero, she was a hero, too. And she *was* a hero: she was about to end the war.

The old man spoke creakingly to her as they walked. He remembered her mother, and he remembered her father. He told her stories of her mother's bravery in the revolution, when he'd been her commander, and she felt her heart race. Valentine was a hero, like her mother. The wizard would win the war for them.

Then they came to his door. The old man didn't need her to point it out. He went and thumped it three times with the butt of his gun.

Ana answered a moment later. She was dressed in old rags and had left behind the cast from her leg, limping to the door on a makeshift cane.

"Hello, comrade," she said. She didn't have her usual accent.

The hero nodded to her. "Comrade Ana." He knew her name, without being introduced.

The wizard came to the door. "Comrade hero."

"Comrade Georg." The old hero shook the wizard's hand. The wizard was wearing rags like Ana's. He had a cunning glitter in his eye and he took in the street, took in Valentine. "Hello, Valentine," he said.

"This girl tells me you have contraband," the old hero said. "It's my duty to come in and search your premises for it."

"Valentine," the wizard said, with unconvincing disappointment. "The food you took from here wasn't contraband. It was my savings." To the hero, he added, "She took the food and I didn't blame her. Surely she was hungry. If I had been a little child in her circumstances, I might have done the same."

Valentine squeezed Trover's hand until he whimpered. She didn't trust her tongue enough to say anything.

They went into the vestibule and then turned left into a flat. Now, until this time, she'd always turned right when visiting the wizard, but now on the right there was nothing but a smooth, unbroken wall. And to the left, there was an entirely different flat, barren of furniture as her own flat, small and dirty and smelling of death.

"Search away," the wizard said. He tried to put a hand on Valentine's shoulder and she shied away and dropped her hand to the waistband of the trousers he'd printed for her, where she'd hidden her mother's tiny sidearm. "You'll find nothing, I assure you."

Valentine could see that they'd find nothing. All the furniture in the room couldn't have concealed a single tin of food. This wasn't even the right flat. With her amazing ears, she heard the movement of the wizard's associates, the documentarians, in the next flat over.

"I hear them," she said. "Next door. This isn't the right flat."

"This is the flat you led me to," the old hero said.

"It's through there!" she said, pointing at the blank wall. "It's a false wall!" She thumped it but it was solid and stony. Tears pricked her eyes. "These clothes!" she said, desperately, plucking at her shirt and trousers. "He printed them for me! He has hardened logic printers on the other side of that wall. He could win the war!"

The wizard shook his head and smiled at her again. His eyes glittered. "Oh, if only that were true. To win this war–"

She looked imploringly at Ana. Ana looked away.

The old hero shook the wizard's hand with his one remaining hand. "I'm sorry to have disturbed you, comrade."

"Nonsense," the wizard said. "Anything for the city."

"Come along," the old hero said. "Let's leave these people in peace."

Trover let himself be led silently into the street and stayed at her side even when she let go of his hand to silently palm her mother's sidearm.

"Your mother would be ashamed of you," the old hero said. "She wouldn't have wasted the city's time on her fantasies and vendettas."

She kept silent. She knew a nearby alley where no one ventured except for people who disappeared without a trace. Though she wanted to shout at him that her mother died for the city that the old hero had just betrayed, she kept silent.

When they passed the alley mouth, she hastily shoved Trover into it. He gave a cry and fell over. She ducked in after him.

"He's tripped! Help me!" she called.

The old hero slowly negotiated his way into the alley and to her side. She was holding Trover down as he struggled to rise, but she hoped it looked like she was helping him up. Maybe it did, for the old hero bent at her side and she stuck the sidearm under his chin and pushed it hard into the wattle of skin there.

"My mother died for this city, you traitorous worm," she said, her jaws clenching with the effort of not shouting the words. "I would kill you right now if I didn't think you could be of use to me."

The old hero's eyes were calm. "Lots of people have tried to kill me, little girl."

"Lots of the enemy have tried. How many from the city?"

"Lots," the old hero said. "Lots of them, and yet here I stand, alive and well."

"I want to go to see the people who fight the infowar. I'll kill you if you don't take me to them."

"You want to do what? You stupid little girl." His tone still wasn't angry. "The wizard there is the city's best friend abroad. He's the only reason our enemies haven't crushed us. You want to betray him?"

"I will win this war," she said. But she faltered. She had thought that he'd just been bought off by the wizard, but maybe it was the case that he supported the wizard's work. Was it possible?

"We will win this war, by cooperating with our friends abroad. We can't afford to expose them to risk. I don't expect you to understand, little girl. This is a very deep game."

The phrase "deep game" enraged her so much that she almost shot him there. It was so–*patronizing.*

She let him lead the way toward the front. Trover was whimpering now–he'd twisted his ankle when she'd shoved him–and she whispered to him to be still.

Her plan was stupid. The old hero was going to lead her into a trap, not to the high command, and she knew it.

"I suppose I should just shoot you," she said.

"Why do you say that?" He was so calm. What kind of man was this?

"You'll lead me to a trap and have me shot or arrested. I have to see the infowar command. I have to win the war."

"You dream big, little girl. I have been persecuting the war on our enemies since before your hero mother was born. The first thing I learned is that war is the art of the possible. It is possible that we will win the siege, given enough time and losses. It is not possible that you will win the war."

"So you'll have me shot rather than try."

"I wouldn't have you shot if I could help it. I owe your mother that much."

"If you keep talking about my mother I will shoot you." She found his calm tone calmed her, too. The soldiers still saluted them, the old people waved, and she supposed that if any of them knew she had the old hero under the gun, she'd be torn to pieces. But she was calm and the day was a sunny one.

"My apologies," the old man said.

"I could have you run away and try to find them on my own."

"You'd never find them."

"I found the wizard. I put a weapon under your chin. I'm fifteen years old and I did that much. I will find them and I'll—"

"You'll what? You'll tell them to go to the wizard's flat to retrieve his technology? I assure you, if that was to come to pass, there would be no technology to get by the time you reached his flat."

They were getting closer to the front. The distant gunfire and zizzing trenchbusters were crystal clear in her amazing new ears.

"He gave some to me," she said. "My hearing aids failed yesterday and he got them back online with hardened logic. I have it in my head."

"You—" The old man stopped in his tracks. She almost shot him by accident, ploughing into him. He turned around, much faster than she'd seen him move to date. "You have it in your head?"

He reached for her and she jerked the sidearm up. Absently he took it away from her in a single cobra-swift movement and dropped it in his shirt pocket. He reached for her again with his one hand and tilted her head, looking for the small scars beneath her jaw.

"He fixed these?"

"Yesterday. I was deaf yesterday morning."

"You're not lying? If you're lying, I will have you shot."

"She was deaf," Trover said, very quietly. "Now she can hear again. My sister isn't lying."

They both looked at him.

"Come with me, little girl," the old hero said, and he struck off.

* * *

Six hours after Valentine left her dead mother behind in their grimy, bare flat, she came to the infowar command.

It was far back of the lines, near the old woods at the western side of the city, and the entrance to it was guarded by five checkpoints. They took away the sidearm from the old hero at the last one, along with several other small weapons the old hero was carrying. They searched and wanded Valentine and Trover and made Trover turn out his pockets. It turned out that he was carrying Valentine's old clasp-knife, which had disappeared some months before. He handed it to the soldier solemnly, and she kissed his cheek and tousled his hair and for a moment, she looked just like their mother and Valentine felt tears behind her eyes.

"We're here," the old hero said. "Come with me."

There were three airlocks to pass through, and then they were put into airtight suits with breathing bottles. They didn't have one that would fit Trover, but the nice soldier who'd kissed his cheek promised to look after him.

Beyond the last airlock, it was like something from before the siege, clean and bold and humming with energy.

"We keep everything that works here," the old hero said. "This is our last cache of material that hasn't been compromised by the infowar. It's a completely sealed space. If a single strand of malware got in, it would turn epidemic and wipe out everything."

His voice sounded like it was coming from a million miles away. Shrouded in her breathing hood, Valentine felt like she was in the first days of a better nation, a time when everything worked and smelled of sharp cleanliness, not rot and ruin. Hooded figures walked past them without a glance.

The old hero led her deep into the maze, then through yet another airlock.

"Comrade," the old hero said. "A word, please."

The hooded figure to whom he spoke looked up from its workbench and peered through the old hero's hood. Then it saluted smartly and hurried to the old hero's side.

"General–" The hooded figure had a man's voice, almost as old as the old hero's voice.

The old hero–the general–touched his hand to his hood and then pulled a retractable wire out of his helmet and presented it to the other. The other patched it into his helmet's collar. Even with her marvelous new ears, Valentine couldn't hear what they said.

They released their umbilicus a moment later and the other one turned to Valentine.

"Is it true?" His voice was choked, like he could barely get the words out.

"In my ears," she said. "Hardened logic."

The other man danced from foot to foot. "It can't be true," he said.

She nodded.

The old man rooted through his workbench and came up with a wand that he put against the back of her neck. It was similar to the wand that the doctor/camera woman at the wizard's house had used to figure out her hearing aids.

"You have it?" the general asked.

"I have it," the other one said. "I have copied it. Whether I can decompile it, whether I can make anything useful from it—well, we'll see."

"Tomorrow, then," the general said.

The other one didn't answer. He was hunched over a terminal on his workbench, fingers punishing his keyboard.

"Now where?" Valentine asked as they shucked their isolation suits, the smell of stink and rot flooding back into her nostrils.

"Now we clean house," the general said. "Get your brother and your gun."

* * *

Twenty four hours after the wizard cured Valentine's hearing, she helped arrest him.

The general knocked on the wizard's door and it swung open. Ana had her cast off again, had her bad cane.

"Yes, comrade?"

"I have business with you and yours. Bring them out here, please."

Ana took in the line of soldiers in the road before her, carrying weapons from knives to old gunpowder weapons to small, floppy sidearms and she went ashen.

"I knew it would be today," she said. She turned to Valentine. "When you came back this morning, I knew it would be today."

"Call them," the old hero said.

"They already know you're here." Smoke emerged from the doorway behind her. "It's all destroying itself. There was never a chance of you getting access to it."

The general shrugged with one shoulder. Valentine wondered if his stump was smooth like a billiard ball or angry and wounded or shriveled like dried fruit.

She gripped her mother's sidearm tighter and watched the wizard emerge. The documentarians. The wizard's eyes glittered.

"It's all gone," he said. "You won't get a scrap of it. What a goddamned waste. We were on your side, you know."

"You were very well fed," the general said.

One of the documentarians sobbed.

"What a pointless goddamned waste. Spiteful, stupid, boneheaded–" The wizard broke off, looking at Valentine. "Her hearing aids."

Valentine smiled. "Yes," she said. "My hearing aids. I'm recording you now. Do you have any words you'd like to say for the microphone?"

The wizard's jaw dropped to his chest and his whole body sort of crumpled, slumping in the grasp of the soldier who held him.

"You little–"

Valentine put a sarcastic finger to her lips and then made a show of covering Trover's ears. She saw Ana smile involuntarily before the woman turned away.

* * *

Three days after they arrested the wizard, the sky-cars lifted off again. They roared over the enemy lines, dropping intelligent motes that zeroed in on enemy soldiers and burrowed up their nostrils and in their ears and in the corners of their eyes and rattled in their skulls until their brains were paste and goo.

Four days after they arrested the wizard, the printers started to supply food and drugs. Clever wormy robots sought out and inoculated the zombies.

Ten days after they arrested the wizard, the buildings started to repair themselves. The lifts all worked again, all at once, in a synchronized citywide *whirrr* of convenience and civilization.

Fourteen days after they arrested the wizard, the siege ended.

Valentine and Trover were in the civil defense bunkhouse. They'd buried their mother that morning, in the woods, in a perfectly square grave that the robots had excavated for them, amid the ranked hundreds of thousands that the robots were digging through the woods, marking each with a small plaque inset to the soil, bearing a name and a date of birth, and sometimes a day of death, and the legend, HERO OF THE SIEGE.

Trover hadn't spoken all that day, but he had tossed in the first shovelful of dirt at their mother's grave. Around them, the survivors had wailed and torn their clothes and shoveled at the massed dead.

The soldiers laughed and sang around them, drinking champagne and eating chocolate. The men hugged them and the women kissed them, even the sour woman from the city.

The general saw them sitting in their corner, Trover's hand in

Valentine's, and he got them and brought them back into the cells. He handed Valentine a key and gestured toward the wing.

"Go and get them. They're free to go now. Tell them to go far."

Ana and the wizard were sharing a tiny cell, the documentarians were in three other cells. Valentine turned the old metal key in each lock in turn.

"It's over," she said. "Victory. The general says to go far."

Ana hugged her so long Valentine thought she'd never let go, but when she did let go, Valentine wished she'd come back.

Valentine never saw them again.

* * *

Ten years after the siege, Valentine got her medal.

The ceremony was a small one. They had almost run out of special medals to bestow on the living heroes of the siege, and children came last. The only times she saw Trover these days was at a friend's ceremony. The rest of the time, he was preoccupied with his studies. He was training to be a diplomat. He still had a terrible temper. Apparently this was an asset at the System Trade Union.

Valentine walked there, but she was just about the only one. Others flew, either in sky-cars or on invisible ground-effect cushions. There were a thousand of them getting their medals today, and she and Trover were placed next to each other in the long queue, which was alphabetical by surname.

"They should have given you the biggest and first medal, Vale," Trover said. His hands were in white fists. "You! You won the war! And *he* knows it!"

On stage, the general shook hands with another medal recipient. He was up to the Cs, and Valentine and Trover's last name started with an X. It would be a while yet.

"His other arm is very convincing," she said.

Trover just fumed.

When they took the stage, the general looked at them and winked. He gave them each a medal, then took her by the shoulders, and then hugged her to his breast. He was still thin and fragile, but he was also still quick and his hug was firm. He pressed his palm to hers and her body told her he was sending her some data, which she accepted with surprise but without comment.

Trover led her off of the stage. She examined her new download. An audio file. She played it, and it played in her cochlea.

I found the wizard. I put a weapon under your chin. I'm fifteen years old and I did that much. I will find them and I'll—

You'll what? You'll tell them to go to the wizard's flat to retrieve his technology? I assure you, if that was to come to pass, there would be no technology to get by the time you reached his flat.

He gave some to me. My hearing aids failed yesterday and he got them back online with hardened logic. I have it in my head.

You—You have it in your head?

She'd never forgotten those words, not in ten years, not through the reconstruction or her years abroad, not in school and not in work. Not a day had gone by without her thinking of it. Lots of people had ears that could buffer now, and hers now had a hundred-year buffer along with all the audio ever recorded on tap for her pleasure, but she never bothered to rewind her hearing. Those words, in her mind, were all the rewinding she needed.

She sat down hard, right there, on the sugary grass.

Trover was at her side in a flash, calling her name anxiously. She was crying uncontrollably, but she was smiling, too. Those words, pulled off of her ears ten years ago, when they'd gone to infowar command. Oh, God, those old friends, those words. The wizard and Ana. It had been so long. Where had the time gone?

* * *

The next day, she met an old face.

"You!" he said. He had a thick accent–the kind of accent that said he'd learned her language the hard way; that he hadn't just installed it.

She looked at him. He was very familiar, but she couldn't place him. Maybe if he didn't have that silly beard, forked into two theatrical points, the way they were wearing them in Catalan that year. She tried to picture him without it. He was grinning like a fool and laughing.

"I can't believe it's you!"

She shook her head slowly. Where the hell did she know this guy from? She was supposed to be going to the cine with friends that night–the new show screened between the trees in the western woods and you walked around through it and drank fizzy elderflower and talked with your friends as the story unfolded around you. It was a warm night and perfect for such things.

"You don't remember me?"

Her tooth tingled. The one that had been knocked out in the trench and resprouted after the siege. Then she recognized him.

"*Withnail?*"

He hopped in place. "Valentine! You remembered!"

She put her hand to her breast and staggered back dramatically, hamming it up. He was still very handsome, and she'd never forgotten her first kiss.

"What the hell are you doing here?"

"I have a layover," he said. "Tokyo tomorrow. But I wanted to stop and see the place–"

"Remember the dead?" she said. He had been the enemy, after all. How many of her countrymen had he shot?

"Remember," he said. "Remember everything."

How many of his comrades had died on the day the death rained from the sky? Surely they had died in great numbers on that day.

The woods were full of her dead. Mata was there. And there was the movie tonight. She touched the medal on her lapel. He had no medal. The soldiers who'd persecuted the siege received no medals.

"You're here until when?"

"Tomorrow," he said, "first thing."

"First thing tomorrow. Come and see a movie tonight," she said.

He looked at her and cocked his head. She wasn't beautiful, she knew, but sometimes men looked at her that way. Something about what she'd done, they could see it.

"I'd like that very much," he said.

She played back a little audio as they walked together, for a terrible silence descended on them as they walked, awkward and oppressive.

Would you have turned us in if we didn't help you?

No one would have believed me anyway.

"Valentine?"

"Yes, Withnail?"

"Thank you," he said. "For the food. And the kiss. It was my very first."

"Mine, too."

"The finest one, too."

She snorted and punched him in the shoulder.

"Shut up, Withnail," she said.

"Yes, Comrade Hero," he said.

She let him kiss her, but only once.

That night, anyway.

About the Author

Cory Doctorow is the author of three science fiction novels, *Down and Out in the Magic Kingdom, Eastern Standard Tribe,* and *Someone Comes to Town, Someone Leaves Town,* and the short story collection *A Place So Foreign and Eight More.* He is the cofounder of www.boingboing.com. "Anda's Game," from this collection, was chosen by Michael Chabon for *The Best American Short Stories 2005.*